# The Professor Who Drove an Aston Martin

The Cat & The Professor Mystery Series

# J. B. Varney

## DEDICATION

*To my Sons*

Who share my love of
Classic Cars, Mystery, History, and Heroes!

# "The Cat & The Professor"

available at amazon.com

# The Cat & The Professor Mystery Series

# Book 3

Such fascinating characters!
I love this series. I don't know who I like more. Russ or Thorndike. It's a draw! Seriously the plots are nicely convoluted. I was completely unprepared for who the bad guy was! And the various sub plots are just as fascinating. Start with the first if you can.

5.0 out of 5 stars - Reviewed in the United States

# CONTENTS

OLD ORANGE BRICK
AWARD
DAN GARN - POET LAUREATE

# CHAPTER ONE
## Bah Humbug

"Hey Russ, did you hear the latest news?"

It was one of his fellow History Professors, Dr. Mariell Thompson. The attractive young woman with shining brown eyes stood in the doorway holding the newspaper.

Russ hadn't watched the news in a week and with the Thanksgiving and Christmas Holidays fast approaching he hadn't even read his newspaper since Monday, and this was Thursday.

"What's new?" he said distractedly, as he put a stack of graded, History 101 papers into his faithful old leather satchel.

"It's your friend, Dan Garn!" She said excitedly.

"Dan" Russ almost shouted, "Is he alright?"

"I'll say" she said crisply, then began reading the front page of the Burlington Free Press newspaper.

"At their annual banquet held last evening the

Adirondack Literary Trust awarded the noted regional poet, Mr. Dan Garn of Eton Falls, in Chittenden County, its highest honor, the annual Robert L. Frost Memorial Award for Poetry. What do you think of that?" she asked.

Russ breathed a sigh of relief. He hadn't seen Dan Garn for several months, not since Garn Construction had finished his large, orange brick garage, and he had to admit feeling a sense of foreboding when Mariell said, "It's your friend, Dan Garn."

The relief flooded over Russ and it was so deeply felt that he actually sat back down.

"Well of course they did" Russ said with an unexpected emotion.

"Is that jealousy I sense, Professor P?"

"No" Russ confessed honestly, "it's more like 'inevitability' I guess. It would be the same thing if you said, 'Oh Russ, did you hear, your friend Dan Garn won the Boston Marathon's men's 55-59 age bracket."

"Well, yeah, that makes so much sense" Mariell said sarcastically. Then she added, "Bah Humbug, and all that, right?"

Russ looked up at Charbonneau's newest History Professor. He remembered not so long ago when he was the college's "newest History Professor." Now he was the battle-tested and beloved "Professor P."

He'd worked with Mariell for just a few months and she'd already shown herself to be a breath of fresh air. She was extremely intelligent and capable but she was also thoughtful, disarmingly funny, and put others at their ease.

"Yeah" Russ said, "Bah Humbug, and all that!"

The two laughed easily together. Then, for a brief and chilling moment, Russ remembered when a young man with a rakish smile, an easy grace, and equally bright eyes, had stood in that same doorway, the same way Mariell was standing.

Marcus Thomas was gone now, at least from Charbonneau College, but thoughts of the young man with an eye for European fashion and a love of black Adidas came to Russ often.

He still remembered the young man's first words.

"I see you made it to Vermont. You must like the cold? How are you settling in?"

The truth was he never forgot a conversation, or a face, or a name, ever. That was Russ's blessing, gift, or curse, even, depending upon the situation. Russ Personette, for better or worse, remembered everything.

And now, seeing the bright-eyed Mariell Thompson standing there had reminded him of Dr. Marcus Thomas. Dr. Thomas had murdered the former head of the Charbonneau College History Department, Dr. R. J. Kaiser. It was the ill-conceived end of a desperate love-triangle and, thanks to the involvement of Russ and his good buddy, the longsuffering Thorndike, it had ended in a stiffish prison sentence for Dr. Thomas and Mrs. Kaiser. Now Russ wondered, as he often did, what Dr. Thomas was doing at that very moment.

"I'll have to send Dan my congratulations" Russ said almost guiltily.

"Yes" Mariell added as she turned to leave, "and don't forget to sign it 'Mr. Scrooge'!"

Dr. Mariell Thompson and Dr. Charles Duncan replaced the two former professors, Kaiser and Thomas, and along with Russ they were competently and pleasantly led by the new head of the department, Dr. Roger Dudley.

Early in his days at Charbonneau College it had been Dr. Dudley's "magnum opus," initially entitled "A People Called the Gullah," that Russ had stolen on one particularly dark and stormy night.[1]

In his fashion Russ had tried to paint the crimes of "breaking and entering" and the accompanying theft, in less offensive terms. Edgar Allan Poe's "The Purloined

---

[1] An homage to "It Was a Dark and Stormy Night, Snoopy", by Charles M. Schulz. I like to add interesting quotes throughout my stories.

Letter" had given Russ an idea for a more "correct" definition than "the Theft of Professor Dudley's Manuscript." Russ dubbed his deed of that dark night as, "The Mystery of the Misappropriated Manuscript."[2]

He had, unfortunately, told Dan Garn, the erstwhile Postman, his theory about "Less-Than-Legal Actions" and the result was a new name for Professor P.

Dan Garn had christened him then and there as the new "Mr. Less-Than-Legal." In Russ's view, what he affectionately called "The Personette Paradigm," the history of criminal theory had missed the mark completely. He argued that by breaking life into the two categories of "Legal Actions" and "Illegal Actions" almost two centuries of criminologists had mislead the world. This, at least, was Russ's opinion.

According to "The Personette Paradigm," there were actually three categories into which the activities of mankind should be broken, criminologically speaking. Legal Actions and Illegal Actions should be joined with a third and nuanced classification Russ called "Less-Than-Legal Actions." Russ pointed out that before identifying something as "purely illegal" the question should first be asked, and answered, whether or not the act is motivated by the benevolent desire to do good, to help. Does the action taken result in doing no harm and much good? If it does, then what was once purely illegal becomes Less-Than-Legal and, perhaps, even praiseworthy.

This was how Russ had seen so many of his adventures over the years. This was also his intention when he engaged in the "The Mystery of the Misappropriated Manuscript." Dr. Dudley had dubbed Russ's theft a "noble endeavor," after the fact. As the book, "Gullah – A People Rediscovered," was being praised as "transcendent," "Pivotal," "Radical," and "A Masterpiece," Russ

---

[2] Magnum opus is the Latin meaning "great work" generally referring to literary work s.  Source: Merriam-Webster Dictionary

considered it a full justification for his "Less-Than-Legal" theory.

"That darned Dan Garn" Russ said to himself as he walked across the beautiful campus. Russ was fully decked out in his "Winter Version," of heavy soled Rockport™ Northfield plain-toed boots, brown Stetson Colton™ felt fedora, Clan MacPherson tartan scarf, and a new purchase, an L. L. Bean® Baxter State Parka™ in Kelp Green Heather, sans hood.[3] The new parka was an upgrade from his former long brown wool coat and a concession to the Vermont winter, the worst of which was yet to come.

Hanging from his shoulder was his battered old satchel. He'd found it at a yard sale in Worthington, Ohio, "many moons ago" and had recognized the name and the quality immediately. It was an English-made "Hanshaws® Briefcase Satchel" from the late 60's but it had hardly been used. The original deep "oxblood" color had weathered to a honey-brown over the decades and Russ had loved it from the start. The fact that he'd paid five dollars for the four-hundred-dollar hand-crafted item made it even more special. He had been, after all, a gentleman of "straightened finances" for several years, as well as a true Scot, and a MacPherson to boot.

"Morning Professor P" came a murmured call from a young man on an old black Schwinn® Voyageur™, still looking good. Russ had been a cyclist in his younger years and owned one of the first-generation of the 15 speed Schwinn Voyageurs, Schwinn's first truly lightweight touring bike. Seeing one still going strong after 30 years or more made him feel almost nostalgic but a crisp northerly blasting down his neck brought him back to his senses.

The golden leaves of autumn were all gone now and it was just a week from Thanksgiving. Snow had already come, and thankfully gone, a couple times and traces

---

[3] Sans means "without." From the Old French derived from the Latin. Source: The Farlex Free Dictionary.

remained in the shadowed sides of Charbonneau's orange brick buildings. Temperatures were now what Russ diplomatically called "brisk" although he acknowledged that for the "natural-born Chittendender" the weather was "quite clement."[4]

"He went and won it." Russ mumbled to himself as he walked along, gloved hands deep in his pockets. "Chittendenders will be popping buttons and champagne corks from Pinesburg and Huntington to Bolton, Underhill, and Milton! That darned Dan Garn."

It was a well-known fact that no Chittendender had ever won the prestigious award and that despite the fact that the founder of the Adirondack Literary Trust was a natural-born Chittendender himself. The eccentric Dawson Langtry had been "hatched," as he put it, in Jericho Township, Chittenden County, Vermont "in the 1880's, or sometime thereabouts". As if to prove the truth of this legend there were still a few of "The Langtry Bunch" roaming around the streets and hills of the county. One of them had become a good friend of Russ's and, in fact, was named Dawson Langtry. Russ's "codename" for his friend was simply "Big D."

"Any relation to 'the' historical Dawson Langtry?" Russ had asked early on.

"Nah, never heard of him."

Dawson, needless to say, was a great joker as well as the great-great grandson of the 'historical' Dawson Langtry. "The historical Dawson Langtry," in fact, wasn't even called Dawson until near the end of his life.

Russ had discovered that many families in Chittenden County in the 1800's and early 1900's, especially in the Starbuck Valley, had followed a complex and complicated custom erroneously called the "Simplified Method".

According to this "method," firstborn sons were

---

[4] A "Chittendender" is an inhabitant of Chittenden County, Vermont, population 156,000, give or take.

typically given their father's first name as their middle name. A second son received a paternal Uncle's first name as his middle name or, in the absence of a paternal Uncle, a Maternal Uncle's name. Vice-a-versa for a third born son.

So the historical Dawson Langtry was named Dawson Robert Langtry, his father being Robert and called "Bob." Then, according to this strange custom, the son would be called by the "diminutive," or "pet name" form, of the father's given name.

The historical Dawson Langtry was called "Bobby," since his father, Robert, was called "Bob." This unspoken and undocumented custom, the "Simplified Method," required the son to continue to go by the "affectionate form" of their father's name until the elder passed on "to the other side," as Starbuckians called.[5] Then it was common for the son to take on the mantel of their own original first name. In this way, the rakish and wealthy New York City newspaperman, Bobby Langtry, suddenly at 55 years-of-age, became the revered "Dawson Langtry".

While this custom was fairly widespread in the Starbuck Valley for well over a century there were exceptions and, often, close friends and relatives continued to insist on calling the elderly gentlemen by their diminutive names. So while the revered newspaper millionaire became Dawson Langtry in New York City, he remained "Bobby" to a handful of siblings and cousins in the Jericho and Underhill areas of Chittenden County, Vermont.

This whole pattern made some form of sense, at least, when it only touched on two generations. The chaos that followed where a grandfather survived well into his "gray days" or where sons were born rapidly to subsequent

---

[5] "Starbuckian" was originally a derogatory term applied by "lowlanders" from urban Burlington, for the inhabitants of Starbuck Valley. By 1850 it had become adopted by the people themselves and used with pride.

generations of a Chittenden County family, was hard to describe.

In order to explain the "method" Harley Shaw, "Folklorist" and great fount of Starbuck County history, once told Russ about the esteemed Baltezore family. This story was so confusing and full of "linguistic pandemonium" that it was almost impossible for Russ to wrap his mind around it, though he tried.

The bedlam surrounding this tradition was taken in stride and apparently without complaint, at least by the few families who still practiced it.

In fact, in getting to know Lara's family, Russ had fallen into the pitfall of this odd custom on more than one occasion. He often bemoaned his embarrassment, for example, at meeting a man named "Mike" only to find out later that he was, in fact, the "Bobby" of several funny stories Russ had already heard.

"I see you met Bobby."

"No, I met Steve, Stevie, Little Stevie, Trig, Tray, Trap, Sage, Kale, Terry, and Mike, but no Bobby! I'm sure of it."

"Well, Mike is Bobby, or rather, Bobby is Mike, Terry is Billy, and Trig is Little Stevie."

Russ had found conversations like these, as incredible as they seemed, common. He'd even secretly breached the subject with Lara.

"Does every man in the county have two names they go by?"

"Of course not, Darling, that would make it consistent and easier for outsiders to understand!"

Lara's humor was one of the many things Russ loved about her, but there were times.

Russ had retaliated in the only way he could, linguistically. He took to calling those men with what he termed as "multi-names," by both names, simultaneously. Mike, or Bobby, depending on who you spoke with, became "Mike-Bobby" in Russ's "new world order."

Terry, or William, became "Terry-Willy." The name order being determined by alphabet. Dawson, or Archibald, became "Archibald Dawsy," Dawsy being the second-generation diminutive form of Dawson. Russ told himself that this was his only hope of keeping the milieu of those who still clung to the odd Starbuck Valley "Simplified Method" naming ritual straight. Interestingly enough, Russ's "Multi-Name System" actually worked fairly well for him, although "it confused the Dickens" out those who were used to the Simplified Method.

So it was that in the strange world of Chittenden County, many Chittendenders had long believed that the historical Dawson Langtry, who had gone on to become a newspaper tycoon in New York in the early 1900's, had put some "secret rule" in the charter of the Adirondack Literary Trust that disqualified residents of Chittenden County from ever winning any of the numerous, prestigious, and lucrative awards given out annually by the august organization which he had founded. Every year that went by without a single Chittendender receiving recognition solidified the idea into legend. After a century, legend had become engraved fact.

Why Dawson Langtry would ever have wanted to punish Chittendenders in this way remained an absolute mystery to them. Russ, on the other hand, had two ideas. Either Chittendenders were just poor writers, at the genetic level even, or Dawson Langtry had created the "secret disqualifying rule" to punish them for using the "Simplified Method" for naming their boys. At least Russ considered these ideas as good "starting points" toward a theory.

When Dan Garn was shockingly announced as the winner of the trust's preeminent award, "The Annual Robert L. Frost Memorial Award for Excellence in Poetry" it sent the entire county on a tipsy and long-overdue celebration lasting almost four days: Thursday, Friday and through the weekend. Garlands from the Fourth of July were brought out again and festooned about the city, almost as if the masses had been planning months in advance. City leaders in Eton Falls, eager to steal the thunder from the bright lights in Burlington, called an "emergency midnight session" and by a unanimous vote passed their "resolution." They declared to a small group of groggy and freezing reporters from WBAX, KLBM, the Burlington "Free Press," the Jericho "Clarion," the Pinesburg "Daily Gristmill," and the "Underhill Utopian," in the pre-dawn hours that, "Henceforth the Thursday before Thanksgiving will be known in Eton Falls as 'Dan Garn Day'!"

The Free Press carried the news in a banner ribbon on the front page of the Saturday paper, "ETON FALLS DECLARES DAN GARN DAY." The city leaders had won. Burlington's belated announcement, that the county had voted to declare "the Thursday before Thanksgiving shall henceforward and forever be known in Chittenden County as 'Dan Garn Day' when public speeches and poetry readings shall be sponsored and widespread" was carried at the bottom of page 4A on the following Tuesday.

It was the town of Jericho that had the final laugh over both its larger neighbors however, when their mayor made the announcement that a life-sized bronze statue of "The Postman-Poet of the North Country" would be erected in front of city hall. The statue would be wearing the Postal Service summer uniform, including satchel, and holding a scroll aloft on which the title of Mr. Garn's most famous poem, "Stopping by the Post Office on a Winter's Evening," would be visible.

The metropolis of Underhill declared they were changing the name of their two-lane main spur-street, Park Street, to "Dan Garn Boulevard, in honor of the Poet Laureate of Chittenden County, Dan Garn."

The township of Milton declared, to no one in particular, that the school's multi-use gymnasium, formerly known simply as "the school's multi-use gymnasium" would now be called "The Dan Garn Building" and these words would be painted in five-foot tall letters, by members of the football team, on the largest exterior wall that faced the visitors parking lot.

Dan Garn, the Postman who had been loved and lionized by everyone on his mail route, including Eston and Greta Phillips, was now lifted to the stature of Hero-at-Large" by the entire county as well, and all the more since he was the first Chittendender in 100 years to receive any recognition from the prestigious trust.

Russ fully expected the first baby boy born in Chittenden County in the New Year to be named "Dan" in honor of the Postman-Poet of the North Country!

Significantly, "The Annual Robert L. Frost Memorial Award for Excellence in Poetry" was also accompanied by a check for one-hundred thousand dollars.

Russ had once told Dan "Your persona was supposed to be 'the-homespun-son-of-the-Vermont-soil' Postman. You really were supposed to be 'Dan the Postman' and 'Dan the Builder.' You really were supposed to blend in and disappear in plain sight. That was supposed to be your persona."

"That darned Dan Garn, Bah Humbug" Russ said out loud. "He always wanted to be a Renaissance Man! Now I suppose Thorndike will insist we give him one of the 'Old Orange Brick Awards,' as if he hasn't been recognized enough already! Postman-Poet of the North, indeed" he mumbled unhappily. Then he had a thought.

"You know, Mariell may be right, I do sound a little like Ebenezer Scrooge!"

The whole idea for the "Old Orange Brick Award" came to Russ in an epiphany he'd had a few months earlier as he was convalescing from the after-effects of a would-be assassin's high velocity bullet. While in the hospital he'd received cards, letters, balloons, flowers, and even chocolate covered raisins and "Kippered Snacks," widely known as two of his favorites, from admirers all over Chittenden County and as far afield as Ohio and Oregon.

Then, belatedly, arrived a gift from one of his dearest and oldest friends, Arnold Williams. It was an old, battered brick with the word "Sanford" pressed into the underside.

Lara had commented on it.

"Arnold left you the orange brick. Is that significant?"

"He...used to call me a brick...said he could always...count on me!" Russ had replied with a sore throat.

Once he was back on his feet and getting around again Russ had put the brick on the mantle at Wildrose. To his amazement he'd repeatedly found Thorndike staring at it and each time he caught him, the big cat would slink away quickly, vanishing out of doors into his Kitty Corral Cat Fence™ jungle gym, as if to escape Russ's inquiry.

"What's wrong with that cat?" Russ thought. As time passed and Thorndike continued his "vigil" over the old brick, as Russ called it, he began to wonder if the brick itself was significant to the cat. Perhaps it had spent the last 60 years in a patch of catnip or, more chillingly, could it have been a murder weapon in an ancient, unsolved mystery. Russ went so far as to smell, sniff, and inspect the brick in its entirety and in minute detail, even going so far as to pull out his old magnifying glass.

"If Sherlock Holmes could see me now" he thought.

Finally he arrived at a shocking conclusion. It was an absolutely ordinary old brick, made in Sanford, North Carolina, and thus stamped in all-caps on the underside "S A N F O R D." In fact, Wildrose itself was made of the exact same orange bricks, even stamped with the same name. For that matter, the team of Garn Construction had scrounged thousands of the same bricks from the ruins of the old Wildrose Post Office that had once stood on the other side of Hunters Lane. It had been just one of the buildings that made up the thriving metropolis of Wildrose Township in its heyday. The crumbling foundations of the train depot, livery, grain terminal, and a few homes were still there too, all hidden in a cloak of trees and bushes now.

Garn Construction used the "reclaimed" bricks, which

were the only ones identical in color to the old Wildrose Schoolhouse, to build Russ's multi-space garage/utility building.

Once Russ had deduced the absolute insignificance of the brick, through his stringent scientific methods, he was even more curious as to why Thorndike continued to pay it such focused attention.

"It's as if he were paying homage to the thing" he'd thought on more than one occasion. Unable to make sense of the matter Russ became almost obsessed with figuring out Thorndike's interest.

"What's wrong with that cat, if he can communicate telepathically then why doesn't he?" he'd asked himself several times during his painful convalescence.

Then one fine day in August, as he nodded off in one of the club chairs at Wildrose, a sudden spike of pain shot through his shoulder where the Israeli-made "boat tail" type bullet had pierced his right deltoid, and he awoke.

Thorndike was sitting on top of a neighboring club chair, his shining amber-eyes staring hard into Russ's forehead. Once Russ awoke the cat went to licking a hindquarter, as if cleanliness were the next best thing to catliness!

"Ah" Russ said out loud, "What's wrong with that cat?"

He'd no more than said this when the epiphany flooded over him. It wasn't the brick that was important, it was what it represented, all that it represented. To the cat the brick could have been the equivalent of an Oscar Award, the little golden man, won by Russ for some magnificent portrayal on the silver screen. That's when the man finally understood the cat.

"Perhaps" Russ thought, "Eileen was correct about his catly intellect."

This was the moment the "Old Orange Brick Award" was born. Once Russ had finally comprehended the "full vision" Thorndike had for the award, he acted quickly.

Russ had stolen, or perhaps he "misappropriated,"

several armloads of Garn Constructions "reclaimed" orange, Sanford bricks, as they finished the garage. At the same time he ordered two dozen hardwood bases and several name plates from the trophy store in town, "Brophy's Trophies."

The first "Old Orange Brick Award" went to Arnold and simply said, "Old Orange Brick Award - Arnold Williams - Friend Extraordinaire."

The second award went to Eston Phillips and said, "Old Orange Brick Award - Eston Phillips - Mechanic Extraordinaire."

The third went to Dr. Dudley and said, "Old Orange Brick Award - Roger Dudley - Author Extraordinaire."

The fourth said, "Old Orange Brick Award - Harley Shaw - Folklorist Extraordinaire."

The fifth said, "Old Orange Brick Award - Eileen Shute - Editor Extraordinaire."

The sixth said, "Old Orange Brick Award - Jim Ramsay - Officer Extraordinaire."

The seventh, said, "Old Orange Brick Award - August James - Detective Extraordinaire."

The eighth award said, "Old Orange Brick Award - Daphne Briggs - Artist Extraordinaire."

The ninth, and up to now the last award, said, "Old Orange Brick Award - Bernadette Langlois - Bond Girl Extraordinaire." The full meaning behind this award was apparent only to Bernadette herself, Vivian Delashmett, Thorndike, and to Russ. Everyone else would only understand a portion of the award's fuller significance. Russ explained to Agent 36 that he simply couldn't put "Spy Extraordinaire" on the award.

"It just isn't done" Russ said.

As significant an award as the "The Annual Robert L. Frost Memorial Award for Excellence in Poetry" was, Russ believed that the "Old Orange Brick Award" was far more important. For one thing, far fewer people had one. For another, "The Frost Award," as Russ insisted on calling it, required $100,000 dollars to give it the significance it garnered. Russ considered this "overcompensation" for the award. The Old Orange Brick Award was accompanied only by a $100.00 dollar gift card to the local Macy's. This, so he argued with Arnold, was because of the "overwhelming significance" of the Old Orange Brick Award itself!

Russ also felt that the scarcity of the Old Orange Brick Award created an elite fellowship of special people, like "The League of Extraordinary Gentlemen" perhaps.[6]

As matters progressed Russ determined that recipients of the prestigious award would gather, with their dates, spouses, or significant others, at what he dubbed "The Orange-Brick Banquet" and being a thoroughgoing Scot himself, he set the date of the great feast for the evening of January 25th of each year. Thorndike, as co-founder with Russ, would be on hand as well, of course. This date, as all true Scots knew, was the birthday of the Poet Laureate of Scotland, Robert Burns. "A Burns Supper," as they were uniformly called, had to have haggis, and was seen by the Scottish community, worldwide, as a celebration of the life and poetry of Robert Burns. Russ envisioned prime rib, steak, or various seafood platters, as acceptable alternatives for those folks who had "not yet acquired" the love of haggis which all Scots naturally possessed.

Now, for so it appeared, a tenth "Old Orange Brick Award was needed. This one would say, "Old Orange Brick Award – Dan Garn – Poet Laureate." "What's a Professor to do?" Russ mumbled to himself. "The last thing Dan Garn needs is more notoriety."

---

[6] "The League of Extraordinary Gentlemen" - A comic book franchise founded by writer Alan Moore and artist Kevin O'Neill. Copyright 1999. Later made into the movie starring Sean Connery.

# CHAPTER TWO
## There's a Cat to Blame!

By the time Lara got into work the next morning, a chilly Friday, she found that Russ had already been there and had gone on to his first class. Yet, since the beginning of their romance her "Young Gentleman" had tried to make Friday's a special day for her. Even when he was on a tight budget he'd worked hard to be romantic and make her feel special. Now that money was no issue for the Author/Spy-turned-Professor Lara had been treated to a long-line of beautiful things.

On her desk she found a glorious ruby red Fostoria® Heirloom™ vase and inside of it, instead of flowers, were three of her favorite Swiss chocolates, Toblerone® Swiss Milk Chocolate with honey and almond nougat bar in the characteristic triangular shaped tubes. The vase and the chocolates were two of Lara's favorite things and the idea of putting the Toblerone into the Fostoria® Heirloom™ vase was a Russ Personette "original."

Lara and Russ had been engaged for several months but she still found herself staring at her beautiful ring at various times throughout her day. She had never expected to fall in love again or to meet anyone as thoroughly wonderful as Russ Personette. He was sweet, thoughtful, and unselfish. He did have some quirks but what man didn't? Among them was a strange theory called "connectionism," dealing with the relationship between cats and humans, and Russ was beginning to believe his own cat, Thorndike, was communicating telepathically with him. Other than this Russ was simply perfect.

"Oh, Lara, how sweet." It was Dr. Mariell Thompson arriving to work and seeing the burgundy-colored vase and the Swiss chocolate. "He is a romantic isn't he? Where is he taking you tonight?" she continued.

"He has reservations at the Sand-n-Sage Lounge" Lara said with a laugh. The lounge was famous, or infamous, in Northern Vermont, namely for the rarity of sand and the total absence of sagebrush, but they had good food and a décor that hadn't changed since 1940.

According to local legend the name of the lounge was the result of an arranged "public relations" stop by a young actor by the name John Wayne. He'd just finished the blockbuster movie, "Stagecoach," and rumors had it that the actor's next film would be another western named something like "The Purple Sage" or "The Sand and the Sage." The restaurant owners had arranged for the stopover and hoped to make the most of the advertising opportunity. Unfortunately for them an airplane problem in New York ended the planned stop and once back in Hollywood even the forthcoming movie failed to materialize. In the end the owners of the already named "Sand-n-Sage Lounge" decided to make lemonade out of their misfortune and mounted glossy photos of John Wayne in various scenes from his many western movies throughout the lounge.

Another plus with the lounge was its location in one of

Russ's favorite local architectural wonders, the Sacagawea Hotel.

"I hope you guys have a great time" Mariell said before going down the hall to her office, formerly that of Marcus Thomas.

"Thank you, Dr. Thompson" Lara said sincerely.

"Oh please, Lara, call me Mars when we not in a formal setting. Dr. Thompson is so stuffy for a 28 year who loves puns, jokes, retro-fashions, and prints by Andy Warhol, don't you think?"

Lara appreciated the new professor's relaxed approach and her self-assuredness. The uptight R. J. Kaiser and the aggressive Marcus Thomas had been a constant tension in the department. Dr. Campbell, the other professor, was less social and outgoing, but he was at least well-mannered and generally pleasant. All in all the new makeup of the History Department was much better for Lara, not to mention that one of the professors was her beau.

When Russ returned to the office after his first two classes he noticed two coats on the pegs.

The first was Dr. Dudley's exquisite Filson® Gray Plaid Wool Packer's Coat with shearling collar and his red and black Field & Stream® Winter Trapper's Cap, with ear flaps that could be lowered for extreme cold, on the shelf above. Two things jumped out at Russ immediately about Dr. Dudley's winter wear. First, the contrast from a year earlier, when Roger Dudley was a part-time History Professor and had been passed over, again, for the full-time position. His "winter" coat then had been unsuitably light for a Vermont winter. Now it was more than adequate and of the highest quality. Being from out west Russ was well aware of the Filson® name, and price tag. The second thing that struck him was Dr. Dudley's Trapper's cap. Russ recognized the clan tartan instantly, Clan MacGregor. More specifically it was called the "Rob Roy" or "Red and Black MacGregor" tartan. In America it was often known simply by the name "Buffalo Plaid."

On the second peg was Lara's classic camel colored long coat. Russ noticed the thinning material at the elbows and was happy he'd already done something about it.

The remaining pegs were empty.

Russ had always noticed odd little things like these. Other people would automatically jettison these kinds of petty details from their memory banks in order to make room for the truly important, but not Russ Personette.

Even before he entered the office he heard the almost imperceptible electronic ringing of a telephone and Lara's pleasant voice answering.

He was a man in love. He had no idea how it had happened and he still found it difficult to believe but there was no getting around it. The Angel seated in the next room, talking on the phone, was wearing his engagement ring. As he ran his fingers through his graying temples Russ was more aware than ever that he was far from the handsome young man who stepped off the train at Oregon State University as a college freshman. Perhaps because of this he was doubly aware that Lara Meredith remained a stunningly beautiful woman.

He still remembered how she had invited him out on their first romantic date. She came into his office and handed him a small leaflet.

"The Burlington Symphony Orchestra is having a concert this Sunday" she'd said with blushing cheeks. "I wondered if you'd like to go."

As Humphrey Bogart had so aptly put it in the movie, Casablanca, "I think this is the beginning of a beautiful friendship," and Russ now realized that Lara's invitation to the Symphony had marked the beginning of their "beautiful relationship."

He stood in the foyer listening until she finished the phone call and then he peaked around the corner.

"I knew it was you, Mr. Nosey, when the door opened and closed and no one appeared after a reasonable interval. I knew then you were either measuring the tread in Dr. Dudley's goloshes or you were rifling through my pockets for a clue to what Christmas gifts I've gotten you!" Lara laughed as he stepped fully into the office.

"I'd never" he said emphatically, naturally defending himself until he realized he had, in fact, done such things before, then he went guiltily silent.

"I loved my Fostoria® Heirloom™ vase and the Toblerone®! You remember all my favorites."

"I can never forget" Russ said with a smile so sincere and genuine that it melted Lara's heart.

While he had gained some unwanted pounds and many gray hairs the one thing Russ didn't realize was the attractiveness of his kind, unselfish personality. Arnold had spoken the truth when he'd called Russ "Nature's Nobleman" and some people, like Lara Meredith, found that simply irresistible.

After a warming hug and kiss, or two, Russ made his way into his old corner office with windows on two walls and a fully operational heating system.

"Ahh" he thought as he came in where the contrast between his chilled body and the flood of warmth was greatest.

Then he saw it. It was a big book and it lay open on the floor. Far back in the shadows under a round table where he kept two chairs for consultations with students. They could put books and papers out and look over then together. The nearest bookcase was 3 feet away. Even before he got to it he knew which book it was. He also knew to which portion of the book it was opened. Despite the heat in his office a chill ran up his spine and set the hairs on the back of his neck standing straight out.

"No" he thought desperately.

"No" he said out loud. If this was what he thought it was, he wanted nothing to do with it. His mind raced as he tried to remember the last time Thorndike had visited the office. It hadn't been recently, he knew that.

"Surely" he told himself as he stooped to retrieve the

book, "this is just a random accident, just one of those things, and nothing of significance."

His life had now been thrown into a topsy-turvy mess on two separate occasions, both by books he'd found lying innocently enough on the floor. In both cases attempts had been made on his life and each time they'd gotten closer to the mark. Granted, it had been Thorndike, that darned cat, who'd saved him both times, but Russ didn't want there to be a third time. The proverbial "third times a charm"!

Russ wanted to have a wonderful, quiet, peaceful holiday season with the woman he loved and the friends he valued. He didn't want another mystery, another murder, more mayhem, dead bodies, and chaos. He didn't want any more midnight meetings with the police or another night in a hospital bed. Above all he didn't want to die just when life was getting good again.

So, as he pulled "Glencoe – Story of the Massacre," by John Ross Prebble, copyright 1973, out from under the table he told himself that this was not one of "Thorndike's books".

"This is not one of Thorndike's Books'!" he insisted unswervingly in his mind.

Then he saw the claw marks in the middle of the page.

"I knew it" he almost hissed, as he tossed the book onto the round table. "There's a cat to blame!"

Russ instantly scratched his head and turned away from the book in one movement. He didn't want to see the book. He didn't want to go closer and he didn't want to see what words had been disfigured by the razor-sharp talons of the giant Maine Coon Cat named Thorndike.

"Genghis Khan if you ask me!" Russ said emphatically and then to his shock he heard Lara's voice.

"Russ, what's wrong dear? I heard the book hit the table all the way out in the lobby. That's not like you."

Russ put his hand over his mouth. He didn't know what to say. He only pointed to the book and shook his head.

Lara approached the book slowly. She too seemed to

share the same trepidation Russ felt. She had once joked about their next mystery and had felt a rush of excitement at the thought they were on another case. This time was different though. She too had experienced fears and terrors she didn't want to repeat and she certainly didn't want to lose her fiancé. The last two adventures had driven home the point that Russ was in real danger.

He still held his hand over his mouth as Lara stepped toward the table. When she saw the claw marks in the page she almost whimpered.

"Oh no, Russ."

Yet, she was drawn to the table almost as if some invisible force drew her to it. She leaned over to read the words that were scarred by the violent gashes of a large cat's powerful and sharp talons.

"You are hereby ordered to fall upon...the old Fox...upon no account escape your hands" Lara read soberly and then she added, "those are the only words in that paragraph I can read, Russ, everything else is torn beyond recognition."

Her gentle voice quavered with emotion.

"It's not like Thorndike to actually hurt a book though" Russ said distractedly. Then, as if it were a second thought, he answered Lara.

"It's alright, I know the words by heart. It was a Royal order given on February 12th, 1692," Russ said soberly. Then he began to quote it without the book.

"You are hereby ordered to fall upon the rebells, the McDonalds of Glenco, and put all to the sword under seventy. You are to have a speciall care that the old Fox and his sones doe upon no account escape your hands, you are to secure all the avenues that no man escape. This you are to putt in execution att five of the clock precisely; and by that time or very shortly after it, I'll strive to be att you with a stronger party: if I doe not come to you att five, you are not to tarry for me, but to fall on. This is by the Kings special command."

Russ sat at his desk, staring at the floor. Lara sat at the round table, with her hand still on the book.

"Who was the order addressed to?"

"A Campbell" Russ said flatly, "Robert Campbell, the 5th Lord of Glenlyon, of Meggernie Castle in Perthshire. He was a commander of two companies of infantry, called the Earl of Argyll's Regiment of Foot."

"And they were the men who conducted the massacre at Glencoe?" Lara asked quietly.

"Yes, they were" was all Russ said and then silence fell on the room.

Lara continued to look back at the book, as if she'd find the terrible words changed. It was a small mercy when her phone began to ring and she was pulled away to answer it.

How long Russ sat there after Lara left remained a question mark to him. His mind was fixed on the same thought over and over, like the needle of a record player stuck in the same groove, going round and round.

As many times as Russ had scolded Thorndike for being a vandal, miscreant, and general scallywag for knocking books down, it really wasn't like the big cat to ruin a book. In fact, other than one word licked to a blurry wetness, it had never happened before.

Why would he do it now? And when had he done it?

When he looked up again Lara was standing in front of him with a worried look on her face.

"Russ" she said gently, "It's time for you to go to your last class."

Time had slipped away from him while he was in his trance and now he'd to come back to reality.

"Thank you, Darling" he said to her, as he stood up.

"We're in this together" she said with grit and determination. "We'll figure it out one way or another."

Despite her very real strength Russ could see the fear in her eyes.

"Yes we will, but today is Friday! And we have a date coming up in a few hours. We'll worry about John Ross

Prebble's book and our next mystery tomorrow, Mrs. Gorgeous, and that's an order."

His words were like a tonic but he wasn't so naive as to think that both he and Lara wouldn't continue to wonder about their new case. Thorndike had struck again!

"That darned cat!"

As Russ headed for his final class of the day snow began falling heavily, propelled, if such a word could be applied to something as fragile as a snowflake, by a "northerly" blowing at about 30 miles an hour.

"At this rate we'll have a white Thanksgiving for sure" Russ thought. He and Lara, as well as her grown children, had accepted an invitation from his best friend, Arnold. and his wife, Rhonda.

They lived several miles north-northwest of Eton Falls on the romantically named "Lone Mountain Road." The name, however, was deceptive. For one thing, the road was bounded on the east by a heavily wooded ridgeline boasting no less than 7 separate, identified summits, called "peaks", making "Lonely Mountain Road" far more accurate than "Lone Mountain". For another thing, there were other roads that ran north bounding the same range. Hunters Lane, in fact, was a parallel, "sister road," on the eastern side of the ridge. From Wildrose to Arnold & Rhonda's home it was almost 14 miles by Mercury Grand Marquis. Down Hunter's lane into the northern end of Eton Falls, across on Old Ox Road, then up Lone Mountain Road. If you put on your hiking boots though, it was just over two miles on a pleasant trail up and over the ridge, but with a rise in elevation of 2,000 feet to the passes the famed Strathmorlick Ridge wasn't a path for the feeble.[7]

The range was, in geographic reality, a "finger range" of

---

[7] "The Courtship of Lord Strathmorlick" was spoken of in the short story "Jeeves in the Springtime" by P. G. Wodehouse, published 1921. In the story the character Rosie M. Banks is named as the author. Strathmorlick Ridge was named for a relative of Lord Strathmorlick.

the "Highlands" north of the Starbuck Valley and it served as the valley's western boundary.

Russ wasn't looking forward to driving out Lone Mountain Road if it was covered in snow. He loved his 1998 Mercury Grand Marquis despite its bland styling, slow heater, and the window wipers that hopped and skipped in a noisy dance across the windshield. The faithful old car had seen him through a lot over the years but there was one shortcoming that Russ had difficulty overlooking.

Unlike the newest generation of luxury cars the old Mercury was one of the last of the rear-wheel drive giants. Blessed with huge motors up front, a wheelbase just slightly shorter than a football field and an empty trunk space that could hold both houses of congress, the cars were notoriously hard to manage in the snow and ice. Everyone was familiar with the driving term "fishtailing," but the Mercury Grand Marquise took this phenomenon to the extreme and Russ couldn't deny the danger.

In fact, when Eston Phillips learned about Russ's purchase of the old Wildrose School he'd almost had a seizure. Few living today understood cars better than the undersized mechanic, and not just their motors.

"You need a four-wheel drive if you plan on living out Wildrose way" Eston had told Russ pointedly, and this from a man whose most aggressive act was saying, "please pass the salt."

Eston loved it that Russ had cared for the Grand Marquise despite its age. Eileen, Russ's Editor, had called it his "antique car," but Eston was adamant that his newfound friend needed something different for the snow.

"The Starbuck Valley is no joke when it comes to snow" Eston had said pointedly.

"Oh, that's very true, Russ" Greta had confirmed. "It was one thing when you lived right here in town, and the little cabin on End Road was very nice" she added sweetly, "but now you'll be driving way out north into the valley, every day."

If Russ had a failing, a true failing, it was his ability to procrastinate when he was busy. He had singlehandedly been able to stave off getting a cellphone for months after it had become apparent to him that he needed one. This was not the skill of a novice procrastinator; Russ was the real MacKay![8] It had taken the combined and intense efforts of both Eileen and Chief Ramsay to finally get him to act.

Eston had been at him for a week to stop by and look at something but now, with the snow coming down hard and the wind biting at his cheeks, he tucked his head down behind his fedora brim and surrendered to his mechanic.

"Alright Eston, you win!"

3 hours and 4 inches of snow later Russ was standing in the center of the Phillip's Shop staring a huge truck.

"That's the biggest truck I've ever seen" Russ said facetiously, grimacing at his little host.

"Ever seen Dane VanWert's 10 Cylinder Ford Triton?" Eston said with a wide grin. "Big green thing? I do all the work on it."

Truth was Russ knew the truck very well and it was two feet higher and longer than the one he was looking at. He opened one of the 4 doors on the quad-cab and found dove gray leather seats, exquisite Black Walnut trim, and all the extras.

"I didn't even know Lincoln made a truck" Russ said.

"They don't anymore" Eston said sadly. "One of the finest vehicles I've ever worked on but they ended the line. They just made them for three years and you got a beauty right here."

Russ looked at the snow-white Lincoln® Mark LT with

---

[8] "The real McCoy" is a corruption of the Scots "The real MacKay", published in Scotland in 1856. Russ knew this and he always made sure to use the "proper Scots" when using the term. Source: Michael Quinion, worldwidewords.org, 2011.

a matching white fiberglass canopy and whistled.

"It's got all the bells and whistles" he said dubiously.

"And lots of chrome too, if you like that sort of thing" Eston added. "Even has automatic side-steps if you turn this button on. Makes it easy to get in, even for a lady in a dress, then it disappears when you close the door."

"Nice" Russ said, finally acknowledging the obvious.

"Like new and low miles" Eston said. Then, with the flash of a perfect set of white teeth that reminded Russ of Dan Garn and Harley Shaw, he said, "And I know the mechanic whose been taking care of it from day one, yours truly" the little man said. "You can't go wrong with this one."

"What will I do with the Mercury" Russ said guiltily.

"Well you got a nice new garage, ain't you? It's not like you're abandoning the old gal along a deserted road. Put her away for the winter, give her a rest through the tough times, she's earned a little consideration, ain't she?"

Russ couldn't argue with Eston's reasoning and he'd decided he'd take it. Greta was right, it was different when he lived in town, and Eston was right, the old Mercury deserved to sit out the Vermont winter.

"Let me ask you a question Eston" Russ said suddenly. "Are you related to Dan Garn?"

"Oh isn't it wonderful?" Eston's face lit up like a Christmas Tree. "His poetry is amazing isn't it? The missus and me, were so happy to see the Trust recognize him." Russ had never seen the words tumble out of the usually quiet Eston Phillips the way these did now. His excitement seemed to mirror the entire community, everyone except for Russ that is.

"Yes" Russ said as sincerely as a man who thought Dan Garn needed the award like he needed a hole in his head. "It is wonderful, but you haven't answered my question."

"What was it again" Eston said distractedly.

Russ understood that just the mention of Dan Garn made everyone think of the day's big news.

"I asked if you were related to Dan Garn, or Harley Shaw, for that matter."

"That's correct" Eston said, "Harley and I are first cousins, Dan is Harley's Nephew and Dane VanWert is Harley's Grandson. We all come down from the MacKean Line through my Great-Aunt Ernestine MacKean-Lyon-Findley and my Grandmother, Agnes MacKean-Phillips. Why do you ask?" he said suddenly serious.

"To be honest, Eston, you all have perfect teeth."

"Yup, we do, that's a MacKean trait for you right there. No hiding it. Auntie Ernestine looked like she'd had her teeth professionally done long before dentists did anything like that. You should be a detective, Russ, if you can figure that all out."

When Russ left Eston standing in his shop it was in a heavily falling snow and behind the wheel of a 2007 Lincoln Mark LT Quad-Cab 4-wheel drive.

The Lincoln had the same spectacularly smooth ride as his Grand Marquis but it also had an imposing height and muscular size to go along with it. It wasn't until he'd sped along the snow-covered Hunters Lane for a few miles that he fully grasped the improved handling of the big 4-wheel drive. Lincoln had done it right, that was for sure.

After parking in his garage Russ walked out toward the house in an atmosphere that could only be likened to a snow globe. Where the winds in Eton Falls had bitten and burned any exposed skin, here in the Starbuck Valley he found no wind at all, and the giant snowflakes fell straight down as if they were in slow motion.

Then it happened.

He caught Thorndike's gaze through the window and the big cat knew Russ had found the book. Thorndike vanished in the massive interior of Wildrose.

"Guilty" Russ said as he unlocked the front door and came in from the cold. Then he reverted to his favorite Shakespearean quote for just such moments. "The guilty mind tis full of scorpions!"

# CHAPTER THREE
## A Complicated History

Thorndike, that courageous cat, stayed tucked away safely in hiding as Russ showered, shaved, and dressed for his Friday night dinner at the Sage-n-Sand Lounge with Lara. Even as Russ was leaving, the cat failed to appear.

"Coward" Russ called over his shoulder as he stepped back outside his warm home and pulled the door shut.

"Cowards die a thousand deaths, the valiant die but once" Russ called out as he tromped up the sidewalk to the garage. He knew a meeting of the minds would be taking place with the big cat, but tomorrow was Saturday and there would be time enough then.

It had taken Russ just two trips on Hunters Lane to conclude that Eston and Greta Phillips were the smartest couple on earth. The 4-wheel drive Lincoln had handled the snow effortlessly and without the least slipping. That same course in the Grand Marquis would have left him exhausted with white knuckles, and several near accidents. After several weeks of procrastinating he now felt very good about making the change.

"Hello Beautiful" Russ said, as Lara opened to his knock. She saw the large, gleaming truck in the driveway

29

and she would have said something about it if Russ had not pulled a large, giftwrapped present from behind him and handed it to her at that very moment.

"It's huge" she beamed.

Once inside she was amazed to have yet another gift, since she'd already received a beautiful vase and her favorite Swiss chocolate that morning. She usually received one gift each Friday from Russ and while they'd gotten substantially more expensive once the "Hollywood People" had gotten involved, she'd never gotten so many before.

Russ was amazed, once again, with how beautiful she was and Lara wasn't simply an attractive woman, she was an elegant lady as well.

"What is this Mr. Personette?" she said with a pleased smile.

"If I told you it would defeat the purpose of the box and the gift wrap, wouldn't it?" he asked mischievously.

"Hmmm" she said, "it's heavy."

When she opened it, in her careful way, Lara found a deep blue Eddie Bauer® Sun Valley™ Down Parka with hood. It was long, to below the knee, and would keep her warm. Some down-filled coats were bulky and made women look like marshmallows, but the Sun Valley was feminine and shapely. She loved it. Then she noticed something in the bottom of the box. It was a pair of gloves and a pair of tall winter boots.

The gloves were black Isotoner® SmartDRI™ Lined Gloves with Faux Fur Cuff and the boots were called Tundra Boots™. The style was called "Mai" and they were a fashionable winter boot that came up almost to the knee.

"My ankles will stay warm" Lara said sweetly.

"Yes" Russ said smiling, "I remembered you said your ankles always got cold."

After kissing him she said, "You are the sweetest man!"

As they made their way to the new pickup Lara asked, "Did my Christmas come early, or what?"

"Oh no! Those were just your Friday gifts" Russ said insistently.

"Wow" she said as they came around the house and she saw the Lincoln up close for the first time. "What a beautiful truck" she said, "and big."

Russ had to agree and when he opened Lara's door to help her in and the side-step came out automatically he was proud to be able to pick her up in such a vehicle. She stepped up and in without the least trouble and Russ said a secret thanks to Eston Phillips.

When Russ got into his side of the truck Lara said, "You make me feel so special, Russ. I don't know what to say."

Russ remembered how much he had loved his late wife and how he had tried to make her feel loved, even when money was scarce, and he said, "You are special, Lara, and truly loved."

The Sand-n-Sage Lounge still had the same décor it had in 1940. It had been kept in good condition and it had been so long since it had opened that the place now was the height of the new "retro-fashion." Round tables surrounded by circular booths wrapping around them, upholstered in Jade colored vinyl, made up most of restaurant. Small, tan lacquered tables with jade green upholstered chairs made up the remainder. Framed photos of John Wayne were scattered throughout, along with a couple old parade saddles, bridles, and a nondescript, rusty "six-shooter."

Russ had recognized the original pistol that had been affixed to the wall as a Colt® Walker™ Model 1847 pistol, which was a collector's item. When he told the restaurant owner he'd pay him a thousand dollars for the old pistol it wasn't long before it was sitting beside him in the booth, wrapped in a brown paper bag.

Russ moved it on to an antique dealer he trusted to represent him and the pistol sold at the Rock Island Auction, a premier auction house for collectible firearms, for $250,000.00. Russ knew his firearms and being who he was, he returned to the lounge and gave the owner, Richey Sugrue, $24,000.00, saying it only seemed right that he get a larger share. It was hard for people to believe the story and Russ hadn't even told Lara about it at first, but afterward he "and guest" always ate for free at Richey's Sand-n-Sage Lounge.

"Hello Lara, you look marvelous." It was Dr. Mariell Thompson and several friends.

"Hello Ebenezer" she said to Russ with a laugh, as the group passed on to the back of the restaurant.

Russ took several minutes explaining the happenings of the previous morning when Mariell had told him about Dan Garn's poetry prize.

"Well, that is quite funny then, Mr. Scrooge!" Lara said this with relish, but she made up for it by kissing Russ sweetly on the cheek then whispering, "Don't tell anyone this, Ebenezer, but someone loves you!"

"Well, I love you more!"

"You better" she said sweetly, then she whispered, "I told Dr. Thompson this morning we were going to come here but I didn't think she'd crash our party."

"She was probably curious what we looked like together, out on the town!" Then Russ added seriously, "She didn't really believe that a beautiful woman like you would be seen in public with a ragamuffin like me!"

"Russ, you're hilarious."

He loved the way Lara said the word "hilarious." She pronounced it as "high-larry-us" and said she'd picked up the unique pronunciation from her mother, who'd been born in Dickey, North Dakota. Whatever the reason for the cute pronunciation Russ found it, and Lara, charming, and he knew he always would.

Halfway through an excellent meal of steak and seafood Lara said what was on both their minds.

"About the book, do you think we could be wrong?"

"Wrong?" Russ thought, how he wished such a thing were actually possible. How wonderful it would be to be wrong.

The first book Thorndike had "taken to" had been a thin volume entitled "Hadrian's Wall" and in the chapter entitled, "Housesteads Roman Fort" the big cat had roughed-up a spot where the word "murder" had almost been obliterated.[9] That word was in a passage that read, "In the age when Roman Legions manned the fort a double murder had been committed and the bodies were buried beneath the floor."

That book, that chapter, that passage, and that very word, had led them to the murder of Lara's late husband and Daphne's mother. It had been a terrible ordeal, especially for those women, but it had also liberated them.

That entire experience had seemed incredible, unbelievable, but even then Russ was reminded of the famous words of Sherlock Holmes, "Once you eliminate the impossible, whatever remains, no matter how improbable, must be the truth."

After everything, no matter how improbable Thorndike's behavior with the book on Hadrian's Wall had been, it had been the one remaining truth he couldn't deny. Thorndike had led them through that quagmire of clues and mysteries until even R. J. Kaiser had been uncovered.

The second book targeted by the cat was "Killers of the Flower Moon." This book seemed to forward an even more chilling reality.[10] The words Thorndike had highlighted were, "The murderer had not acted alone but had been part of a conspiracy orchestrated by a band of local citizens." This revealed a "Murder Ring" at work in Chittenden County. The shock waves and trials from that scandal, which had taken 4 lives and would have taken one more, were still reverberating through the community and

[9] Hadrian's Wall, by David Breeze, published by English Heritage.
[10] Killers of the Flower Moon: The Osage Murders and the Birth of the FBI, by David Grann, published by Knopf.

had affected 20 or more of the county's highest leaders and wealthiest people. Russ had thought it was inconceivable at the time and he'd said so, but it had all been proven true.

Now there had been a third book and a third passage, more unsettling and frightening than anything he and Lara had seen before. As if to emphasize the violence and the scale of this crime Thorndike had viciously ripped most of the passage to tatters, leaving only a fragmentary message on the mutilated page. It was only the fact that Russ had memorized the infamous "order" long ago that allowed him to recite the entire thing for Lara. The difference was that Thorndike had never actually destroyed a book before. Now he had.

Could they be wrong?

"No, I don't think we're wrong" Russ said with resignation in his voice, "but I sure wish we were."

"Then I think we need to get the Chief and Detective James involved, first thing." Lara said with a pleading in her eyes. She was right, of course. Russ hadn't thought of it. His mind had been numb since the moment he saw the book under the table really. Now Lara's words were waking him up again.

"Yes, yes" Russ said, "Of course. I should call them tomorrow."

"I've already done that" Lara admitted awkwardly.

To her relief Russ wasn't upset by this, in fact, he seemed thankful.

"Well, that's done then" he said smiling, but it was only the mask. "I guess there's no turning back now" he said as he unconsciously rubbed his right deltoid. Somewhere deep in the vaults of Russ Personette's mind he was wondering where this case would lead, and what it would cost them, all of them.

Saturday morning came far too early for Russ and he wondered why Lara had arranged for an 8 AM meeting at Wildrose. There was a foot of fresh snow across the valley and far more up on "The Strathmorlick" as locals called the long ridge. The sky was a clear and perfect blue. The calm after the storm.

"Wouldn't 9 AM have been okay?" he hollered out through his vast new home, apparently now void of any of any other life forms. He knew Thorndike could hear him. He'd seen the cat's shadow the night before when he returned home. It had flitted through the darkened living room like a shadow in an old Boris Karloff movie, but Thorndike, that great soul, had remained aloof.

"I know you're lurking around here somewhere!" Russ hollered again, "Unless Benjamin Disraeli's been visiting and eating your Smalls™."

Smalls™ pet food was all Russ had been getting Thorndike for some time. Bernadette, the indefatigable Agent 36, had converted him to the brand with her enthusiasm for the product and her celebrity endorsements. Her own pet, a coal black Siamese cat named Lucifer, and Vivian Delashmett's little Westie, the aforementioned "Benjamin Disraeli," had both given Smalls™ their "paw of approval."

Russ prepared a pot of Stash™ Orange Spice tea, one of his favorites, and a pot of Folgers Classic Roast™ coffee for his soon-to-be-arriving "Cohort." He expected Lara, the handsome young detective, August James, and Eton Falls Chief of Police, Jim Ramsay, to start arriving at any minute, so he put some of "Bernadette's World-Famous Cinnamon Rolls™," as Russ insisted on calling them, into the oven.

The little "Puree Maker – Spy" would often drop off treats for Russ and Thorndike because, of course, Russ looked like he needed more treats! For this purpose, Agent 36 had drafted Dan Garn into building her a little lockbox of oak, with a cooler inside, next to the side-door at Wildrose. This way, if Russ were away she could put her treats into the lockbox and when Russ returned he'd be able to retrieve them easily. The two of them each had a key so whatever she put inside would stay secure.

Her "World-Famous Cinnamon Rolls™" were now warming up nicely and giving Wildrose an irresistibly homey scent.

Detective James was the first to arrive, parking his unmarked black Ford Crown Victoria, license plate AJV 804, at the farthest end of Russ's long parking lot, the end closest to the lake.

"You've got a beautiful Christmas tree there, Russ" he said as he shook himself from the cold. "We haven't even put ours up yet, my wife says there's some rule that no Christmas decorating can ever happen until after Thanksgiving. Never! Crazy, right?"

He wiped his feet twenty times on the floor mat inside the door and then, seeing Russ staring at him, he said, "What?"

"You're Mother raised you right, I'll say that for her" Russ laughed, "anyone who wipes their feet twenty times or brushes their teeth for two minutes or more, they were raised right."

"Well, I don't know how you do it" the Detective said, "but my Mother is one in a million and she did it right! That's for sure!"

"Here's your Folgers™, just the way you like it" Russ said as he handed the dashing 6' 3" detective his slightly cooled coffee. "I poured it out an hour ago to let it get cold!"

"Hallelujah" said the young man, "I don't know how you can drink that scalding brew, straight from your three-legged cauldron!"

The two men laughed together easily even though the detective had once suspected Russ of being a diabolical mastermind. As it had turned out, the late R. J. Kaiser had been the evil mastermind and Russ and Thorndike had helped prove it. The men had joined up and become part of a good, if unorthodox, crime-solving team. Russ, in time, had even discovered that August James had an eidetic memory. That was the formal way of saying the young man had a photographic memory and could remember things, even pages of text, indefinitely.[11]

"Before the rest of the gang gets here I wanted to thank you Russ."

For once there was no teasing in Detective James words or voice. He was sincere.

"What am I being thanked for?"

"Well, those Hollywood People seemed to like my screen-test and I've been given a part in an upcoming movie."

"That is fantastic" Russ said, shaking August by the hand. "I couldn't be happier for you."

"I owe it all to you, Russ. God knows I'd never have done anything like this without your encouragement."

"You are a natural, kid, with your Rudolph Valentino/young John Wayne good looks and" then Russ paused, "and your photographic memory, can you imagine memorizing lines?"

"I know" the young man said, showing his true excitement for the first time, "I've already gotten the entire script memorized."

"What kind of movie is it?" Russ asked seriously.

"In the 60's there was a comedy movie made that was called 'That Darn Cat'. The new movie has nothing to do with it, but the working title is called, 'That Darned Cat.' They want me to play a police detective from small-town America."[12]

"Congratulations" Russ said sincerely. "You are going to be a real hit, though I don't know how people will take to a movie about a cat!"

At that moment Chief Ramsay's Dodge Charger,

---

[11] From the Greek noun "eidos," refers to the ability to recall images, sounds, or events accurately. Merriam-Webster Dictionary.

[12] "That Darn Cat!" starring Hayley Mills, Dean Jones, and Roddy McDowell, 1965. A comedy movie based on the 1963 book "Undercover Cat" by Gordon and Mildred Gordon.

painted in the neon green, white, and black checkerboards, pulled in.

"You let them in and I'll get the cinnamon rolls out of the oven."

"Just one thing, Russ, don't say anything about this yet, okay?"

"You've got it Detective, it's your news!"

Russ knew Lara was going to be hitching a ride with Chief Ramsay, that had been his idea to deal with the snow-covered Hunter's Lane. At least, that was his excuse. The fiendish truth was sitting in Russ's garage, next to his pick-up. It was a new garnet-red Kia® Telluride™ 4-wheel drive, with a big red bow on it, and this time it *was* Lara's Christmas present. The front license plate said, "My Girl."

When he brought the platter of Cinnamon rolls out to the large, open living area of Wildrose and saw Lara bundled in her new coat, he was speechless.

"I love the way you look at me." She said, then gave Russ a warm kiss that made him feel thawed out despite the cold onset of a Vermont winter.

"Great tree you've got there, Russ" Chief Ramsay said, as he tried to help change the subject. "What is it, a Blue Spruce?"

"Yes" Russ said, "and all I can say is, never get a Spruce for a Christmas Tree. I gave a pint of blood on those sharp needles just decorating it." As he sat the cinnamon rolls down he added, "here's your treat and there's coffee and tea on the side-board, so make yourselves comfortable."

Everyone got their drink, a lovely gooey cinnamon roll, and found a chair arranged around the stylish Rosewood coffee table, then a sudden "thud-thud" announced the arrival of Thorndike to the proceedings. The big cat showed himself for the first time since Russ had found the mutilated history book, jumping to the arm of Russ's club chair.

They were all familiar with Thorndike's size, presence, and beauty, but Lara couldn't help to sing his praises again.

"He's more gorgeous than ever, no wonder Princess Charlotte loves him."

Princess Charlotte was Lara's little "Shelter Kitty."

"Okay, now that the Chairman has arrived, what kind of 'Cockamamie Soup Story' have you gotten us into this time, Professor?" Chief Ramsay said accusatorily. Then he added, "These cinnamon rolls are out-of-this-world!"

"Aren't they?" Lara said, "Did you know they are Bernadette's secret recipe?"

"I'm glad I'm not around cooking like this" Detective James said, "I wouldn't be able to resist it."

Russ had given up the effort of educating the two officers of the law on the subject of Scottish Cock-a-leekie Soup. He'd tried. Heaven knows he'd tried, but the two men simply couldn't resist making jokes about "Cockamamie Soup!"

"Alright you two ne'er-do-wells, if you can forget about the cinnamon rolls for a minute here's how I see our next mystery."

With this he brought out the book from under the Rosewood coffee table and opened it for all to see.

The claw marks were clearly visible in the middle of the page, looking like a tattered war zone. Everyone leaned in toward the book slowly. Thorndike looked away, clearly suffering from a sense of overwhelming guilt, Russ told himself.

"It remains difficult for me to believe Thorndike did this" Lara said, "but there seems to be no other alternative."

"This is definitely all Thorndike" Russ said in a tone of resignation, "either that or a Mountain Lion got loose in the History Building."

"I can't make many words out" Detective James admitted.

"Nor I" said Chief Ramsay, "although I'm ashamed to say that Scottish History isn't my strong suit."

The Detective lifted several pages gently then said,

"Your Gypsy-Fortune-Teller's talons have gone through twenty, twenty-four pages here. Whatever his plan was, he did it with feeling!"

Russ said, "The text quotes a Royal Order. It says, 'You are hereby ordered to fall upon the rebells, the McDonalds of Glenco, and put all to the sword under seventy. You are to have a speciall care that the old Fox and his sones doe upon no account escape your hands, you are to secure all the avenues that no man escape. This you are to putt in execution att five of the clock precisely; and by that time or very shortly after it, I'll strive to be att you with a stronger party: if I doe not come to you att five, you are not to tarry for me, but to fall on. This is by the Kings special command."

Silence followed Russ's quoting of the order.

"And you believe the Royal Order is a message from Thorndike, right?" Chief Ramsay said, looking from Russ to Lara and back again.

"Based on how he has communicated with us in the past that's what we believe" Lara said plainly.

"This order was given to Robert Campbell, commander of two companies of the Earl of Argyll's infantry regiment on February 12th, 1692, and they were the men who carried out the massacre at Glencoe, as ordered" Russ said.

"How terrible" Lara said quietly.

"So, there's a Campbell somewhere in the county and we have to stop him from killing MacDonald's. Is it really that straightforward?" Chief Ramsay asked.

"If only" mumbled Russ.

"If only? What do you mean?" Lara asked. "It is that straightforward isn't? Like the Chief said."

"I'm afraid it's a little more involved" Russ said wearily. "It's a complicated history, a really complicated history!"

Everyone's attention turned to Russ, and Detective James said, "You know, these cinnamon rolls really are fabulous, aren't they?"

"You bet" Chief Ramsay agreed, "addictive!"

Lara was about to say something when Russ raised his hand and, knowing her sense of humor, volunteered the information himself.

"Did you know they are Bernadette's World-Famous™ Cinnamon Rolls?"

Everyone laughed and Chief Ramsay shared a morsel with Thorndike, who seemed to know where the best odds of a handout were to be had.

"Yeeoww yip-yip" Thorndike added his proverbial "two-bits" to the conversation.

Russ just shook his head.

"That darned cat, whether it's bacon, Salmon in Lemon & Dill, or Bernadette's World-Famous™ Cinnamon Rolls, he gets his share."

After a moment Russ continued but the tension had been broken and he spoke much more freely.

"Although the order was to kill 'the McDonalds of Glenco,' the people who lived there were actually known as Clan Iain Abrach, or Clan MacIain for short."

"Then how's it considered a massacre of MacDonald's then?"

Chief Ramsay was on point.

"I've heard of the massacre of the Glencoe MacDonald's since childhood and I've never heard of Clan MacIain."

"Well, you're right, Chief. Few people look deeply enough into the massacre to get past the surface. That's why I said it was a complicated history. All the clans were made up of numerous families or lines. Some married into a clan and some joined themselves to a clan for protection, by swearing an oath of loyalty. All the families who joined through marriage or confederation are called the 'septs,' or members of the clan. Some branches of a clan were established by sons, as they received their own areas and offspring and septs developed around them too. This is the case with Clan MacIain. The clan descends, many generations earlier, from Iain, also called John, who was the great-grandson of the original Donald, from whom all the MacDonald's take their clan's name. Iain was given two nicknames, Fraoch, meaning 'of the Heather' and 'Abrach,' the root of the word Lochaber, the area where he spent many years.

"Your own clan, Clan Ramsay, had several distinct branches even as early the 1200's. The Ramsays of Dalhousie remain to this day and the Chief of Clan Ramsay is a man with your exact name, James Ramsay, of Dalhousie. Other branches included at that time the Ramsays of Clatto, of Auchterhouse, of Forfar and of Banff."

"So the Chief's namesake is the head of the worldwide Ramsay Clan?" Detective James asked.

"Exactly, the MacDonald's were a huge Scottish Clan too, with several branches in different areas, and the MacDonald's of Glencoe were actually members of Clan MacIain, the descendants of Iain MacDonald, called Fraoch, as I said."

"You're right Russ, it is a little complicated isn't it?" Lara said with her bewitching smile.

"So" Chief Ramsay started again, "there's a Campbell somewhere in the county and we have to stop him from harming the MacIains. Is that it?"

"Ick-ick-ick" said Thorndike emphatically, before abandoning them completely and vanishing silently into the branches of the old oak high above.

"Either the Gypsy Fortune-Teller just developed allergies or he disagrees with my summary, Russ. Which is it?"

"Eileen calls that sound a 'chirp' but I think you're right Chief, I think Thorndike is telling us were still not getting it."

Detective James had been digesting the words and looking over the pages of the book constantly since Russ had first shown it to them. Now he said something that shocked everyone.

"I have an idea I want you all to think about" the young man said soberly. "First, we know Thorndike has never destroyed a book before, and this book is definitely ruined. But what if he didn't do it to express violence or anger? What if it were the only way he could communicate with us this time. If he only wanted us to see certain words this would be the only way to actually highlight them?"

Here he paused and looked around the table.

"Listen" he continued, "if what I'm saying makes sense, this is the actual message Thorndike was trying to make. These are the only words that survived his destruction, 'You are hereby ordered to fall upon...the old Fox...upon no account escape your hands.'"

At that very moment a loud "Yeeoww" of obvious affirmation echoed through the branches and cast-iron rafters overhead.

"There's no mistaking that" the Chief said.

Russ looked at Detective James with an expression of reverence.

"Brilliant Detective."

"But what does that mean?" Lara asked. "Does that mean we have no names to go by at all, just 'the old Fox'?"

"If that's the case, then we don't stand a chance" Chief Ramsay added.

"I think Detective James is right, completely" Russ said, "but I believe we still have to assume the names in the order apply to our mystery. So that means, until we know better, that our criminal is a Campbell and our victim, called 'the old Fox,' is a MacIain."

"The only problem is, there are no MacIains listed in Chittenden county." Detective James said as he looked up from his smart phone.

"None?" questioned the Chief.

"Not one" emphasized the Detective.

"How many Campbells?" asked Lara.

"Over a hundred."

"How many 'Robert Campbells'?" Russ asked. "That's

who carried out the order."

"This will take a minute" the Detective said, and he meant, literally, a minute.

"Five" he said promptly. "Robert Campbell, Sr., 70 years old, Burlington. Robert Bob Campbell, 56, of Underhill. Rob Roy Campbell, 32, of Charlotte. Robby Campbell, Jr., 50, of Eton Falls. And last but not least, Robert M. Campbell, 43, of Milton."

"Well, it's a starting point, and it's a lot more than we had an hour ago" Chief Ramsay said with satisfaction. Then he remembered something, "Oh, I almost forgot." He got up and retrieved something from inside his coat.

"A Christmas present from the missus and me. Something to put under that spectacular tree of yours."

The gift was obviously a book of some sort. Russ could feel it was a paperback, a thin volume, maybe 150 pages. His guess was a book on some point of local history or a fiction, most likely a mystery.

"Thank you" Russ said sincerely as he rose out of the club chair. "I've got a little something for you too, Chief."

He went to the mantle where he had several Christmas stockings and digging deeply in one he pulled out two envelopes.

"I hope this will make your Christmas a little merrier" he said, as he handed one to each of the law enforcement officers he counted as friends.

"You must have given me Detective James by mistake, Russ, this says 'numbskull' on it" Chief Ramsay laughed.

"Hahaha" the Detective said, "Russ sure got that right!"

When they were preparing to leave, each with a bag of cinnamon rolls, August James said, "I'll do a full investigation of the names we've discussed and get back to you."

After they left, Russ said mischievously, "Now we have to go to the garage for your present!"

# CHAPTER FOUR
## The Trouble with Names

"Hey Russ, did you hear the latest news?" It was Dr. Mariell Thompson, Charbonneau College's newest History Professors. She stood in the doorway just as she had the week before, only this time she wasn't holding a newspaper.

"What's this, déjà vu?" he said curiously.[13] "Didn't you ask me the same thing last week?"

Mariell laughed but continued as he watched her.

"It's our boss, Dr. Dudley!" She said excitedly.

Russ sat at his desk just as he had the previous Thursday when she had told him about Dan Garn winning the big poetry award. This time he was paying full attention.

---

[13] A French phrase meaning "already seen". Source: wikipedia
*The clan tartan shown above is generally called "The MacDonald of Glencoe Tartan" today. "It was found on the bodies exhumed" years after the massacre for reburial in consecrated ground. Source wikipedia – see MacDonald of Glencoe.

"No" he answered the question she asked the week before, "I haven't read the paper." Now he said, "What about Dr. Dudley?"

"He proposed to Suzanne and she said 'yes'."

"Really?" Russ said in shock. "That's wonderful."

Having gotten recently engaged himself, Russ could immediately identify with Roger Dudley. Their "boss," as Mariell had referred to him, had suffered several setbacks before Russ came to Vermont. Roger had been passed over numerous times by their former boss, the late and infamous R. J. Kaiser. When Russ's friend, Arnold, had selected Dr. Dudley to head the college's History Department the older man was nearly speechless. Russ couldn't have been happier for him. Roger, however, had quite erroneously laid the credit for all his good fortune at Russ's door and, say what he might, nothing could change the new boss's view.

"What are you planning on doing for them?" Russ asked Mariell.

"Me?" she said surprised, "I'm the new kid-on-the-block. I should be asking you that question."

That was true enough, but Russ hadn't wanted to step on her toes if she'd already had plans in the works.

The Thanksgiving Holiday had begun the prior Friday afternoon for students and some faculty. Dr. Charles Duncan, the last member of the Charbonneau College History Department, had flown out of Burlington International Airport that night. Dr. Dudley had left on Saturday, apparently in company with his new fiancé, to be with his family in Bennington. Lara had the week off.

Russ had come in bright and early Monday morning to finish all his grading and recording and to prepare his upcoming finals tests. He planned on being off the remainder of the week.

"Well, I'll get him a lottery ticket" Russ said with a laugh.

"I've heard of your magic with lottery tickets and if you

ever want to get one for me I'd be happy to accept."

"I'll bet. If I know odds I could probably buy another thousand tickets and not get one five-dollar winner."

Mariell was pleasant company and the two laughed easily together at Russ's joke. That was when Russ heard a familiar voice down the hall. It was Nathan Williams.

"Hello" he said to Mariell. "Do you know where I could find Professor Personette's office.

"I can go you one better" the young woman said casually, "I can show you the Professor and his office." She said, while pointing her index finger in toward Russ.

Nathan was instantly attracted to the young History professor and while thanking her he took the effort to introduce himself. When Mariell asked him what he did Nathan didn't hesitate.

"I'm a writer" he said. "In fact, I have my first three books right here if you'd like to see them."

"I would" she answered matter-of-factly.

The two young people were both in their latter-twenties and though they knew nothing about each other, Russ knew they both shared many of the same interests. Both were academically minded but casual, with great senses of humor, they enjoyed history, writing, learning, the outdoors, and snowmobiling. These were just a few of the facts Russ had gleaned from Dr. Mariell Thompson in the short time he'd known her, and all this matched with Arnold and Rhonda's eldest son.

"Hi Uncle Russ, I brought you your Christmas presents early."

"Uncle?" Mariell said surprised. "And here I had Professor P marked down as a moody-loner with an eye for the ladies."

"No way" Nathan answered with a winning smile, "he's always been my hero."

With this he opened his backpack and pulled out a plastic bag full of books.

"This is my first one" Nathan said proudly.

"Platinum Blonde – An Autobiography, by Vivian Delashmett with Nathaniel Williams." Mariell read out loud, then she said, "Impressive cover and about 400 pages, wow."

"Eileen says sales are brisk, Uncle Russ."

"That's wonderful, Nathan. How's Vivian taking the news?"

"She's happy about it, you know, but not like she was in the beginning. In fact, I don't think she's feeling very good."

Nathan said these words without thought, without suspicion, but Russ was immediately worried and though he had no bracing chill race up his spine to settle in his neck, he knew he'd be contacting Vivian soon.

"What's next?" Mariell asked.

"This is the next one" Nathan said, "The Delashmett Legacy – Tribute to an American Family."

"So it's out now, huh?" Russ said with satisfaction. "Congratulations Nathan, you've been busy."

"And Vivian has signed all of them for you, Uncle Russ."

"I'm honored."

"Well, maybe a girl could check one of them out sometime, just to see your writing style."

"That would be fine" Russ said. He was always glad to share books with people who loved to read.

"Eileen sent me an author's copy of the last one, it won't be out for a couple months." Here he laid the largest of the three books on the table.

"It's called an oversized portfolio or coffee-table book with beautiful photographs of the manor house and the estate grounds" Nathan said, as he stepped backward so they could look at it more easily.

"Caledonia: An American Estate," by Nathan Williams, Photographs by Daphne Briggs." Mariell read out loud.

"That's great, you got Daphne to do the photographs" Russ said happily.

"Well, you know, she's a great painter so she has a real eye for what will make a good photographic composition."

"Those pictures are spectacular" Mariell admitted with a tinge of surprise in her voice. "When you said 'coffee-table book' I had no idea the photographs would be so breathtaking. What an incredible place. And this is around here?"

"Yeah, about 7 miles as the crow flies" Nathan said, pointing south, "straight out Whistling Duck Road."

"Whistling Duck, really? Wouldn't Quacking Duck be more accurate?" Mariell laughed.

"Exactly" Nathan agreed wholeheartedly, "that's just what I said to Vivian, word for word."

The two young people stood staring at each other for a moment, surprised to find another person who thought the same way.

"And your text is bold enough to be easily read, Nathan. What font is it?" Russ asked curiously.

"The publisher recommended 'Calibri,' but I chose 'Baskerville Old Face.' I didn't want the modern look, you know?"

"To Russ" Mariell read from the inscription in the front of "Platinum Blonde." "The man to whom I owe my life, a man who can be trusted and entrusted! A thousand thanks. Vivian Q. Delashmett" she finished.

"That is an amazing inscription. You don't read that kind of thing every day." Mariell said sincerely. Then she boldly asked, "Are all the stories about you true?"

Before Russ had an opportunity to play down rumors Nathan blurted out, "And then some!"

To the young man's credit he caught himself immediately but there was no way to "un-spill" the milk.

"Has Daphne seen this yet?" Russ asked, letting Mariell's prying question go with Nathan's answer alone.

"Oh yeah, she helped with the set-up and lay-out. I could do the writing but I wouldn't have made it nearly as nice without her help. And Vivian has adopted her too."

When Nathan left and Mariell returned to her office Russ put the books into his old English-made "Hanshaws® Satchel and thought to himself how impressive the three books were.

Russ had helped Dr. Dudley and Nathan get their works to Eileen, bless her heart, but they'd done the real work. He had been proud when Roger's book had been chosen for publication and he was even prouder now with Nathan. The fact that Daphne had done the photography thrilled Russ. He knew that successes like that were so good for the young and he knew better than most how much Daphne had gone through in the past.

Daphne was in New York at the moment, staying as Eileen's guest in a fine high-rise apartment overlooking Central Park. As he drove home that evening he was thankful that success had come to two of the young people he'd tried to help. He determined then and there to send the young woman a surprise congratulations and he also promised himself he'd reward Eileen appropriately, at long last, for all her efforts.

She had done so much and with the sale of movie rights for his second book, "Emancipator – The Heroic Life and Tragic Death of a Civil War Soldier," he had what felt like unlimited resources.

With his growing bank account Russ rebuilt Wildrose and purchased the big Lincoln Mark LT pick-up. He'd also purchased the little cabin he and Thorndike used to live in, the place on End Road. He now rented it to Lara's son, Charlie, at a good price. He bought Daphne's 8 x 6-foot painting of the snow-capped Elkhorn Mountains in Northeast Oregon, which now hung in his living room not far from the portrait of Thorndike that had been taken when he won a blue ribbon at the Vermont Fancy Felines™ Cat Show. The purchase of the painting had been accomplished by Russ's alter-ego, Donald Frobisher, but too many people had become aware of Mr. Frobisher's true identity.

Russ needed a new alias now and it had to be someone nobody could connect with him. This latter task hadn't proved easy. Russ's connection to Mr. Frobisher had lasted decades and was far more sentimental than he had realized. His first thought was to create a Mr. MacPherson, which was his original Scottish Clan, but there were some who knew about this connection too, and it wouldn't be difficult for them to put two-and-two together. He told himself it would have been perfect though. George MacPherson was his 6th Great-Grandfather. He had fought in the Jacobite Risings to restore Scotland's deposed King James to the throne and when the rebellion was crushed he had been the man who'd changed the family name to Personette. Russ thought he would have been a good choice for an alias, if others didn't already know about the MacPherson connection. George's cousin, Ewan MacPherson, who'd gone down in history as the famous outlaw "Cluny MacPherson," would have been an even better choice. It was a pity that neither of these alter-egos were an option.

Russ had been looking into the possibility of purchasing the old Sacajawea Hotel. His attorney, Alexis Stonecipher, had notified him regarding the opportunity. The family who'd owned the beautiful old building for over fifty years had not been reinvesting in its upkeep, with the result that business, and profits, continued to dwindle. The family was ready to sell and he'd promised Alexis a new alias soon, so the purchase could be made incognito, as it were. Ronald Fernsby had come to mind, out of the thin-blue as it were, and Russ felt a strong pull to the name mainly because there were only 21 Fernsby's left in the whole world. It seemed a tragedy to let the name vanish without some final, grand flourish. It was just this kind of sentimentality in Russ that surprised people.

As he drove north up Hunters Lane in the growing darkness he again gave thanks for the big truck with sure traction and made his decision.

"Ronald Fernsby it is!"

It had begun snowing heavily again by the time he arrived home and when he unlocked the door and walked in he hollered, "Ronald Fernsby is home."

He laughed at his own joke, as he so often did, and saw the shadow of his roommate flit across the room.

"Oh yeah, you big coward. You were okay when all your friends were here. You could come out then."

At that moment Russ's phone went to buzzing in his coat pocket.

"Hello" Russ said facetiously, "is this the party to whom I am speaking?" He knew full well that the caller was Detective James.

"Not a MacIain to be found anywhere" the Detective said with the weary voice of a man who has looked under every stone in the county. "But I've got Campbell's jumping around me like Nebraska Jack Rabbits!"

"That's a problem" Russ admitted. "How about criminal records on those Robert Campbells?" Secretly Russ had already concluded that their killer would be one of the Robert Campbells and likely in the 30 or 40 age group.

"Squeaky clean."

"Squeaky clean" Russ repeated, "nothing?"

"Nothing Professor, any ideas where we go from here?"

In the beginning it had looked straightforward. Thorndike's clues had pointed at a Campbell villain and MacIain victims. Now he didn't really know where to go next.

"Let me look at it again, Detective, and I'll send you a text if I come up with any brainstorms tonight."

After he hung up his mind was uneasy. What was it? He wondered. As he put the tea water on, filled Thorndike's clean bowl with some Smalls™ pet food, and sprinkled it with bits of bacon, one word came to his mind.

"Nebraska."

What was it with that word? Nebraska. Russ remembered telling Arnold that he was surprised R. J.

Kaiser had hired him because he only had my master's degree and everyone else was a doctor.

"They're like jack rabbits in Nebraska" Russ had said.

Now, out of the blue, Detective August James had made a similar reference.

"That can't be a common saying here in Vermont, out west, yeah, but not back here. They don't even have Jack Rabbits here."

Then two things happened virtually simultaneously. First, Russ noticed that Thorndike wasn't eating, he was just sitting on the kitchen floor staring at him. Second, a chill ran up Russ's spine so powerfully he actually shivered.

Russ ran to the large living room of Wildrose, where he'd left his phone. Detective James' mention of Jack Rabbits had triggered something deep in Russ's brain and, if he was right, Thorndike had used their telepathic connection to complete the message.

"Detective, you don't have Jack Rabbits here in Vermont, do you?"

It was probably the craziest question Russ had ever asked anyone.

"No, we've got Cottontails in the valleys and shoreline and Snowshoe Hare in the forests and highlands. What's this all about Russ?"

"Well, I thought I was being clever identifying MacIains instead of looking for MacDonald's, but your talk about Jack Rabbits, and a little help from Thorndike, made me realize that names are different wherever you live. Names change and develop. What I'm trying to say is, while I had you looking for MacIains, I already knew of a whole bunch of MacKean's right here in Chittenden County. Harley Shaw told me he was descended from the MacKean Line."

"But are they the same clan, Russ? The names are nothing alike."

"Yes, the names look very different, but if you sound them out they're the same name, and the same clan. I should have thought of that. As the MacIains moved around the world their name was spelled other ways. MacKean, McKean, MacKeen, even McCain, and MacKane.

"Well, like you said, we've got MacKeans all over the county. I'm married to one, in fact."

"I know" Russ said, "and I should have thought of it, names develop and change."

"But there's only one MacKean I've ever heard called a fox, Russ. If we're still going with the words Thorndike left legible in your history book."

Detective James voice was troubled. Russ could hear the fear, as if he were afraid he'd be too late. Then he quoted the words again.

"You are hereby ordered to fall upon...the old Fox...upon no account escape your hands."

"Who have you heard called the fox?" Russ asked.

"You said his name, Harley Shaw. You know he's an amazing dancer right?"

Russ had heard something of Harley's dancing skills but nothing had prepared him for what he saw from the diminutive Octogenarian during the night he and Lara celebrated their engagement. Harley and his wife, Fiona, were the stars of the dance floor that night, and Russ could honestly say he'd never seen a smoother dancer than Harley Shaw.

"That's why they call him 'the Fox,' for his dancing."

"Detective" Russ said soberly. "I think you'd better have someone check on Harley."

"I'm on it!"

When Russ turned, Thorndike was sitting in the doorway to the dining room staring at him.

"Buddy" Russ said sadly, "I don't want to believe that."

If Russ's senses were right, Thorndike already knew they were too late. He struggled with the possibility that Harley Shaw was dead. One part of him argued there was no way Thorndike could know such things. It reasoned that telepathy was impossible, regardless of what Edward

Thorndike may have said, and Harley Shaw would be the last person anyone would want to kill. Another part of him knew better than to doubt Thorndike. It argued that the big cat had already provided too many proofs to be questioned.

As he made his tea he paused. If he'd only remembered sooner that Harley's "MacKean Line" was the same as Clan MacIain, they would have had time to save the treasured historian/dancer/wind surfer/friend.

Even the cheery combination of his brightly lit and decorated Christmas tree, the beautiful music of a Mannheim Steamroller's® "Christmas Extraordinaire" album, and a relaxing cup of Stash's™ Orange Spice tea wasn't enough to lift Russ's spirits.[14]

He sat in the large living room looking out into the darkness of a Vermont winter evening, with the snow falling gently past the soft yellow light of the colonial lampposts that lit the front of Wildrose.

Thorndike sensed Russ's turmoil and quietly joined him, jumping up on his lap. For a moment, the cat and the man considered each other in silence, and then the cat lifted one large front paw and placed it on Russ's chest. It was something Thorndike had done before, early in their friendship, just before a murder.

"He's missing" was all Detective James said, when Russ answered the phone.

"Missing?" Russ stammered in disbelief.

"Fiona, his wife, said he went windsurfing this morning. He's always home before dinner."

"Windsurfing?" Russ nearly shouted. "Are you kidding me, with snow coming down?"

"It's Harley we're talking about, remember? He's the oldest member of 'The Starbuck Valley Polar Bear Club' you know. They call themselves 'The Plungers' and a Polar Bear holding a bathroom plunger is the Club Logo!"

---

[14] Mannheim Steamroller, "Christmas Extraordinaire" Album ©2001

Russ knew this already. He'd purchased one of "The Plungers' sweatshirts at a fundraising dinner to support their charity efforts.

"Did Fiona know where he was going?"

"She gave us his usual spots but nothing has turned up. He's overdue getting home and that's not like him."

"Oh no" Russ said.

"He could just be late, flat tire or something, you know."

Russ realized Detective James was right. So many things could have caused Harley a delay. A flat tire, sliding off a snowy, icy road or getting stuck. It still seemed crazy to Russ that Harley would windsurf in Northern Vermont during the week of Thanksgiving, but there too the Detective was right again. They were talking about Harley. He was the antithesis of an elderly man in virtually every way, and not just in his continued interests and hobbies, but in continuing to find new adventures too.

Russ remembered his initial shock when he found Harley hunched over the motor of an Aston Martin DB5 right there on his farm near Jericho. Even when he was a younger man Harley was willing to buy a car with a steering wheel on the wrong side and a motor no one in Vermont had ever worked on.

In the end he called Lara and while Thorndike slept on his lap, Russ sipped his Orange Spice tea and discussed arrangements for Thanksgiving with the love of his life. He would pick Lara and Veronica up at 6 PM at Lara's house, they would swing by the rental cabin on End Road and get Charlie, then drive out Lone Mountain Road the Arnold and Rhonda's. Russ was looking forward to it and having the Lincoln Mark LT pickup meant that driving around in Vermont, in the winter, was no longer a worry. Russ made sure he said nothing about Harley Shaw. No matter what he didn't want to trouble Lara.

"Tomorrow we can cross whatever bridge we have to" he told himself. "For now, let her have all the peace she can."

"Je t'aime" Lara said in her lovely French accent. It meant "I love you" and Russ always replied, "Je t'aime," although he was more than aware his pronunciation left a lot to be desired.

After hanging up, and still trying to keep his mind from worrying about Harley, Russ pulled out one the books Nathan had given him that morning. "Platinum Blonde – An Autobiography, by Vivian Delashmett with Nathaniel Williams" he read out loud to Thorndike. "It has impressive cover and about 400 pages" he continued, trying to quote Mariell Thompson's comments from that morning as closely as possible.

"Chapter One, Humble Beginnings" he began reading. He was surprised by how humble Vivian's beginnings really were and he found Nathan's writing style refreshingly direct but also informative.

Thorndike stretched when he heard that Vivian had begun cooking at a mining camp in Idaho when she was only 15, but he didn't open his eyes, not even when Russ read about a mine collapse. "I'll read you one chapter a night" he said to the cat who was feigning sleep. He knew Thorndike so well that he could tell when the big cat was hooked and the book, "Platinum Blonde," had captured Thorndike's curiosity.

"I wonder if it's the subject matter or the writing style that gets him?" Russ thought to himself. "Or is it just the sound of my voice?"

"We're still getting snow" Russ said as he rose and sat Thorndike back in the warm club chair. He stood looking out on the mesmerizing scene, almost carried away by the Holidays and the beauty of northern Vermont, even on a dark winter's evening. His students were all home with family for the Thanksgiving break and Russ, who'd spent several of the last Thanksgivings alone in Ohio, would be spending it with his new and growing family. A lot had changed in a single year. As he stood looking out the tall windows of Wildrose he was suddenly aware of how much he had to be thankful for.

He'd come to Vermont with his 1998 Mercury Grand Marquis, a trunk full of his last remaining possessions, some books he couldn't give up, clothes that were almost all a decade old but still looked and fit nicely, two boxes of cherished photographs, the last evidence of his former, happy life, and a couple thousand dollars. Not much to show for a long life and yet, perhaps, his wonderful memories made him among the richest of men.

"Who can take it with them in the end, anyway?" he said philosophically. Yet, there was no reassuring "yip" or throaty "yeeoww" from Thorndike, no warm hand or comforting word from a loving wife. There was just the quiet music in the background and the sound of silence outside.

Russ turned and looked out every window in Wildrose's expansive living area and the view was identical. Snow fell vertically, the unbelievably large flakes falling so slowly it almost seemed like a reduced gravity environment.

"We're living in a snow globe" he said to the soundly sleeping Thorndike. "I said, the Starbuck Valley is a Snow Globe! Greta was right about this place!" he repeated loudly. The quiet, melodic music continued on.

"You really are a great listener" he said facetiously, staring down at his big buddy, roommate, partner-in-crime, and on-again-off-again tormentor.

Russ Personette had worked hard not to think about his friend, Harley Shaw, and he had succeeded surprisingly well, at least for a while. Harley had "adopted" Russ from the first time the two men met at the Eton Falls Senior Center. Russ had been "volunteered" by Lara's Great-Aunt Virginia "to help serve," but he soon discovered that the experience had served him far better than anything he did for his elders.

The amazing people he'd gotten to know and the many fascinating life-stories he'd heard on that first visit kept him coming back whenever his schedule allowed.

Harley Shaw, folk-historian-extraordinaire, was also a square dancer of wide repute, as Detective James had already confirmed. He was also a Lake Champlain "ice sailor" who held the DN ice-speed record. The single-seat, tri-runner, handcrafted sailing "boats" were called "DN's" for some reason that no one could, or would, tell Russ.

A blurry Polaroid photograph of the little man in a bright yellow, neoprene wet suit holding a surfboard still hung near the front door of the Orchard Café, proof of his undisputed skill as a windsurfer.

One of the interests the two men shared was scuba diving. While Russ had usually plied the warmer waters of the world, Harley had mastered the chilly environment of Lake Champlain.

"You know I've been diving here since the 50's, when the first good wetsuits came out. One of these day's I'm gonna find a sunken treasure!" Harley had beamed that perfect smile and said, "Golden Doubloons, 'tousands of them'!"

Those last three words, "tousands of them," was another line from "The Quiet Man" with John Wayne and Maureen O'Hara. It was one of Russ's all-time favorite movies, but it was Harley Shaw's undisputed favorite. In fact, the little man peppered his speech with constant bits and pieces of the movie's best-known lines. His most-used line was "a good stretch of the legs," which was John Wayne's line when Maureen O'Hara left him behind and he was forced to walk five miles home.

Russ had found the little man to be absolutely amazing and even though the coming year would have been his 96th birthday celebration, the proud member of the "Jericho Chapter" of the Green Mountain Nonagenarian's Club™, had absolutely no intention of slowing down.

When Russ had gone to see Harley at his farm the diminutive "Jack-of-all-trades" had told him and Thorndike, "Yeah, once I get this car running, my next challenge is to jump out of a perfectly good airplane."

The "car" Harley spoke of was a 1963 Aston Martin DB5, the "James Bond Car", as Russ called it, and less than 60 seconds later it had been Thorndike who fixed the car. Harley's whole body shook as he laughed at his luck.

"I'm gonna be the laughingstock of Starbuck Valley! They'll say I'm that Blue Grass Seed Farmer who needed the big cat to fix his foreign car."

With the car running Harley had kept his word before the end of summer, when he jumped out of a perfectly good 1961 Cessna® 185 Skywagon over the Pine Valley.

When Russ once asked Harley his secret for staying young the great-Nephew of Ernestine MacKean-Lyon-Findley said, "Never stop movin,' you gotta keep on goin' as fast as you can, as long as you can! Keep trying and learning new things. Humans are just like Sharks, Russ, you know this. If we stop movin' we die."

Russ had indeed heard that some species of shark had to keep moving in order to get oxygen from the water but he'd never researched it to find out how true it was.[15]

Despite his wonderful memories of Harley, the reminiscences failed to comfort him. "Russ's trouble," as Eileen called it, was his impatience for news. He had always liked to have his Christmas presents early and wanted to know what was going on as early as possible. He found it difficult to wait for news.

It was almost 10 PM when Russ's phone began buzzing and he braced himself for what he was about to hear. He already knew it would be tragic, it would be the details of the thing that would drive home the horror and the wrongness of it all.

Even as he picked up the phone he thought to himself,

---

[15] This is indeed true. "Two dozen of the 400 identified shark species are required to maintain this forward swimming motion" in order to breath. They will literally "drown if they stop swimming." Source: animals.howstuffworks.com.

"What reason would anyone have to Kill Harley Shaw?"

"Russ" came a loud voice across the line, "is that you?"

"No" he answered roughly, "It's Mark Twain!"

Russ invariably used Mark Twain for moments like this. Whether it was Eileen, Arnold, or Detective James, if they asked that question they would find themselves talking to Mark Twain. Why Russ did this no one knew, least of all him.

Another of his "telephone habits" was when making a call he'd say "Hello, is this the party to whom I am speaking?"

His was a strange mind in many ways but he told himself he was different; in that he had the good sense to admit it.

The loud voice continued without pause, backed up by a symphony of sirens and heavy wind.

"We found him, Russ!"

"Here it comes" Russ thought.

"Silly guy took the backroads home. He was at Sand Bar State Park and headed back through Cozy Corner. He was headed for Long Pass, just north of you, when he hit black ice. He's okay though."

"Harley's alive?" Russ was in total shock. Everything he'd gotten from Thorndike had made him certain of the outcome.

Detective James was almost yelling over the noise around him. "Yeah, he's cold and hungry, says he missed his wife's dinner, but he's okay, Russ. Can you hear me?"

"Bring him here, Detective." Russ hollered through the phone. "If you're near Long Pass, then I'm the closest help. We'll get him warmed up and fed. I'll call his wife and let her know he's okay."

Russ couldn't believe it. Harley was okay. He rushed through the house getting everything ready but Thorndike was nowhere to be seen.

He took a container of the "Portage LaPlatte Hearty Beef & Barley Stew" he regularly purchased from the Old Homestead Pub and began heating some on the stove.

This was the same stew he enjoyed with Arnold and Rhonda when he first arrived in Vermont and he knew it would warm his friend up fast. He also laid out his heavy US Navy, dark blue and yellow sweatshirt and sweatpants and a pair of his Wigwam® Merino Comfort Socks on the bed in the guest bedroom. An extra pair of Sorel® Men's Dude Moc™ slippers sat on the floor by the bed. Russ put one of the white terrycloth robes he reserved for visitors in the adjoining bathroom.

By the time he returned to the large living area of Wildrose and put another log on the fire in the orange brick fireplace, a police Dodge Charger pulled in.

A Deputy hustled the small man wrapped in a gray wool blanket into Wildrose and Russ thanked him.

"He's all yours Professor, Detective's orders!"

"I've got him, Officer, thank you."

Harley was bedraggled and shivering but he was alive and Russ was happy to see it. He had been in such turmoil, fearing the worst about his friend, and now he was just thankful to be wrong. He still didn't know how he'd misunderstood Thorndike but that deliberation would be for another day. In the meantime Russ led Harley straight into the guest bedroom and showed him the shower.

"Fiona knows you're alright, Harley" he said. "Now you take a long, hot shower, you're chilled to the bone."

Harley only nodded but Russ could hear his teeth chattering.

Russ couldn't help himself. His curiosity was just too great, and so he asked his friend, "Harley, what on earth could make you go windsurfing today?"

With great difficulty Harley Shaw replied, "I thought...it would be...my last chance...with open water!"

That kind of summed up Harley's whole philosophy of life, Russ thought, and as he closed the door he just shook his head.

"I hope when I'm 90 years old I'm half the man you are Harley!"

Forty minutes later the little man came sheepishly out of Russ's guest suite and made his way to the dining room.

He looked like a caricature of a man who'd shrunk inside his clothes as Russ's sweatshirt, pants, and slippers were all far too big for Harley, but he was warm and dry.

"Thanks for your hospitality" he said, his old humor returning after his near-death experience.

"Our pleasure" Russ said, as he pointed to the table where Thorndike sat in the chair at the end.

"Now have a seat and I'll serve you up some of the Old Homestead's Beef & Barley Stew."

Harley hadn't been eating long when Detective James' unmarked black Ford Crown Victoria, license plate AJV 804, pulled in to Wildrose parking lot and slid to a stop.

"Come in Detective, how much snow did they have up on Long Pass?"

"Two feet and still falling" then, as he wiped his feet he saw Harley eating in the dining room.

"You were a lucky man to survive that crash, Harley, I'm afraid I can't say the same for your S-10 though."

Russ was still shocked that Harley was alive. He was confused by Thorndike's apparent mistake, the first Russ knew of from the big cat, but there was something bothering him. Was it truly an accident or was it an attempted murder gone awry? That was what Russ really wanted to know. This information would tell them all if Harley was truly safe. If not, there would be a "next" attempt coming. Detective James seemed to know exactly what Russ was thinking.

"It was a 2003" Harley said matter-of-factly. "Gave its life for the cause, I guess." Then he added, "This is some good stew, Russ, I need to take the missus to the Old Homestead more often."

"Can you tell us if your truck was acting normally before the accident?"

"Yup, no problems there, Detective, until I hit that ice. I should've gone home on Interstate 89. It goes right down to the University of Vermont Jericho Research Forest and I live just beyond, up the Onion River Road then right on Skunk Hollow. I would've been home four hours ago and still had a truck, and I wouldn't have worried my wife and everybody."

"These things happen" Russ said, "we're just glad you made it out alive."

"That's right" Detective James said, "a truck is a small price to pay, under the circumstances. When I saw the cliff you went over and your Chevy upside down in the river I thought you were a goner for sure."

From his seat at the head of the table Thorndike had been staring at Russ for several minutes.

"Hey Harley, I don't mean to be a snoop but I was wondering if you have any MacKean relative your family calls, 'the Fox'?"

"You mean, besides me, Russ?" Harley chuckled and his whole body shook inside the large US Navy sweatshirt. Then he said, "There's just one, although they have a lot of other names for him too."

# CHAPTER FIVE
## Death Knocks Twice

"I could've told you about John MacKean" Chief Ramsay said, staring over his Lismore™ Crystal Whiskey Glass by Waterford®. Neither Russ nor the Chief were heavy alcohol drinkers but they both enjoyed the husky feel of the traditional Irish whiskey glasses, filled with ice and the Old Homestead's Orchard Cove Cider™.

"I'd say he's two-parts crusader and one-part scoundrel, but that's just my personal opinion. I guess, under the circumstances, I should say 'he was'".

The official line between law enforcement and Russ Personette had been blurred out of all recognition, and not just with the Eton Falls Police. The FBI was in no position to point fingers either, having utilized the services of Russ, and Thorndike as well.

So it was that Chief Ramsay's first stop on Tuesday

morning was Wildrose, where enlightened conversation and an excellent glass of "cider on the rocks" were always on tap.

"It looks like suffocation. The preliminary examination shows both bruising around the mouth and nose as well as bloodshot eyes. The blood test will confirm it by noon, or so they're telling me."

"And the whole time I was thinking it was Harley" Russ said emphatically. "Thorndike, bless his longsuffering heart, did everything he could do to show me who it would be and I still managed to miss the signals. Lucky I don't work for the railroad I guess."

"Well, the science of, what did you call it again?"

"Telepathic Animal-Human Communications" Russ said wearily. He knew very well how much his theories sounded like the "Cockamamie Soup" to the two men who loved making jokes at his expense.

"Yeah" the Chief continued, a broad smile playing about his strong face, "the science of Telepathic Animal-Human Communications isn't really, well, off the launchpad yet is it? So you have to give yourself a little room to maneuver, Russ."

The Chief was right, of course he was, and he knew it.

"Yes" Russ said, "but if all I do is look at the history book Thorndike vandalized I should have known. The Chief of Clan MacIain wasn't named 'Harley Shaw.' He was named Iain MacIain, and 'Iain' in Scotland at that time is 'John' in English. John MacIain, or John MacKean in our case, was the man Thorndike identified."

"That's the trouble with names, Russ. That's what you're always trying to teach Detective James and me about, right?"

A shrill "Yeeoww" came the branches above, providing Thorndike's proverbial "two-bits" in the conversation.

"Yeah" the Chief said happily, "like Thorndike says!"

"I guess so" Russ said awkwardly. "I know I'm thankful to be wrong and I'm glad Harley is still with us."

"I think we could all second that, Russ. If this community had put it to a vote between Harley Shaw and his cousin, John MacKean, it would have been unanimous."

"So he was killed in his sleep?"

"Well, yes, he fought back as best he could, but you have to remember, he was Harley's cousin and, at almost 90-years-old, he couldn't have been much trouble. It looks like he had blood and skin under some fingernails though, so he might have scratched his attacker. They're running tests but it won't be quick."

As the Chief put his coat and trooper's cap on to leave Russ said, "You know, I got the Lincoln pickup to get around more safely in the Vermont winter."

"I know" Chief Ramsay said with a smile, "a smart move too, you saw what happened with Harley and he's been in this country his whole life. He put five or six sandbags in the pickup bed and thought that would compensate for a rear-wheel drive vehicle. I see it with the Old Timers a lot."

"Well, the reason I brought it up is because Detective James is driving around in the same rear-wheel drive Mercury Grand Marquis I put away in my garage, only his is the Ford-version. He really needs something better."

"Not really my department, Russ" the Chief said honestly, then added with a touch of resignation, "but I'll look into it, since it can be put down as a safety issue I might get some traction!" The chief emphasized the last word, "traction."

"Good pun, Chief!"

Russ's late wife had loved puns and Chief Ramsay was almost her equal in weaving them into his conversations. In a final parting shot the Law Enforcement Officer said, "See you around, Mr. Gorgeous!"

Lara had given Russ the nickname several months earlier and now half the community seemed to know him as much by it as they did the longer known moniker, "Professor P."

As Chief Ramsay's neon green and white checkerboard Dodge Charger drove out, Russ turned to Thorndike.

The big cat was sprawled atop one of the club chairs in a pose Russ likened to an exhibit of Modern Art that would have been entitled, "Roadkill."

"Alright you Rapscallion! What am I going to do with you? I know I messed that up completely but you don't need to rub it in. How on earth did I get so far off-track? I knew the Clan Chief's name as well as I know my own, now you won't let me live this one down!"

With that Thorndike spun to a sitting position in a movement that defied gravity and gave an authoritative double-yip, twice.

"Yip-Yip, Yip-Yip!"

It was Thorndike's very justified effort to emphasize the point that it had been Russ who'd made the mistake, not him. After all, Thorndike had a reputation to watch out for.

Russ stared at his roommate and Eileen's words raced through his mind.

"Unfortunately, you are the greatest obstacle to the communication between you and young Thorndike. You are the weak link Russ."

Russ had protested, as anyone of sound-mind would have done, but now he was beginning to think that perhaps the longsuffering E had been right in her earlier assessment. He couldn't tell her that, at least not right now. Maybe, in time, he thought to himself, but not right now.

"Our human intellect is just not as advanced as is that of our feline counterparts and anyone who truly knows their cat, already knows what I'm saying is true. We humans must develop our skills in order to understand a cat's simplest communications."

Nevertheless, as intelligent as Russ believed he was, Eileen's words carried a sting. Now he was guilty of thinking Thorndike had made his first mistake when it was really Russ himself who'd missed an obvious clue.

"Treats" Russ said, as he hurried to the kitchen. Still,

the "Amazing Thorndike," as Eileen continued to refer to him after he'd taken a blue-ribbon at the Vermont Fancy Felines™ Cat Show, got there first!

"How does he do it?" Russ thought to himself. The incredible physicality of the big cat never ceased to amaze even Russ.

"I know you love Rocco & Roxie's™ Jerky Stick treats as much as Benji does, so here you go. Even Thorndike's catnip ball didn't merit the kind of response "R & R's" got. One of Russ's quirks or eccentricities was his habit of shortening names or giving "codenames." One example of this was a fellow sailor named Arthur Nugent. Russ had codenamed him "Wingnut" and after that he remained "Wingnut" for the duration of his Naval enlistment. Russ had only taken a few minutes to turn Thorndike & Benji's beloved Rocco & Roxie's™ Jerky Stick treats into "R & R's." Now hollering "treats" brought both the intelligent, dignified creatures scurrying like simple pets, all thanks to "R & R's."

The magnificent cat ran off into the living area with his treat just as if he were a lion with its favorite feast on the distant Serengeti.

"I've got Brunch with Vivian, Benji, and Winston, so I'm going to get ready" Russ said without receiving any acknowledgement. "I'll give them your kind regards!" These last words were added facetiously, as Russ's way of getting even with Thorndike for all the perceived slights the cat bestowed upon the sensitive-natured man.

"That darned cat" Russ thought as he headed to the master bedroom, "he sure has it made." He hung his Baturina™ Navy Blue Paisley Silk Pajamas up next to his matching Dressing Gown. The set had been "a gift of appreciation" from Vivian after the arrests of the Chandler Gang had insured her safety. It was an incredible gift, just the kind Vivian would give, and the first silk pajamas of Russ's long life.

The morning was clear, cold, and bright, with not a

single cloud in the Vermont sky. Behind the substantial mass of his new Lincoln Mark LT pickup, Russ took the back roads down the Onion River Road, just a mile south of Harley Shaw's farm on Skunk Hollow, through the Jericho Forest and into the beautiful landscape of the Pine Valley. Whistling Duck Road had packed snow but the 4-wheel-drive had no problem with it and as he enjoyed the spectacular view he thought back to the comment Dr. Mariell Thompson had made.

"Whistling Duck, really? Wouldn't Quacking Duck be more accurate?"

The greenish verdigris of Caledonia's aged copper roofs and her gray stone-towers were much more visible in a winter's forest, void of foliage. They stood out strong and tall, three perfect circular towers and one giant square one, along a rolling ridge in an ancient hardwood forest backed by a mountain of pine and fir. It was indeed a magnificent place and an incredible estate and even in winter it shined like a diamond.

The paved road on the property was clear and dry, obviously plowed early and often, and even the large, paved parking lot surrounded by majestic Sugar Maples and towering Black Walnut trees, was bare and dry.

Russ had been to Caledonia often enough now to be seen as "a regular" by the staff. Among the others, including Bernadette and fifty or so "charity" and "club" ladies who were in the same organizations with Vivian, Russ was the lone "Gentleman Regular" who visited solely for social reasons. The "Manor House," as Vivian called it, still inspired awe in him but was no longer strange and forbidding.

"The Vivacious Vivian," or "VV" for short, as Russ called her, always welcomed his visits as a rare treat. Nathan continued to work full-time for her and she had become used to being called "Viv" by him. Once the three "main books" Vivian wanted written were finished, the young man focused on organizing Vivian's personal papers and cataloging her many possessions, including books.

"Your trees are majestic even in the middle of winter" Russ said in reverential tones. "It's always a pleasure to visit you."

"My dear Russ, you are so sweet, but I'm far from my dotage, so tell me the real reason for your sudden visit."

"Sudden?" Russ countered as best he could.

"Yes, 'sudden' is a suitably accurate word, wouldn't you agree? Since you habitually provide Benji, Winston, and me a week's notice but today was less than 24 hours."

Russ was caught dead-to-rights by the bright little woman whose attention to detail had been heightened to an extreme by what the press had taken to calling "The Chandler Conspiracy." Vivian had the somewhat chilling distinction of being characterized as the "sole survivor" of the conspiracy which had now indicted over 20 local business, government, and political leaders.

"Tell me the truth now, Nathan said something when he delivered the books, did he not?"

Russ saw no further use in denying the purpose of his visit.

"He might have let slip that he didn't think you were feeling well." Russ reluctantly confessed.

"Yes, indeed" she said, as she transferred her Irish Shillelagh walking stick to her other hand and took the crook of his arm.

"I left Benji sleeping in front of the fire in the library and snuck away, so let's walk that way. He'd never forgive me, you know, if I didn't include him in your visit. You do spoil him though, and Winston also. Winston just loves the Parrot Treats you bring him, they are quite his favorite, you know. I've never seen him take to something that way."

Vivian was speaking of a brand known as "Caitec®" which Russ stumbled upon by sheer luck. He visited the local pet store in Eton Falls, it was called "The Blue Iguana & Friends," and, of course, featured a Blue Iguana named "Felix." One of the employees, an attractive young woman named Kelly, with long, straight sandy-brown hair, was knowledgeable about all kinds of pet-related information and she was the one who introduced him to the Caitec® Oven-Fresh Bites Mixed Berry Cookies Parrot Treats.

"They also come in a wide variety of flavors" she'd added helpfully, "there is Peanut Butter and Baked Almond, although I can't recommend the Hot Chili Flavor, myself, having no experience with it."

The Mixed Berry Cookies had catapulted "Uncle Russ," as Vivian referred to him on behalf of Winston and Benji, to the pinnacle of popularity with the notoriously picky Parrot.

"Those two characters just adore you; you know?"

Behind their backs Russ called Winston and Benjamin "The Odd Couple" and "Churchill, Disraeli & Company," but he adored them just the same and in his own characteristic style, he fussed and cooed over the two "characters" even more than Vivian did.

As they neared the Library, Vivian's voice must have woken the little snow-white Benji because he came hurtling down the hallway lined with pictures, paintings, chairs and sideboards, as well as statuary.

"Ben-ha-meen" Russ said in a nebulous Middle Eastern accent, "my little Chutzpah!" Chutzpah was a Yiddish word, a language Russ had little familiarity with, but he loved the way it sounded. It meant, basically, audacious or cheeky, but no matter it's "official meaning," one thing about Russ Personette was he simply couldn't resist a word if he liked the way it sounded. It had been the same way in his younger years when he'd often just spout off, "Fenêtre Livre," which, in French meant quite nonsensically, "Window Book." When his late wife, who spoke French fluently, asked him about this "habit" he simply said, "I like the way it sounds." No further defense or justification seemed necessary so long as Russ liked the way something sounded.

"Ben-ha-meen, my little Chutzpah!" he said again,

greeting the little Westie with some energetic petting and adoration and, of course, the prerequisite Rocco & Roxie's™ Jerky Stick treats.

"He can't resist you, or your 'R & R's' for that matter!"

"Well, as Miss Fanny Fern said in 1872, the way to a man's heart is through his stomach" Russ said coyly.[16]

"I believe John Adams is credited with the first version of that saying" Vivian said with satisfaction, "but I must say, in my experience, it was proven true. I was a cook at the Lucky Lad Mine in Idaho in 1945 when I met my husband."

"Thorndike and I read that last night" Russ said, the thrill in his voice obvious. "You worked the Pistol Creek Mining District for a guy named Lafe Johnson."

"That's right" Vivian said with a tranquil smile, as if the memory had taken her back to her own youth.

"Say, Vivian, what was the name 'Lafe' short for, anyway?" Russ's natural curiosity, if truth were to be told, was no less than Thorndike's. The cat and the man were, in fact, very similar in nature and well-suited to their friendship.

Vivian laughed at the question, recollecting the time nearly 80 years earlier.

"Lafayette Fauntleroy Johnson" she said with another laugh. "He hated his name" she confided with a smile.

With this Russ stopped petting young Benjamin and gave him his reward of one Rocco & Roxie's™ Jerky Stick treat. The little Westie did circles before running back to his warm fireside with his favorite snack.

"The Lucky Ladd Mine was spelled incorrectly at first" she reminisced, "English wasn't quite so uniformly taught in those days. Lad was spelled with two-D's at first. Only later, in the history books, did it get corrected."

They walked into the immense, two-story Delashmett

---

[16] "Wise Words and Wives' Tales" by Stuart & Doris Flexner, Avon Books, New York, ©1993.

Library, where Winston watched from his brass stand near one of the tall windows while Benjamin gnawed and wrestled with his R & R treat.

When he saw Russ the big bird lifted in flight. With two powerful strokes of his broad wings he came zooming toward the man who still found the experience nerve-wracking. Vivian had instructed Russ from the beginning, "Just hold still!"

Anyone whose been the landing-pad for a full-grown, mature African Grey Parrot can tell you that standing still and waiting for them to land is easier said than done. Russ had found out that despite the awkward look of the bird at rest, in flight Winston was a masterful aviator. When he landed on Russ's shoulder the big bird hardly made any impact at all. The long, razor-sharp talons had never hurt him and he was unexpectedly light for his large appearance.

"Well now, Mr. Churchill" Russ said with the same sense of relief that followed every such successful landing, "are you ready for your mixed fruit treat?"

"Hello, Hello" the majestic bird said, and Russ handed him the Caitec® Oven-Fresh Bites Mixed Berry Cookie Parrot Treats.

"He used to be in an office" Vivian said the first time Russ met the Parrot. "Hello, Goodbye, and even the ring of the telephone are on the top of his repertoire."

When they sat down in opposing Chippendale wingback chairs Vivian texted for "tea and scones for two in the library." Vivian had spoken about John Adams earlier but Russ knew the Chippendale chairs had been purchased from the estate of John Quincy Adams. The chairs, newly upholstered and regularly used, were historic pieces, like so many of the furnishings at Caledonia. Plaques on many items told of their provenance but Vivian rarely mentioned these.

"It's so much more convenient to text" she said looking up at Russ. "I never liked ringing the bells anyway."

Russ laughed, but in a home as big as Caledonia was it

made sense to use every modern convenience possible. In fact, Russ had learned a trick or two from Vivian already. She had purchased a "robot vacuum" for all five floors of Caledonia and the first time he saw one buzzing by he felt like he was in a Star Wars™ movie, with the little wheeled-delivery bots running around on the Death Star.

He was shocked to see how Vivian had embraced technology to help with the running of her estate. Once he had her endorsement of the iRobot Roomba S9+™ it wasn't long before one was running around Wildrose. The little vacuum did all the floor surfaces and even emptied and recharged itself automatically.

Mrs. Tibbetts came in each Tuesday and Thursday to do cleaning at Wildrose and although she was skeptical at first, after her first week she had become what her daughter, Docherty, described as a "Botvert," a convert to the robot culture.

Even the vast lawns at Caledonia, acres of them, were cut throughout summer with robot lawnmowers. Vivian had purchased ten Husqvarna 435X All-Wheel-Drive mowers. The 435X could climb and cut all the rolling hills and as well as the trim around the dozens of flower beds that decorated the estate grounds. The sight of three or four mowers going at once in various areas was startling at first but Russ adopted this advancement too and it wasn't long before two Husqvarna 435X mowers were seen taking care of the twenty-plus acres of Wildrose.

Fresh Twining's Irish Breakfast™ tea and warm, "Caledonia-Raised Blueberry" scones, Russ's undisputed favorite scones, were rolled into the room on a cart covered in a snow-white tablecloth within minutes. It was left between the two chairs for Vivian to "pour out."

"It looks delicious" Russ said to the young woman.

"Thank you, Sir" was all they ever said to Russ, but he felt they welcomed his appreciation.

"You have the best scones I've ever tasted, Vivian."

"Mrs. Dale has been with me for almost twenty years,

she's a jewel" the little woman said sweetly, but Russ saw a twinge of sadness pass over her face. In a moment she was Vivian again, happy and upbeat.

Their time passed enjoyably, the way it does with two friends who have reason to trust each other deeply, and Vivian had refilled Russ's Lenox® Chelse Muse Fleur teacup twice.

"Alright Vivian" he said seriously, "what aren't you telling me?"

It was all Russ needed to say. Nathan had been wrapped up in the writing and designing of three books and even he had noticed.

"I don't think she's feeling very good" the young man had said.

In light of the threat to Vivian's life from the Chandler conspirators Russ had just two questions. Was Vivian being poisoned, or was something else going on? These had been on his mind since he'd heard Nathan's comment the day before, and Vivian was right about one thing. Russ wasn't about to wait to find out the answer and so, within 24 hours, he'd come to visit.

"Oh sweet man" she said in a voice that filled Russ with dread. "I'm dying my dear friend."

Russ stared at her in disbelief. The stylish, energetic, classic lady who had been her own force of nature through a long and challenging life seemed above such things.

"How ironic it is that so many powerful people who wanted me dead, only needed to wait a couple more months and they would have gotten their wish."

"I don't understand" was all Russ could stutter.

"Of course you don't understand" Vivian said sympathetically, as if it were Russ who was suffering. "In your noble mind good always triumphs, truth always wins out, and those you love never come to harm. How much you've been hurt by life, Russ. I've seen it in your eyes so many times, the deep, abiding sadness. Our loved ones may die, my dear, but the memories never do. You have been such a blessing to me at a time when I needed one desperately. Now, my end is near. A brain tumor, undiagnosed by my last doctor for over a decade, will now be the cause of my demise. I'm only telling you and I think you'll understand why, when I say that I've been given two weeks or two months, but little more."

Russ looked to the Persian carpet where young Benjamin still enjoyed his treat, then he looked to the perch, just a few feet from where he sat. Winston looked on, blinking slowly, just as if he'd understood every word, but was sworn to silence.

"I told you I needed someone to trust, and to entrust" she said. "I've never known anyone who could fulfill those needs better than you have, and will, Dear Russ, and I've never needed that person more than I do now."

Vivian now looked from Benjamin to Winston.

"They've both known only me, all these years. They'll be lost without me at first." She stopped for a moment, the sadness catching in her throat.

"Of course, Vivian, I will take care of them and love them, just as I do Thorndike."

"I know you will" Vivian said with a heavy sigh, as if she felt all of the weight of the world on her shoulders at that moment. "And they will need you. They both adore you, I can see that, and they will be safe and cared for with you. Of that I have no doubt. And this is what I meant when I said I needed someone to entrust."

Russ reached over and took her small, frail hand in his large, powerful grip, and they sat in silence like this for a half hour.

"I believe this will be the last time I see you, Russ."

He couldn't believe this. Vivian, and Arnold, had both measured Russ correctly. He was a man of hope. Always he hoped for the best, even when things were the worst. He said nothing but he wanted Vivian to be wrong.

"I believe this will be the last time I see you, dear friend, and so I want to thank you for the friendship and care you've given to me since the first moment we met. You took me seriously from the very beginning and I know I owe you, and Thorndike, that special animal, my life. I don't want to say 'good-bye.' I've sensed you hate 'good-byes' too. So I'm going to get up and wish you a wonderful Thanksgiving, and then I'll take Winston and Benji with me. You'll be alright seeing yourself out this time, won't you?"

Vivian's upper lip had quivered as she finished speaking and her eyes welled with tears but, by some force beyond Russ's skill to know, she kept from crying.

"Of course, Vivian" Russ said, and then he stopped. He would have liked to have said more, he had so much he wanted to say, but he knew he didn't possess the same strength the little woman did.

She took Winston from his perch and with Benjamin at her heels the trio disappeared. Benji looked back from the door, as if he too wished there were some way to avoid what was coming.

Russ sat in the Delashmett Library at Caledonia and wept in a way he hadn't done in years.

# Thorndike & Company™

## The Great Cat Official Fan Club Member

Eton Falls - New York - Paris - London

# CHAPTER SIX
## Operation Golden Doubloon

When Russ pulled in to Wildrose he saw Thorndike looking out one of the windows from his perch on a club chair.

Somehow he knew that the cat knew about Vivian. Telepathy was the only possible answer but few were willing to believe it. Even Russ struggled with the idea.

Thorndike joined him at the door when he came in. It was something the cat had never done. In fact, Thorndike had mastered "playing-hard-to-get" and the big cat's usual reaction was to ignore Russ completely. However he'd done it, Thorndike knew Russ was nearly overcome with sadness.

Russ sat on the bench beside the door and took his

boots off.

"I stopped at Fitzgerald's Flowers & Gifts on the way home and Julie's sending a dozen, long-stemmed red roses to Daphne in New York. It's to congratulate her on publishing her first book of photographs. I signed our card 'Thorndike & Russ' just in case she was in doubt as to which one of us gets top-billing."

Thorndike's "Yip-Yip" seemed almost celebratory.

The small talk helped Russ and having Thorndike to talk with helped too.

"I hope Daphne's having a good time" he continued, "but it will be nice when she gets back home.

"Yeeoww" said Thorndike in agreement. Of all the visitors Russ & Thorndike received, Daphne was among the big Maine Coon Cat's most adoring fans and Eileen was, of course, the President of the "Thorndike Fan Club™."

Russ put his boots away, hung up his coat and MacPherson tartan scarf, and put his fedora on the shelf above. The routine helped him and yet his mind still reeled at the devastating news Vivian had shared with him, and him alone.

He didn't know what to do or how to move ahead. In the end he and Thorndike settled down and started reading the second chapter of "Platinum Blonde." It was called "Moving Fast" and told of Vivian's two-week whirlwind courtship in the high mountains of Idaho and Montana and of the simple country girl going east on the train to meet her new in-laws, the Delashmett's of Caledonia Estate.

"What a life's story" Russ said as he closed the book. Thorndike once again feigned sleep and, very shortly, Russ was asleep as well. The news he'd received that morning had been a shock and sleep came as a welcome respite from continued sadness.

He woke from a deep, dreamless sleep an hour and half later. It was 3:30 PM and the shadows of Strathmorlick Ridge were falling over Wildrose when Thorndike rose and stretched. Russ's eyes focused slowly and his mind woke even more slowly, but gradually a vehicle in the parking lot took shape. It was strange and unfamiliar to him but as he regained full consciousness he recognized Chief Ramsay and Detective James coming toward the side door, which, for all practical purposes, had come to serve as the main entry.

"Hello" Russ said, trying hard not to sound like a man who'd just woken up from a deep sleep.

"Our people were able to lift one footprint from the snow outside John MacKean's home. It's probably a dead end but knowing you the way we do we thought it was worth the trip."

"That, and we wanted an excuse to try out my new rig" an excited Detective James said, pointing over his shoulder to the black and white SUV. "It's a brand-new Ford Interceptor™ the Chief got for me. 4-wheel drive too."

"It's a beauty" Russ agreed, "and it will be a lot safer on the snow and ice."

Once inside the men laid out newspaper on the kitchen counter and pulled out a plaster cast nearly a foot and a half long by a foot wide.

"What do you think of that Russ?" Chief Ramsay said without much enthusiasm. "What have you got for us?"

Russ pulled up one of the stools and sat down to inspect the plaster cast more closely. He turned it in silence, taking note of the smallest details.

"Not easy to make a plaster cast in the snow, or so we were told."

"No, Detective, I wouldn't imagine it would be, but your people did an admirable job."

"Well, what's the verdict Professor? You got anything for us?"

"I'm not sure where to start so I'll just jump in" Russ said flatly. The truth was, his mind was still only operating at about half-speed, but he was waking up fast. The Law Enforcement officers looked at him in shock. Despite seeing Russ in action many times before they were finding it difficult to believe he could have much to say about the cast.

"First off, it's an Australian boot. Tasmanian to be more exact. It's made by John Blundstone & Sons Manufacturers in Hobart, Tasmania, since 1870."

Chief Ramsay looked Russ straight in the eyes and said, "You just make this stuff up as you go along, don't you, Tasmania? Are you serious? Tasmania, as in the other side of the world?"

"That's right, Chief, Tasmania."

"So, let me get this straight, Professor. We've got a victim of Scottish descent, killed by an Australian wearing boots made in Tasmania?"

Russ laughed for a moment.

"Not quite, Chief. The boots are made in Tasmania, that's true enough, but the boots, called 'Blundstone® 500 Chelsea Boots', are sold through L. L. Bean® and Company so anyone, virtually anywhere, could have purchased them."

"And you can tell all of this from this one blurry plaster cast?" Detective James asked.

Russ nodded in the affirmative.

"Incredible" said the Detective, shaking his head.

"So we aren't looking for an Australian? That's a relief" said Chief Ramsay.

Russ looked at the two men for a moment longer.

"What's more, I can tell you quite a bit about the man who wears these boots."

At this point Chief Ramsay pulled out a chair from the dining table and sat down.

"I gotta hear this sitting down" he mumbled half to himself, "I don't want to fall down, that's for sure."

"Dr. Charles Duncan is one of my fellow History Professors at the College. These are his boots" Russ said confidently.

"You're telling us" the Chief started to speak, then he

paused and started again. "Let me get this straight, Professor, you want me to believe that the perpetrator of the MacKean murder is another Charbonneau College History Professor? The guy who replaced the last Charbonneau College History Professor we convicted of murder a year ago?"

Chief Ramsay often called Russ "Professor" when he was getting his input on a crime. Otherwise, he called him "Russ."

"I'm not making this up, Chief. Believe me, I know it sounds crazy. What's even more difficult to believe is that Dr. Duncan flew out of Burlington International Airport last Friday evening bound, supposedly, for Mobile, Alabama, to visit his parents for Thanksgiving."

"Russ" Detective James interceded, "on a scale of one-to-ten, how certain are you that these boots are Dr. Duncan's?"

"Twelve" Russ said flatly. "Same boot, same size, same depth of wear on the outside-rear of the left heel, and a cut in the right instep, fairly definitive."

"So what you're saying is, Dr. Charles Duncan loaned his Tasmanian boots out to a murderer, then flew to Mobile, Alabama? Or the murderer stole Dr. Duncan's Tasmanian boots once he was gone, I guess, to frame the good Professor? You can't make this stuff up." The Chief was shaking his head in utter disbelief.

"Or Professor Duncan wasn't on that flight and he is our murderer" Detective James added.

"All possibilities" Russ said, "but surveillance footage from the airport and the DNA results from the flesh and blood under the late John MacKean's fingernails should tell you which it is. My own hunch is it's Dr. Duncan."

"Why do you say that?" Detective August James asked.

"You remember the Massacre at Glencoe?" Russ asked. "Well, Captain Robert Campbell was the man who carried out the bulk of the infamous "order," but the man who wrote the order, and who arrived later but still in time to see to some additional murders, was a man named Major Robert Duncanson."

"So, because a man named Duncanson participated in the massacre in 1693."

"1692" the Chief interrupted, "it rhymes with 1492, when Columbus sailed the ocean blue!"

"So" the Detective began again, "because a man named Duncanson participated in the massacre in 1692, you believe that Dr. Charles Duncan is the actual perpetrator of our murder."

"That's right" Russ said simply, without elaborating further. A part of him already knew how crazy so many of his "Thorndike-Inspired-Ideas" seemed to others, and there seemed little point in trying to make a crazy idea sound sane.

"I could retire" the Chief said quietly to himself. "I have enough years in, I started with the Department when I was 25."

Russ looked at Detective James and the two men laughed.

"I came out here to stump Professor P" the Chief continued, "And I have to hear a Cock-a-leekie story about Tasmanian shoe company founded in 1492 by Marco Polo and how Columbus landed in Mobile, Alabama?"

"Don't you mean 'Cockamamie' Chief?"

It was the first time Russ had really gotten a little of his own back on the quick-witted, pun-master and Chief of Police, and he was enjoying it.

"Oh yeah, Mr. Gorgeous" the Chief said with satisfaction, "and if this all pans out the way you tell it, no one is going to trust a History Professor at Charbonneau College again, right? Ever! How many of your professors can we put in jail before someone says 'enough'?"

"He has a point, Professor, and Eton Falls has a great record of solving homicides."

"Partly thanks to the involvement of Thorndike & Personette, LLC., right?" Russ said with a broad smile.

"Well, yes, now that you mention it" Detective James admitted.

"His point is, we aren't the 'Unsolved Murder Capital of America' and sooner or later Charbonneau College has to come up with a better way to screen their History Professors" the Chief said, finally regaining his composure, then he laughed.

"So no retirement then, Chief?" Russ couldn't resist rubbing it in.

"Well, History Professors aren't the only ones who can retire!"

As the men were preparing to leave with their plaster cast, once again heavily wrapped in paper and back in its cardboard box, Chief Ramsay turned to Russ.

"Well, Professor, I don't know how you do it, but you never cease to amaze me." As he went out the door he was mumbling unintelligible words under his breath.

"He means 'thank you'!" Detective James said, shaking Russ's hand. "And thank you too, Thorndike, we all know you're the real brains of the operation!"

"Yeeoww!" said Thorndike happily. He and Eileen couldn't have agreed more with the young Detective.

"You don't have to crow about it" Russ said with feigned indignation.

As Chief Ramsay reached Detective James' new Ford Interceptor he turned back and hollered.

"Thanks a million, Mr. Gorgeous!"

Twenty minutes later a giant, metallic green, 10 Cylinder Ford Triton Crew Cab 4-wheel drive pulled in to the Wildrose parking lot.

"It's like Grand Central today" Russ said to Thorndike as he put his spoon down on dining room table next to his soup.

It was his young friend, Dane VanWert. Dane was a mountain-biker, among many other hobbies, and had overpowered and captured Russ's would-be assassin several months earlier. In gratitude Russ had replaced

Dane's English-made Cotic RocketMAX™ mountain bike
and his Zéfal® HPX high pressure tire pump, both of
which had been damaged in Dane's rescue. Then Russ
insisted on paying for the engine rebuild costs on Dane's
Triton engine.

Russ was surprised to see the diminutive form of Harley
Shaw tumble out of the back door of the 4-door behemoth.
Dane came next and then three others came around the
back of the pickup. Russ noticed little things, odd things,
like handwriting, hats, shoe tread patterns, and last names.

At this moment Russ realized Harley was the same
height as the top of the wheel-well on his Grandson's big
Ford.

"Incredible really" Russ murmured as he opened the
door and welcomed the noisy group in.

Four men and one girl came in out of the cold and a
bustle formed around the door as boots, coats, and caps
came off and everyone dipped into the vintage galvanized
20 Quart milk-can with large letters "GREENWOOD
DAIRY – La Grande, Oregon". It was a well-known fact
that Russ kept the milk-can by his door so that anyone who
wanted could get a pair of slippers, hand knitted by a
woman named Corinne, to wear around Wildrose.[17] Each
pair was a different color, a bright yellow or stately blue or
deep red, all with a thick knitted sole of black yarn.

Once the entourage was colorfully "befooted" Dane
emptied a bag of gifts under Russ's Christmas tree.

"Thank you" Russ said sincerely, "but it looks like Santa
went on a crash diet." Everyone laughed as Dane VanWert
was lean and tall. He didn't even have an extra pound.

"Great tree, Russ" Harley said thoughtfully. He'd been
in shock after his accident and had no memory of seeing
the tree. "Never saw a Blue Spruce used as a Christmas
Tree before but it sure is pretty."

"Harley said you saved his life" a husky, dark-haired

[17] See: etsy.com/shop/TricotDeCordela, $21.95.

man said. "Name's Griff, heard a lot about you."

"Wow, what a beautiful cat" the girl said. She was Dane's 13-year-old daughter, Taylor. She knew Russ but had never seen Thorndike before and, as usual, it was love at first sight.

"He is a handsome animal" Dane chimed in, "you know he even has his own fan club."

"No way Dad" Taylor said dismissively.

"Russ?" Dane said in a pleading voice, wanting him to corroborate his statement.

"You all make yourselves comfortable" Russ said, "I'll be right back with the evidence."

Shortly after Thorndike's amazing performance at the Vermont Fancy Felines™ Cat Show, Eileen, in conjunction with the generous funding of the ubiquitous Donald Frobisher and the attentive legal help of Russ's attorney, Alexis Stonecipher, had created the "Thorndike & Company™ Fan Club LLC." She soon had hundreds of lavender sweatshirts, in all sizes, printed with Thorndike's unmistakable silhouette in black and the words "Thorndike & Company™ The Great Cat Official Fan Club Member." Underneath the silhouette were the names of several cities, "Eton Falls – New York – Paris – London." The only color on the shirt was a large, bright blue ribbon, raised in 3-D gel and looking like the real thing, which Thorndike had won. It was affixed to the neck of the black silhouette of the cat on the shirt, exactly where it was in the actual portrait taken at the Cat Show. The overall effect was stunning.

Eileen had given two dozen out throughout Chittenden County, largely with the help of her "accomplice," Lara, as the two women had formed a fast friendship.

Lara's Great-Aunt Virginia and their dear friend, Gracie, both wore theirs proudly the 29th of each month, as all "official fans" knew the 29th was the day Thorndike had won his blue ribbon. "Thorndike Day," as Eileen had dubbed the 29$^{th}$, would see Bernadette and Lou donning their own "Thorndike Shirts", as well as Rhonda, Daphne, Ben, and Vivian.

Even in distant New York, Eileen assured Russ that Vincent, and all his associates at Ramadi's Gallery, faithfully wore their own "Thorndike Shirts" on the 29$^{th}$. Vincent, for all this classicism, had embraced "The Thorndike Phenomenon" from the very beginning. In fact, he had even hung the giant portrait of Thorndike and his blue ribbon at Wildrose.

"The Gallery does a brisk trade selling Thorndike Shirts to their distinguished customers and all the proceeds go to the printing costs of additional shirts" Eileen had proudly said. "It's become quite the popular fad in the Big Apple" she admitted.

When Russ came back to the large, open living area of Wildrose, everyone was relaxing in the club chairs he had arranged around the rosewood coffee table Chief Ramsay had given him, and Taylor was petting Thorndike with gentle caresses.

"This should fit you perfectly" Russ said, as he held up the lavender sweatshirt.

"Oh I love it" the girl said excitedly, "and it's my favorite color too."

Russ and Dane served up coffee and tea for the adults and the Old Homestead's Orchard Cove Cider™ for Taylor, then took their seats.

"Thank you for the Thorndike Shirt, Russ" Taylor said dutifully.

"I'm glad you like it" Russ said, ever the good host. The truth was, as much as Russ had come to love Thorndike, and he truly did, there was a part of him that was jealous. It was just a little sliver of jealousy and he never said anything about it to anyone. In fact, only Thorndike knew about it but that was because Russ couldn't hide much of anything from his roommate and Little Buddy.

"Why not 'Russ Day'?" he'd said to the big cat one day,

"or a 'Russ Shirt'? I'd like mine to be cardinal red with the white silhouette of a tall, handsome man in a fedora."

At this Thorndike had yipped in an especially disgusting way and flipped onto his back in what Russ called his "Death-Pose" position. "You look like a statue in a modern art exhibit called 'Roadkill'."

"Russ Day" had never caught on and now he was passing the time handing out "Thorndike Shirts" to Chittendenders across the county.

"We didn't mean to interrupt your meal, Russ."

"It's no problem, Harley, I can heat it up easily enough later on."

"We want to talk to about something serious" the husky, dark-haired man who introduced himself as "Griff" said.

"It has to remain a secret, Russ" Harley said conspiratorially, "there's a lot of competition."

"I understand" Russ said, although he understood nothing more than a need for secrecy. "What's important enough to bring you all out in the cold a couple days before Thanksgiving?"

"My name's David Gaertner" the fifth member of the company said. He was a tall, middle-aged man with a crew cut of bristling dark gray hair. "I'm a builder. I know Dan Garn, he did a good job on this place. About 11 years ago Harley got us together and told us about a crazy idea."

"We didn't take him seriously at first" Griff said flatly, "I mean, what did any of us know about scuba diving, or sunken treasure back then?"

"Sunken Treasure?" Russ had no idea where this was leading but the talk of sunken treasure had sure captured his attention.

"Well" David Gaertner said, "I've got a boat, a 27' Eastern® Islander, the 'Miss Cindy', with two Honda 250 horsepower motors, so Harley brought me in for that."

Russ liked David's down-to-earth way and nodded his head. "Makes sense" he said.

"I'm a hobby-historian" Griff said bluntly. "No degree and no letters after my name but I know all about our local history, especially Lake Champlain, and since the treasure Harley wanted was sunk during the American Revolution, he thought I could help out on that front."

Russ could feel the defensiveness in Griff. After all, the man was talking to a bona fide College History Professor so a little sensitivity could be expected.

The truth was Russ could identify. He remembered what he'd said to Arnold just a year earlier.

"I've taken the job of history professor which kind of surprises me because everyone I work with is a Doctor of this, that, or the other, but I've just finished my master's degree and I've never taught before."

"A piece of paper doesn't prove much" Russ said to the man's point about a degree, "but since you guys are here today I take it that you haven't had any luck."

"That's right" Harley said in exasperation, "and we know there are at least 4 other teams trying to find that treasure right now."

"Harley, would I be right to assume you weren't out 'windsurfing' yesterday" Russ said gravely, with a knowing expression.

"Well, we've got to strike while the iron is hot."

"But try as we might, nothing has worked" David said matter-of-factly.

"When Dane said we should talk to you, well, what did we have to lose, really?" Griff said with a defensive edge in his voice.

"Just another equal share in the treasure, right Griff?" Russ said, and the dark-haired, self-proclaimed hobby-historian choked on his tea and nearly upset his cup.

"That goes without question, Professor" David acknowledged. "If you're able to help us find the gold, after 11 years of fruitless searching, you'll more than deserve it."

"What part does Dane play in all this?" Russ asked.

"He's helped us out now and then" Harley said, "like a

good Grandson."

"And he's an equal partner too?" Russ asked.

"No" Griff said gruffly. "He just helps out, now and then, like Harley said. The rest of us have been at this every spare minute for closer to 12 years than 11."

"And what is an equal share of zero, divided by 12 years?" Russ asked seriously. Even though his point was logical he guessed Griff would take offense.

"I didn't come here for this" Griff said angrily and put his cup down to go.

It was Harley who made him reconsider.

"Now don't go getting all hot and bothered Griff. Russ is right if you'll look at it for a minute. We've got nothing to show for all the hours, all the work, all the fuel money, equipment. We're out, what, $60,000 easy, among the three of us. Twenty grand each, and we're no closer to a payoff than we were 12 years ago, just as you say."

Griff stood at the door with his hand on his coat, staring out into the cold Vermont winter.

"Well, I don't know" Griff said, trying to find a way to back down without losing face.

"Listen" Russ said, "I'm not criticizing you men, I'm interrogating you with an eye out for our best chance at success. You three have been an equation that seemed to have all the necessary parts, but you haven't found the treasure. So, rather than plow the same field over and over, I'll tell you straight. You have to change your equation. You need new minds and not just a little free armchair-advice from a history Professor on a cold winter's day. I know Dane's mind and I know mine. I know Harley pretty well. You two," here he looked at David and Griff, "I don't know, but I'm impressed you've had the grit to stick with it this long. The way I see it, one fifth of a vast fortune is better than one third of nothing, am I right Griff."

"You'd be right, if bringing you two in on for equal shares was a guarantee for getting the treasure, but no one knows better than the three of us that there are no sure things in this business."

"Okay then" Russ said simply, "you stay the course and hope one of the other teams doesn't beat you to the punch, is that your plan."

Griff remained standing at the door in silence.

"You were glad to have Dane's help for free and you were happy to come out here for some free advice, if it could help you find fame and fortune. What you have to decide on is are you willing to pay for what you get, because that's the only fair way to go about it."

"Dane never told us you'd play hard ball" Griff said with resignation, as he returned to his seat.

"It's only fair. You add two new members at equal shares and we look at the problem again, or you stay the course. What's it to be?"

As Russ watched the three men talking among themselves he realized he was doing all of this for just one reason, it was taking his mind off of Vivian and all she had told him that morning.

"Alright, even partners" Griff said with obvious disappointment. "Now what?"

"Alright then" Russ said, "then let 'Operation Golden Doubloon' begin. I want to see all your maps and see where you've already searched. Do you have that with you?"

David and Griff went to get the dozens of rolls of lake maps and documents they'd hauled around for over a decade and Dane pushed two of Russ's 10' long library tables together under the balcony to make a huge work surface.

"Don't think too badly of Griff" Harley said with a little chuckle, "he's an intense guy and he's really disappointed that we've had to come to another historian. He feels like he failed."

"I don't blame him at all" Russ said, "if I'd been at this for 11 or 12 years with nothing to show for it, I'd probably just throw it over and take up stamp collecting."

Harley laughed and Thorndike said, "Yip."

"What does 'yip' mean?" Taylor asked.

"He said that it would've taken far less than 12 years, in my case. He's a real Smart Alec."

"I told them you'd be able to figure it out, Russ, and fast. You know, you'll be able to see where they went wrong" Dane said confidently.

"Well, yeah" Russ replied, "Don't make it easy for me, partner. Why not say I could lasso them the moon."

This last line was a reference to George Bailey, a character played by a young Jimmy Stewart, in the movie "It's a Wonderful Life." It was one of Russ's favorite movies and he loved the fact that the late Jim Henson had named two of the Muppets™ after the cop and the taxicab driver in the movie, Bert & Ernie!

"I can't believe I'm a full partner" Dane continued. "I don't feel like I deserve it."

"Let me tell you this while our friends are outside" Russ said with a wink to Harley. "When we find this treasure, who do you think is going to be doing most of the work to bring it up?"

Dane stared directly at Russ.

"I assure you it won't be me" Russ said, "and I have the notion it won't be your Granddad."

"Not me" said Harley, "I've already paid all my dues!"

"I see" Dane said soberly, "so you were already calculating who be doing the heavy lifting?"

"That's right my young friend, and by the time you're done you'll agree wholeheartedly that you did more than your fair share!"

"It's getting real cold" David said. "The lake will be freezing fast tonight."

As the men delivered the rolls, maps and documents to the tables, Griff looked straight at Russ.

"David said I was being a real jerk to you, which he said was a real pity since I'm not normally such a jerk in everyday life, so I'd like to apologize. The husky historian held out his hand to Russ. The men shook hands.

"No problem Griff, Harley told me you could get a little intense."

"A little?" questioned David with a laugh. "That's the understatement of the year, no, the century, no, the millennium!"

"It's not that" Griff admitted honestly. "It's my Cousin, he never shuts up about Professor P. He's read both your books and he's always saying, 'Hey did you know this or that about Jericho, or Underhill, or the Civil War. Blah, blah, blah. When I finally met you I almost said, 'Russ Personette, the man, the legend'!"

Everyone laughed but Russ was curious.

"Who's this mysterious cousin of yours and where'd he get my books?"

"You should know" Griff said flatly, "you gave them to him, his name is Louis Langlois!"

"Good old Lou" Russ said in disbelief.

"Not my idea of a cheerleader either, but he's definitely one of your biggest fans" Griff said, and, with the first show of a good nature, he chided Russ.

It fell to Griff, the hobby-historian, to summarize the story of the sunken treasure and the team's reasoning regarding their years of action. Harley and David helped by sorting out the maps to show Russ and Dane.

"It was 1777" Griff started out, clearly in his element. "England's brash young General, Gentleman Johnny Burgoyne, was stamping south from Quebec with all the tact of a bull in a china shop. It looked, at that moment, like nothing would be able to stop him so, his overlord, Sir George Germain, ordered the troops pay be forwarded by ship down Lake Champlain. This would keep the soldiers' morale and fighting will in good form and prevent grumbling and disturbances."

"On August 16th or 17th of 1777" Griff continued, "the weathered sloop, the Morning Star, commanded by Captain Israel Johnson and a crew of a dozen sailors ran aground off the mouth of the Lamoille River. The ship was carrying 10,000 English Sovereigns and, no doubt was riding much deeper than usual. I believe this was the reason for the unexpected grounding."

"A contingent of the Green Mountain Boys, with some of the Lewis Boys you wrote about in your book, came upon the foundered vessel and despite a reported distance from the shore of well over a hundred paces they fired upon it. Captain Johnson was killed outright and the sailors who didn't take their chances with the lake were killed in turn. The unmanned sloop heeled over according to a later report and only its mast and riggings remained visible to the soldiers from the shore. No search of the vessel was conducted at the time and no sign of it was visible a week later. That was the end of the Morning Star."

David Gaertner then showed Russ and Dane a large, detailed map of the mouth of the Lamoille River with hundreds of grids drawn in and "x" marks to show it that grid had been searched. The vast majority bore the "x" marks.

Russ took a ruler and pencil and drew out a shape on a piece of paper.

"Do you have a bathymetric map of the lake, showing depths, underwater terrain, that sort of thing?"

"Sure do" David said without hesitation, as he went to rummage through rolls of maps.

"Taylor would you be willing to cut me out five shapes just like this one?" Russ said as he held up his first drawing.

"Sure, Russ." She was a helpful girl and Russ wanted her to feel involved.

"How about I put something on for supper, it won't take long."

There were a lot of comments that it wasn't necessary but the long shadows of Strathmorlick Ridge and Beulah Mountain, the main peak along the ridge just above Wildrose, were almost touching Scottish Princess Peak on Highland Ridge across the valley to the east. Darkness would be falling soon.

When Russ got back everything was ready. He put the depth charts next to the grid maps and, with everyone crowded around his seated form he took the small objects Taylor had cut out.

"Watch carefully" he said with a tinge of suspense. Then Russ Personette put the five shapes, each identical to each other, in five of the few remaining empty grids, almost on the shoreline.

"This shape is the exact scaled size of the sloop, Morning Star. This is how it could fit into each of the remaining grids."

"But, Russ, you've put them all along the shore."

Harley probably spoke for everyone when he shared his confusion.

"Yes" Russ said confidently, ignoring Harley's point. "Now look at the area from this grid, over here on the bathymetric-depth chart. Tell me what you see in that area" Russ said as he pointed to a strange shape in the detailed underwater map.

"Well I'll be a Monkey's Uncle" Griff said as he turned away in absolute disbelief.

"That's, that's not possible" David Gaertner said as he put his face so close to the underwater map that it nearly touched. "That is the exact shape of the sloop."

"Yes, it is, isn't it?" Russ said with deep satisfaction. "And what's the depth in that area?"

"Ten feet to sixteen feet" Dane said, "it's only 20 feet from the shore there, can that be it?"

"Look at the shape" Russ said, "the question is a mathematical one, what are the odds that Mother Nature would create that shape, in the exact dimensions you gave me for the sloop, Morning Star."

"Those are some long odds, Russ" Harley said, "real long odds!"

"Mathematically that would be almost impossible" Taylor said sincerely.

"That's right Taylor, and because of that, I say that's where the treasure of the Morning Star lies to this day."

After dinner, which Russ and his friend and stalwart mechanic, Eston Phillips, would have called "supper," the company returned to the large, open living room of Wildrose and settled into their chairs each cradling a large cup of Ghirardelli™ Premium Double Chocolate hot cocoa.

"Dane told us you'd be able to figure it out, and fast, but I still can't fathom it" Griff said. "How'd you do it, Russ?"

"It isn't done yet" Russ reminded everyone, "and as Griff said earlier, there are no sure things in this business. So, until we're all holding gold doubloons in our mitts let's just assume we're in for another 'Goose Chase,' okay."

"But how'd you come up with it, and that near the shoreline?" the soft-spoken David Gaertner asked.

"If you look at your grid map there are only a dozen sections you men haven't inspected in the past twelve years. Some of those are between 100 and 200 feet from shore, five of them are on or near shore. So, with my background in the maritime environment I know how delta's form, mature, and change. The Sandbar National Waterfowl Management Delta sits where the Green Mountain Boys once fired upon the sloop, Morning Star, right? Wrong! It doesn't. The remaining empty grids sitting out there between 100 and 200 feet from shore are the right distance, for 1777. I know our nation's rivers were all deeper before settlement. Development, farming, roads, construction, and human activity put far more silt into the rivers and lakes than ever occurred before settlement."

"That means the Sandbar Delta today, two-hundred and forty-some years after the sinking of the Morning Star, is much farther out in the lake than it was in 1777. In other words, those empty grids sitting out there between 100 and 200 feet from shore would have been 400 or 500 feet back then. Checking any of those grids would be an absolute waste of time and energy. All the other grids have been checked by you three. The fact that you were unsuccessful doesn't tell me you're bad at what you do, it tells me the ship wasn't there. So where can it be?"

"In one of the five unchecked grids along the shore" Taylor said proudly.

"Yes" Russ said, "or perhaps even under dry land today, in the Sandbar Management area itself. That's why I did the shape-search for our sloop. Since I know it sank in shallow water two-hundred and forty-some years ago I would expect it to be in even shallower water today. A shape-search, if it could reveal any matches in the unchecked grids, was the quickest way to find our object. We call this a 'quick and dirty' inspection in the business world. We basically cut-to-the-chase. Now, Mother Nature does a lot of strange things. I've seen shapes on the bottom of the ocean you'd swear were sunken ships, and it turns out to be silt-drift built up over hundreds of years behind a single insignificantly sized rock. Our shape-search, however, had the exact measurements of the sloop. If it still survived underwater, in the shallows, it would still be its original size. It wouldn't shrink. So when I saw grid Alfa-23 with a ship-like formation and the same exact size as the ill-fated Morning Star, I knew the odds were good that we were looking at the same treasure-ship you men have spent the better part of twelve years searching for."

"Absolutely incredible" Griff said, with a sincere, open admiration.

"Yes, well, like I said, It isn't done yet."

"No" said David Gaertner, "but it will be, bright and early tomorrow, agreed?"

# CHAPTER SEVEN
## The Best of Times

Despite all the heroic stories Arnold told about Russ Personette, and there had been many, Russ hadn't done anything truly crazy in a long time.

Taking up a collection for the widow of a fellow sailor killed in an accident was a noble idea. Jumping ship at 2:30 AM with all the money in a plastic bag, and swimming across a busy shipping lane to get to the shore of Sri Lanka, in order to buy Black Market sapphires and rubies, was, in hindsight, absolutely insane. The fact that the resale of those gems back in the states provided the widow with ten times more money than the original contributions would have, was both brilliant and highly illegal. Dan Garn may have been right to call him "Mr. Less-Than-Legal," but no one could argue that Russ Personette meant well.

The theft of Professor Dudley's original manuscript, what Russ insisted was "more of a misappropriation of property than anything," was another example of the dizzying array of behaviors he was capable of justifying.

The Mystery of the Misappropriated Manuscript had resulted in a New York Times bestselling book for Professor Dudley, as well as a busy tour schedule of high-end speaking engagements across America and Europe.

Yet, while the devil-may-care heroics and the awe-inspiring daring-do of what Ben and Nathan had called "a modern mix of Sherlock Holmes and Captain America" had always worked out for Russ, getting up at 4 AM, donning a diver's dry suit, cutting through 14" of ice, and jumping into the frigid waters of Lake Champlain, the day before Thanksgiving, was a little much, even for him. He was just glad he wasn't going to be the one in the water. He was the brains of the operation, or so he told himself.

As he crunched through the frozen snow and tall tussock grass along the shoreline, leaving his warm Lincoln Mark LT pick-up behind in the parking lot, he felt the cold Nor'easter send its sub-zero chill straight down his coat collar and thought to himself, "What am I doing?" In the back of his mind Russ knew he'd welcomed this whole adventure much more easily since receiving Vivian's news. Even though this was easily one of the craziest things he'd done, it had already helped him to deal with the approaching loss of someone who had become very dear to him.

He parked next to Dane's Ford Triton and across the lot was a huge, bright yellow, 1956 Dodge Power Wagon™ with shiny black fenders and running board. It was proof positive that earlier generations had their "big truck aficionados" as well.

A white Chevrolet Crew Cab was parked not far from the boat ramp and Russ could still see the tracks leading out onto the ice and going away north into the inky blackness of early morning. Operation Golden Doubloon was off and running and it had already been a busy morning for the other members of the Golden Doubloon Team™.

He could hear voices on the wind, snippets of clear conversations vanishing as soon as the wind changed. His vision was blurred by the ice crystals driven by the high winds swirling and blasting straight off the lake. Yet, he could see a dozen lights, movements, and the sound of a portable generator in the distance.

It was like a little city on the ice and as Russ gingerly tested the ice for traction he was surprised how sure his footing was.

He'd gone ice sailing with Harley the January before and had found the ice often rough and bumpy. The winds, storms, and varying temperatures made for a strange combination of ice conditions.

"Hey Russ" came a welcome from Harley as he buzzed up on one of the strangest contraptions Russ had ever seen.

"Morning Harley, what's that you're driving, or riding?"

"Yup, I know, what will they think of next?" the little man chuckled despite the black coldness and the churning vortex of extreme weather. "It's a DTV® Shredder, an S200-UT dual tracked vehicle with the utility trailer. I've got two of them out here" he said as he pointed behind him. When Russ looked he saw Harley's great-granddaughter, Taylor, whiz by.

"Come on Grampa, they need the supplies" she hollered.

"Gotta go, the boss is calling" Harley said with another chuckle and with that the two "dual tracked vehicles" disappeared south toward the parking lot at a surprising speed.

What looked like a utility trailer, sunk up to its axle in the ice, sat in the darkness, illuminated by a bright LED light on each corner.

As Russ hurried to get inside and close the door he saw Griff coming at him with a large block of ice.

"Hold the door, would 'ya Russ, I've got Dane right behind me."

The two men sat the blocks off a dozen feet next to a

stack of bright orange boxes.

"Ain't this the greatest morning to be alive?" Griff said, holding his hands aloft to the sky as if he were basking in the golden rays of the sun on a warm Caribbean beach.

"I know what you're thinking" Dane said as he came in and Russ closed the door, "crazy, right?"

Russ laughed.

"You guys have been busy" he said.

"Not every day you make $10 million, you know?" David Gaertner said as he stood up stiffly.

"Well" Russ said quickly, "it's like I said, this is a longshot, so don't get your hopes up prematurely."

"Yeah, sure, right Buddy!" Griff said as he elbowed Russ with a broad grin. "We're ready to hit the Mother Lode!"

Russ stopped trying to reason with them, the new team members and the belief that they would soon be multi-millionaires had energized them almost like some kind of drug.

"I've cut two holes" David said to Russ. "That one is 3' x 4' for entry and egress, that one is a little smaller, for the pump."

What looked like a swing in someone's front yard hung from a winch over the larger of the two holes. Thanks to Russ's time in the Navy he recognized it as a Boatswain's Chair. This would be their method of getting into and out of Lake Champlain in their dry suits.

"What are you pumping?" he asked David.

"Silt, dirt, along with water. You'll use the head like a vacuum and what you pick up will be brought up here and then discharged down this tube Dane will stretch out 100' to the southwest, the current will take the load away from you two and your visibility should remain perfect."

"My visibility?" Russ said with a laugh, "I'm not going down there."

The three men immediately stopped what they were doing and stared at Russ in absolute silence.

"What do you mean, you're not going down there?" Griff asked seriously. "You were a Navy diver, right?"

Russ looked at the stony faces and thought suddenly of Mount Rushmore.

"I was in the Navy and I was a diver, but that was thirty years ago."

"Just like riding a bike" Griff said with a firm slap on Russ's shoulder. "You'll get the hang of it once your back in the saddle, brother, believe me!"

"I don't doubt that" Russ said, "but I still have no intention of getting 'back in the saddle'."

Griff was losing his patience and Dane wasn't sure how to handle Russ's refusal. Like Griff, he'd assumed that Russ was going to captain the underwater salvage.

David stepped in during the tense silence and said something that made Russ's blood run cold.

"I'm afraid you don't understand, Russ. It isn't that we don't appreciate the brainstorm you had yesterday. Dane was right about you, and we've all got our fingers crossed that you were right, but, well, this isn't an option for you." David said these words without emotion. He wasn't trying to threaten, cajole, or persuade Russ, he was just stating a fact.

"You see, you can't have your share of the treasure until you've been baptized by Lake Champlain. That's the gist of what Griff has been trying to say. Right now you're just a Landlubber with a good idea. Once you go down into that icy water you'll be a 'born-again Lake Champlainer' and you'll be worthy of your share of the treasure!"

"Yeah" said Dane with a cruel grin, "and then you'll have something to complain about."

"My dry suit will fit you perfectly" Griff said with a happy grin, "and I'm glad to share it with you."

As Russ and Dane sat down and started putting on several layers of thick wool socks, sweatpants, and sweatshirts, Russ asked about the trailer.

"It's a Yetti™ 8' x 17' with a hydraulic axle lift system,

custom built." David said proudly. "With two hatches in the floor. We've used it before Russ, just never 30 feet from shore. We never imagined it would almost be on the beach."

"What kind of helmets do you have?" Russ asked as he looked at the icy water lapping at the edges of the holes David had cut.

"Kirby Morgans" Griff said matter-of-factly. "Overkill at this depth but they'll keep you high and dry. You'll have a 500-041 SuperLite® 27 Commercial Helmet, no worries."

Russ knew Kirby Morgan, KM, made great helmets but still, he thought to himself that he had plenty of worries.

With the help of David and Griff they were ready to go in about 40 minutes and Russ could see the sky outside the Yetti's little windows beginning to brighten.

Dane went first, bravely Russ thought, and disappeared in a rush of bubbles into the dark depths of Lake Champlain.

"You'll be fine" David said, tapping on Russ's helmet, "You've got two lights on your helmet and I've got a camera running. We'll see what you see. We are directly above the Morning Star. You've got this."

Russ was breathing easily inside the KM and he nodded confidently despite his anxiety.

"What would Thorndike think of me getting wrangled into this fine mess?" he thought as the dry suit and all the extra clothes were pressed tightly to his body by the encroaching water. As his torso vanished into the whole he felt a definite chill, but thankfully it wasn't as bad as he thought it would be.

"T'was the day before Thanksgiving, and all through the house, nobody was making a fuss, except for poor, old Russ!" This was Russ's last thought before his feet hit the bottom.

He imagined he could almost hear David and Griff laughing above and thought, now I'm a "born-again Lake Champlainer."

Russ was a self-contained unit, free to move where he wanted to, with two powerful waterproof lights shining down on him and identifying the hole in the ice above. He didn't move his feet, instead he searched his surroundings with his high-beam helmet lights and camera. When he made out the shape of the sloop he was standing dead center. Everything was covered in a fine mix of sand and silt between 3 and 6 inches deep but it was all clearly visible to him. He looked and pointed to his right, toward the bow. He reached out and touched the 3 feet of remaining "main mast" near the center of the ship, and pointed aft, to the telltale stub of the helm.

This was a sloop and Russ was amazed. Now he just hoped it was "His Majesty's Ship," the Morning Star, from 1777.

Dane appeared out of the dark nothingness and handed Russ the long, rake-shaped front of the vacuum nozzle and gave the "thumbs up" sign.

Russ knew computers, shoe-treads, handwriting, knot-tying, and historic ships. He believed the hatch would be a raised lid, 4' x 6' or 7' on a ship the size of the Morning Star, and it should be located somewhere between the mast and the helm.

The vacuum proved more powerful, or the silt-load on the two-hundred and forty-some year-old ship was not hard and packed. He moved freely toward the rear of the ship while Dane carried the main weight of the trailing vacuum line that rose to the pump above.

To Russ's surprise the ship's surface was in far better condition than he would have thought and soon the aft hatch appeared for the first time in over 240-some-years.

Russ had believed "from the math" that this grid held the long sought-after treasure-ship. To actually be standing on her deck and watching the hatch appear out of a bed of sand and silt was another matter altogether. Russ was now as excited as Griff had been earlier. What Russ Personette couldn't know, and wasn't thinking about, was the jubilation that was exploding in the Yetti™ trailer above. David, Griff, and Harley, the original "Die-Hards" who'd pushed for 12 years to find this ship, were gathered around the computer monitor with young Taylor, screaming, jumping, and celebrating the momentous occasion.

Russ handed the underwater vacuum back to Dane and then knelt stiffly to lift the hatch. It came up easily, smoothly even, and Russ peered into a ship's hold that hadn't seen the light for as long as there had been an America. Then he gave Dane a "thumbs up" sign and signaled they wouldn't need the vacuum and line any longer.

Russ counted 20 boxes below and then he entered the hold of the Morning Star. The chill was beginning to penetrate his body and he hoped that the moment-of-truth that now lay before them would prove all they hoped.

Every crate was heavily built with rusted iron bands and locked shut. Russ bent and lifted one. Even underwater the box was heavy. He sat it back down and turned to Dane, who'd followed after him with a flat Vaughan® Superbar™ crowbar.

Even without much force the latch held shut by the lock pulled free of the old wood and Russ moved the metal out of the way so he could open the lid. When he did a burst of bright, yellow light exploded out of the box. The combined four halogen headlights of the two divers reflected off of the box full of English golden Sovereigns and filled the small hold of the sloop with a golden radiance.

Dane patted Russ on the back, a congratulatory, brotherly gesture. Above the celebration was so raucous that Harley, as fit as he was, had to sit down to catch his breath. Griff ran screaming from the trailer and, arms flailing, raced joyously across the ice and into the bright rays of the morning sun.

The original boxes were still strong enough to transport the coins and the work of two hours saw all twenty boxes hoisted up to the trailer, carried to the DTV utility trailers and transported, by Taylor and Harley, to Griff's Dodge Power Wagon™, where it was secured under a heavy-duty locking pickup bed cap made of stainless-steel Diamond Plate™.

Russ was in good condition but when he was hoisted into the trailer again, his body was so spent all he could do was roll out onto the floor and wait for help.

It was 2 PM when the white Lincoln Mark LT pickup truck pulled into Wildrose again. Operation Golden Doubloon had been a success, but for now silence had been the chosen course.

As Russ walked slowly to the front door, his tired muscles rebelling at the effort, he was reminded of a line from Charles Dickens' story, A Tale of Two Cities.

"It was the best of times; it was the worst of times."

Here were his 4 friends celebrating the greatest discovery of their lifetimes, a take worth $10 million, or two million each for the 5 of them. The best of times. Meanwhile, in another valley not far to the south of him was another friend, Vivian, living her final days, the result of an inoperable brain tumor. The worst of times.

There was something more locked deep in the vaults and recesses of Russ's intricate mind. It was a room of great sadness and one he tried hard to keep closed and locked. It was filled with memories of lost loved ones who had gone before their time, unexpectedly, and without warning. Without "goodbyes." The memories of his late wife and their daughter, of their fatal car accident, were kept in that locked chamber and those who were getting to know Russ more deeply knew he wasn't as tough as his rugged frame suggested.

It was in this mindset that Russ had heard Vivian say, "I believe this will be the last time I see you, dear friend, and so I want to thank you for the friendship and care you've given to me since the first moment we met."

"I believe this will be the last time I see you, dear

friend."

He played it over in his mind. 13 words total, 12 words of one syllable, 1 word of two syllables. Not a complex sentence. In fact, almost as simple in structure and form as it could be, but what those 13 words conveyed, the volumes that could have been written from them, were cataclysmic.

Russ noticed things. Chief Ramsay had been immediately impressed by his attention to details and his surroundings. Russ had honestly told the two Law Enforcement Officers, "I pay close attention to a lot of things. I've tried to develop my skills of observation and reasoning as much as I could."

He noticed coats hanging in the hallway, the presence of white hair and dandruff on one coat, whether someone's handwriting was made with a left hand or right hand, what brand of shoes someone wore, how a knot was tied in a rope, what kind of hat someone liked, and last names.

Russ Personette also noticed words, even the shortest words in a language. Sometimes the simplest sentences said the most profound things. An old friend had once described him as a "Wordsmith."

What Vivian was really saying was, rather than wait for this condition to destroy her, she was going to act. While she was still well enough to function as she always had she would set her world in order, see to the future care of her two much-loved companions, Winston & Benjamin, say her "goodbyes," just as she had with Russ, and then she'd leave this life on her terms and at her chosen time.

All this is what Vivian had said. She didn't just "believe" their visit would be the last time she would see Russ. She "knew" it was the last time because she was in control, and she undoubtedly knew everything, the how, the when, and the where.

Russ had read the third chapter of her autobiography, "Platinum Blonde," to Thorndike the night before, while the cat pretended to sleep. Chapter three was called "Long Live the Queen" and it told of Vivian's sudden and unexpected coronation, at a mere 19 years of age, with the death of her husband, to the head of the Delashmett Empire. The young woman who had been cooking at the Lucky Ladd Mine in Idaho just four years earlier, was now in charge of one of America's greatest family fortunes.

From the very beginning she saw herself as a steward of her beloved husband and his parents, and she brooked no opposition. Soon she was known as "The Queen" as she oversaw the mining, business, and agricultural operations of her sprawling kingdom. During an age when family-owned mines were failing or being swallowed up by madly expanding and unrestrained corporations, the little woman had steered her great ship through the troubled times with a steady hand. She was in control then, and Russ knew she would be in control until the very end.

That was what she meant when she said, "this will be the last time I see you, dear friend," and Russ knew it. It was a dark thought, destined for the locked chamber in Russ's mind, for he had come to love and admire Vivian, and he would feel her loss keenly.

"It was the best of times, Thorndike; it was the worst of times" he said as he closed the door behind him.

There was no beautiful cat sauntering through the vast living area of Wildrose, no sassy "yip" from the upper balcony, "the cheap seats" as Russ referred to it, or the high branches of the old oak tree, and no feisty "Road-Kill" pose on the back of one of the leather club chairs.

There was only a cold wind and a drift of snow on the floor in the corner of the Wildrose living area. Then Russ saw the broken window and the dark, red blood on the windowsill, and his heart stopped.

"Thorndike!" he screamed, and his eyes searched everywhere.

"Thorndike!"

Again and again he called for Thorndike. He raced through the house, up onto the balconies and around on every bookshelf, behind the club chairs, the bedrooms, bathrooms, in the kitchen, and under the dining room table.

The cat had scared Russ before, terribly, and it always made him realize how much he had come to care for the magnificent animal. Russ couldn't even begin to explain how he felt. Thorndike wasn't a pet, he was a friend, a confidant, a trusted companion, and even a lifesaver. The relationship the two shared was complex and, for outsiders, difficult to understand. Lara understood best and she loved the fact that "her two boys" were best of friends. Chief Ramsay, bless his pun-spinning heart, insisted he didn't believe a word of Russ's "Cockamamie Soup." Yet, the offices of "Thorndike & Personette, LLC" were always among the Policeman's first stops when there was a puzzle to solve.

Detective James admitted that he was lost at first, when Russ proved not to be one of the lead characters in "Villains I Have Known." It had taken the young man a while to see "The Cat and the Professor" for who they really were. Now, he saw Russ and Thorndike as Vermont's version of "Bat Man and Robin" with Thorndike filling the lead role, a kind of "Cat Man and Ruskin." This never thrilled Russ. To add insult to injury, instead of "The Caped Crusaders," August James, the soon to be Hollywood "leading man," said he saw them as "The Cat Crusaders" fighting crime in all its forms in Chittenden County!

When Russ returned to the broken window he saw the cat. He was outside, sitting in the deep, Starbuck Valley snow, in the middle of a trail of blood that led up through the trees toward Hunters Lane.

Despite his exhaustion from the morning's adventure on Lake Champlain, Russ ran out through the traditional double, front doors of Wildrose, as fast as he could. At the sound of his voice Thorndike turned slowly and gave a faint "Yip." Russ knelt in the deep snow without thought and took the cat into his arms.

Someone had obviously tried to break in to Wildrose while Russ was away. They must have thought that even with Wildrose's sophisticated security system they'd be able to get what they wanted and get away before the police had a chance to get there. It probably would have worked too, had it not been for the vigilance of "The Cat Crusader."

"Are you hurt buddy?" he whispered.

Russ didn't doubt Thorndike's incredible strength and his agility was absolutely mindboggling at times. What he could do defied physics.

As he looked into Russ's eyes though, it seemed the cat was confused by his experience and when he collapsed in Russ's arms, he rushed with the big cat, back into the house.

Thorndike was covered in blood and almost unconscious when Russ laid him on a towel on the kitchen bar where there were bright lights pointing downward. He searched over the big cat's body with his fingertips, inch by inch.

"Mah-yaow" came softly from Thorndike several times but, despite the blood, Russ could find no wounds. The fact that there were no wounds didn't mean Thorndike wasn't injured, only that the blood wasn't his.

Russ called Police Dispatch and reported the crime, but he didn't wait at Wildrose. Despite the coming of another big winter storm and a thick veil of falling snow, twenty minutes later he pulled the big Lincoln Mark LT 4-wheel drive into Dr. Debbie's Veterinary clinic. The Purple Parrot™ Veterinary Clinic took care of all kinds of small animals and it had the distinction of being the only facility that would care for birds in a 4-county area of Northern Vermont.

"Do you smell that?" Doctor Debbie asked.

Russ leaned down over the cat and sniffed around his nose and mouth.

"Disinfectant?" Russ asked, then, realizing the

significance of this he fearfully said, "Did Thorndike get into my cleaning supplies?"

"Chloroform" the pretty veterinarian said curtly.

"Chloroform?" Russ repeated without understanding.

"Chloroform leaves a disinfectant smell."

Thorndike, in his sedated state, lay on a white towel on the examination table while Doctor Debbie checked all his vitals and then examined the big cat head to foot.

"Someone chloroformed him" she said, "based on what you've told me it obviously wasn't enough to be immediately effective and this big guy put up quite a struggle."

Thorndike made some of the sounds Russ had called "Drunken Sailor Noises" when he'd brought him in during the summer.

"Why would anybody want to chloroform a cat?"

"Catnapping is a crime, Russ."

"Catnapping?" Russ said in a state of disbelief.

"The kidnapping of pets, especially high-end, valuable pets held for ransoms, has exploded in the last five years alone" she said sadly. "Up 30% in the last year. That's why I was so happy when you wanted to do the microchip for Thorndike."

"You mean you think someone was really trying to take Thorndike for a ransom?"

"Based on what you've told me, yes."

Russ was speechless. When Eileen had first mentioned the idea, a year earlier, he'd not even considered putting a chip in the cat. It seemed ridiculous. It took him six months or so, and a lot of encouragement from Eileen, to be able to finally do it. Now he was being told that someone, in Chittenden County of all places, had really tried to conduct a "Catnapping" on his little buddy. It was incredible.

"One of the earliest petnapping's in America was a dognapping" Debbie said as she continued her minute examination of the handsome cat. "A group of fraternity boys from Harvard successfully dognapped the Yale mascot, a beautiful bulldog by the name of 'Handsome Dan,' in 1934, if you can believe that. Since then such crimes, for ransom though, have become all too common."

"He seems to be fine and uninjured, no wounds, no broken bones, and his heart rate and breathing are normal and steady. There was likely enough of the chloroform on his face and head to render him unconscious, especially when he stopped moving. The fact that he passed out in your arms tells me the crime had just occurred. The person or people who did this were likely only a short distance away from you at the time, perhaps still on your property, even as you cared for Thorndike."

Driving home Russ was overcome by waves of emotion. Anger, indignation, disbelief, and frustration at his own naivety. His inaction and passivity to Eileen's warnings had put his little buddy, roommate, partner-in-crime-solving, and friend, at risk. As Russ looked down at the peacefully sleeping cat he knew it was a miracle Thorndike wasn't dead or, at least, missing and in the hands of catnappers.

"Is he going to be okay?" Detective James asked when Russ returned home, placing Thorndike in his Mila™ cat bed.

Russ straightened up slowly. The adrenaline of his nightmarish experience had faded and his aching muscles were screaming at him.

"He will, thankfully, and I've had a real wake-up call. It was pure luck he isn't dead or the prisoner of some catnapper."

Russ's voice betrayed the anger he felt at himself for not having taken stronger security measures. He knew one thing for certain, money had not been the obstacle. His own slowness to listen to Eileen and take her warnings seriously now weighed heavily upon him.

"Well, Russ, I hate to disagree with you but I'm afraid it might be a little more than 'pure luck'."

"What do you mean?"

Russ's mind was a blank. He had no idea what Detective

James could be talking about.

The Detective pointed out the window.

"Do you see the spot in the snow where you knelt down with Thorndike?"

Russ nodded.

"Well, did it strike you that the blood trail was very heavy?"

"I don't think I was focused on that." Russ admitted.

"I understand, Russ, but just beyond that small pine tree, not 15 feet from where you knelt down, is a dead body."

The words instantly froze Russ in place. He didn't move, didn't blink, and didn't even breathe. Finally he gasped.

"A dead body?"

Detective James nodded.

"Do you feel up to identifying it?"

Russ took a deep breath. A part of his mind couldn't believe any of this was real. The box of golden Sovereigns he'd opened just that morning, now seemed to be an experience from another life, in another time and place.

As they stood over the body, Russ was stunned to see a face he knew well.

"Do you know him?" the Detective asked, routinely.

"I bought a motorcycle from him last summer" Russ said in little more than a whisper. "He said he wanted to become a veterinarian."

"There's only one wound."

"Then how is there so much blood?" Russ said in shock.

"It looks like Thorndike got just one swipe and he got the jugular" Detective James said, "This was found near the broken window."

It was a ransom note that said, "$150,000 to see your cat alive again. Directions will follow. No cops - or else."

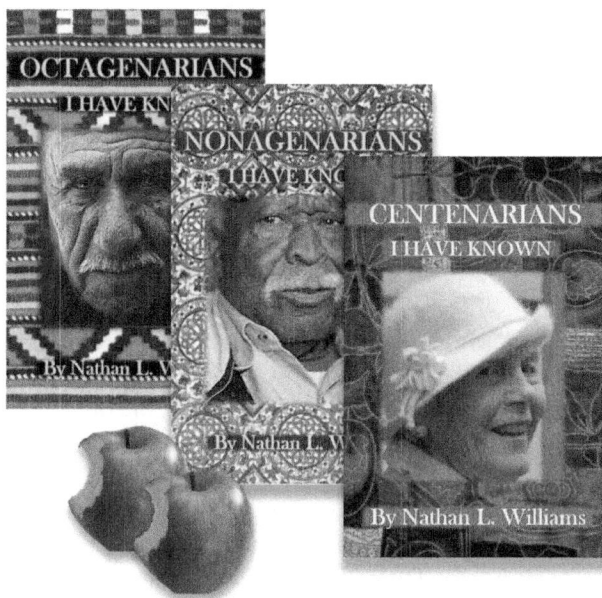

# CHAPTER EIGHT
## 3 Books & 2 Bad Apples

"Happy Thanksgiving to Russ and Thorndike in the Great White North, from the prettiest girls in the Big Apple." Laughter punctuated the video of Daphne and Eileen holding the dozen, long-stemmed deep-red roses Russ sent to Daphne to congratulate her on publishing her first book of photographs.

The elegantly dressed women ended their short movie-quality message with proclamations of love and adoration, for Thorndike of course, and lots of laughter, presumably for Russ.

"It was 9 AM on Thanksgiving morning and the message helped lift Russ's dampened spirits. The day before had been challenging, to say the least, and Russ needed a pick-me-up.

He saw a second message on his smartphone and he took a deep breath before he checked it.

"I hope this is a good one too" he said to Thorndike, who sat imperiously at his favorite chair at the head of the table.

He instantly recognized the quavering voice of Lara's Great-Aunt Virginia. Her message was given as if she were writing a letter.

"Dear Russ" she said stiffly, "this is Virginia and Gracie and we want to thank you so sincerely for the beautiful 'early Christmas presents' that were just delivered. We wouldn't have opened them until Christmas, of course, but your message commanded us to open them first thing, so we did. We don't know what to say, the gifts are the most lovely we've ever received. I love my Biddy Murphy® Irish Ruana.[18] Now it's your turn Gracie. Hello Russ, this is Gracie. I adore my Tiffany™ Peacock Feather Shawl. We will wear these today when we go to Vivian's for Thanksgiving Dinner.[19] Thank you again."

"Yeeoww" Thorndike said insistently.

"Don't complain" Russ said, "I put your name on the cards. I always do, 'Thorndike & Russ,' you always get top billing."

Russ had seen the ladies at several events and Gracie had always worn the same pale green shawl. So he'd decided to find them each the most exquisite gifts he could and he hoped it would make them feel special on one of the most important holidays of the year.

After breakfast Russ wrapped a dozen or so presents for different people. He planned on delivering many of them during the afternoon of Christmas Eve, a pleasant surprise

---

[18] Biddy Murphy Calzeat™ Irish Ruana, made in Biggar, Scotland. See: amazon.com

[19] Louis C. Tiffany™ Peacock Feather Shawl. See: store.metmuseum.org.

for each recipient. He always enjoyed giving nice gifts and loved to make people feel special.

Lara, of course, had gotten her "big" Christmas present already, the garnet-red Kia® Telluride™ 4-wheel drive, with a big red bow on it, with a front license plate that said, "My Girl". Her shock and joy had been so satisfying to watch. Her little Ford had so many miles on it that she just kept praying it could make it to 200,000 miles.

Russ had never dreamed of finding love the second time around, but he was on Cloud 9 to have Lara. She loved it when he called her his "Cat's Meow."

He'd never forgotten what Bernadette had once said to him.

"Old Blue Eyes says, 'Love is lovelier the second time around'."[20]

The "little" gift he'd gotten her was a yellow gold Celtic Claddagh Ring, called a "Caged Heart" because his Garnet birthstone was contained in the heart area of the ring. He knew it would look wonderful on her beautiful hand and it was hard for him to wait for Christmas to give it to her.

He was happy that Virginia and Gracie liked their gifts so much. He knew they lived on a tight budget and made do with very little extra. In the back of his mind he had the beginnings of a plan forming whereby a newcomer to the county, a man by the name of Ronald Fernsby, would play a leading role.

As Russ cleaned up the table he heard the familiar revving of a snowmobile motor. It wasn't the powerful machine-gun sound of the new motors, more a smooth running, older model.

When he rounded the corner into the living area and looked out the windows he saw Lou Langlois's "swimming pool green" 1971 Johnson Skee-Horse with the long, blaze orange vinyl seat. Russ had grown up with snowmobiles out west and "the Johnson," as they commonly referred to the

---

[20] Second Time Around, Frank Sinatra, Reprise Records, ©1960.

machine, was a perennial favorite of his.

It wasn't Lou climbing off the machine though. It was a much slighter built, younger man. Russ knew Nathan had been living with his grandparents since the successful completion of what he had called "Operation Cheesecake" and the end of the Gordon Parrish Gang. They had been blackmailing Nathan and with Russ's "classified" help their days of extortion were over for good. Afterward Nathan never returned to Bennington and his dental hygienist career.

"Hey Uncle Russ, hi there Thorndike, looking good my man!" Nathan's casual, easy-going ways reminded Russ of one of the first History Professors he'd ever worked with, Dr. Marcus Thomas. Dr. Thomas had murdered their boss, Dr. R. J. Kaiser, and was doing life in the State Penitentiary as a result. Russ and Thorndike had played a behind-the-scenes but significant role in the exposure and capture of the young man, but try as he might, Russ had never viewed Dr. Thomas as a true villain or bad man. As Russ saw it, the young man had gotten caught up in an affair with Dr. Kaiser's alluring young wife and one thing led to another. Russ often wondered about Marcus Thomas. He was a clever young man and would have gone far if he'd been able to focus his energies on his career.

"What brings you out on a cold Vermont Thanksgiving morning, Nathan?"

"You know you're a really smart person, Uncle Russ, and I've finished all my cataloging work for Vivian. She paid me well and I've got a good nest egg, plus, I get a percentage of her sales on "Platinum Blonde" and I get all the royalties from the other two books. So I'm in good shape as far as that goes, but I was wondering what I should do now. My mind is, like, numb though and I can't think of any ideas. Grandma said to ask you. Do you have any ideas for me?"

Russ looked at his adopted Nephew with appreciation. His spunk and openness were two things he liked most about him. He got Nathan a cup of his favorite coffee, Folgers Classic Roast™.

"Let's sit over here in front of the fireplace" Russ said casually.

Wildrose had a large, open living area and Russ had thought about a huge, central square arrangement of the big, non-descript, rectangular sofas that were so popular. His interior decorator, Samantha Uptheroad, had other ideas though and recommended arranging several, more intimate sitting areas in various locations.

There was the circle of club chairs around what had increasingly come to be called, "The Ramsay Rosewood Table™," in the same way someone might say, "The Wedgewood Dining Set," "The Chippendale Chair," or "The Tiffany Lamp." The Ramsay Rosewood Setting was closest to the side-door of Wildrose, which, for all practical purposes had become the main entry because of its nearness to the parking lot.

There was another circle of club chairs closer to the original front, double doors with thick beveled and etched glass, and it was just beyond this grouping where "Thorndike's Spot" had been located. It had turned out to be the area above the body of a man who had been attacked in the 1800's and had crawled under the floor of Wildrose to hide. His injuries proved fatal and he died there.

A circle of wingback chairs were partially under the cast iron balcony that ran around the room. They were closest to the corner window where the unfortunate young intruder had recently broken the window.

Lastly, was a half-circle of wingback chairs arranged around the large, orange brick fireplace, with Thorndike's magnificent portrait hanging above the mantle.

"I have a couple ideas" Russ said sincerely.

"Well, I'm sure glad to hear it, my mind is blank."

"You were a natural with Vivian" Russ said to Nathan. "You communicated well and formed a sincere friendship, which is increasingly rare between the generations."

"Yeah, I owe my Grandparents for that" the young man said frankly. "Growing up with them I don't even notice age, you know. People are all people to me, we all have our lives to live and stories to tell, and you can't judge a book by its cover. I mean, look at Viv for a minute. A little woman in her 90's who likes the finer things in life and controls a multi-bazillion dollar empire, and she started out at 15 as a camp cook for a bunch of rough, tough miners in the Rocky Mountains. I mean, who'd ever guess that?"

"Exactly" said Russ, "exactly, and you have the gift of getting their stories out of them. Let's face it, that's your gift. So here's my idea."

Russ spent the next thirty minutes describing a labor-intensive project requiring lots of travel, interviews, notes, photographs, and editing. He called it the "I Have Known Project" and it would take advantage of Nathan's gift with his elders.

"Imagine" Russ said to the young man, "not one book, but a series of three books built on the biographies of elders throughout our Vermont communities. People like Harley Shaw, Lara's Great-Aunt Virginia and their family friend, Gracie. People just like Vivian, with their own stories to tell, punctuated by spectacular photographs just like your portrait book on the Caledonia Estate."

Russ could see the young man was captivated by the idea.

"One book would be the biographies of elders in their 80's and would be called 'OCTAGENARIANS – I Have Known' by Nathan L. Williams. The next book would be the biographies of elders in their 90's and would be called 'NONAGENARIANS – I Have Known' by Nathan L. Williams. The last book would be the biographies of elders over 100 and would be called 'CENTENARIANS – I Have Known' by Nathan L. Williams."

"I love it" Nathan said exuberantly. "I mean, I love it Uncle Russ. It's brilliant, and later on it could lead to a whole bunch of other books, like, 'BOATMEN – I Have Known,' or 'PLUMBERS – I Have Known'."

"Or even 'POSTMEN – I Have Known'." Russ said with a laugh.

To his surprise Nathan said, "Or 'PROFESSORS – I Have Known'."

An hour later as Nathan sat on the bench by the side door and put his boots on he couldn't contain his excitement.

"I'm going to start with Virginia and Gracie, I'll bet you they have had incredible lives but no one knows about it. And I'll put Virginia's face on the cover. Can you imagine how much the world has changed since they were my age?"

He gave Russ a huge hug and told him how much he appreciated everything.

"Thanks a million, Uncle Russ, you're the best!"

Not long after, the purring of the Johnson Skee-Horse could be heard as Nathan headed south and then east toward his Grandparent's farm on the Middle Fork of the Starbuck River, which was more correctly and more confusingly called, "The West-Middle Starbuck," though no one would or could tell Russ why.

Speaking of names, Lou and Bernadette's farm was called "Nut Run Farm." Supposedly this was because of a grove of Chestnut Trees that stood along a section of rapids in the little West-Middle Starbuck River.

Arnold said that was only a cover for the real reason, that Lou was a real nut and was still on the run. "Nut Run Farm," in this second explanation, never failed to make Russ laugh, and Lou's wonderful sense of humor went right along with it.

"Someday they'll come for me. Until then, I'll party like a Rock Star" said the retired flute-player-music teacher-turned-organic barley farmer!

Russ didn't have to pick Lara up until 6 PM so he showered and shaved, then put his heavy US Navy, dark blue and yellow sweatshirt and sweatpants on. This was one

of his most comfortable outfits. Over this he wore his
Baturina™ Navy Blue Paisley Silk Dressing Gown. The
unexpected gift from Vivian had been like none he'd ever
received and made him think about the dear woman. She
was entertaining several of the older women of the
community at Caledonia. Among them were Virginia and
Gracie. It had been one of Vivian's Thanksgiving traditions
for many years and only Russ knew this would be her last
one. He shook his head. The Chandler Gang was now
believed to have murdered as many as 7 wealthy
Chittendenders with their conspiratorial assassinations,
claiming vast fortunes in the aftermath. One of the
conspirators was Vivian's own Doctor, and while the Gang
had failed to kill the doughty little woman, her doctor had
managed to give her a death sentence by not diagnosing her
condition in time to save her. They would probably never
know if it was the result of the man's incompetence or his
indifference but it was too late now. Either way, the result
was the same. The inevitable death of Russ's friend.

Finally he put his Sorel® Men's Dude Moc™ slippers
on and headed to the kitchen.

In his loudest baritone he began belting out one of his
favorite tunes. Few knew the song and fewer still knew
where it was from. Even fewer enjoyed his singing and
apparently Thorndike was one of these, as he scurried
away to hide in the highest branches of his old Oak, in the
living room.

"Lazy, I want to be lazy, I want to be out in the sun, with
no work to be done, I want to be lazy!"

Russ thought he sounded good and he loved the tune
and the words of the Irving Berlin song, but Thorndike's
agonized "Yeeoww" let him know his singing was not
appreciated.

"Everybody's a critic" he huffed as he poured out
another cup of hot coffee and marched to the living room
to harass the big cat.

"I'll have you know that song is a classic, it's from the

1942 movie 'Holiday Inn', starring the incomparable Bing Crosby and the flawless footwork of Fred Astaire, so there."

Thorndike's silence was deafening.

"Okay, Thomas De Quincey!" Russ hollered.

De Quincey had been a 19th Century English essayist famous for his criticisms of other writers and poets.

Russ sat down painfully in the wingback chair. His muscles were still sore from his labors of the day before, but he was comforted to know that the treasure from the sloop, Morning Star, were securely ensconced in Harley Shaw's vintage bank safe. Harley had purchased the "Hall Lock & Safe Company™" bank safe from the City of Underhill, probably for the same reason he purchased the 1963 Aston Martin with the steering wheel on the wrong side. The safe had been the newest, "state of the art" safe available in 1889 when it was installed in the First International Bank of Underhill, just in time for the bank's "Grand Opening". The Underhill Ledger/Beacon newspaper said "330 persons" had attended the Grand Opening, although their reporter admitted that "some of that number were children" and, therefore, not old enough to open a new account.

Now the safe graced the basement "Museum" of the amazing little man who had collected so many vintage items of local historical importance that he was referred to as the "Historian Laureate of Starbuck Valley."

Russ had overdone it but he meant to rest before the big Thanksgiving Shindig at Arnold and Rhonda's.

"And you're coming along" Russ said to the cat in the shadows high above.

A quick "Yip" in protest said otherwise but Russ was having no arguments.

"The window is only fixed with duct tape and Dan Garn won't be able to fix it until tomorrow" Russ said in his most convincing voice, "and if you think I'm leaving you here for the next Catnapper, your mistaken young man!"

Then, feeling imperious, Russ swished his hand as if he were an ancient, High-King wielding a scepter, gold no doubt.

"I have spoken" he said regally.

Then his phone began it buzzing and he answered Detective James.

"Hello Detective."

"Happy Thanksgiving, Russ. I'm sorry to bother you today, of all days, but some of us are still working."

"I understand" Russ said sincerely. "I wish you didn't have to."

"Thanks, I wish my wife was that understanding."

"I get it" Russ said, "I had a job like that once too, no murders, but lots of hours."

"Anyway, I'll be quick about it so you can get back to the party."

Russ laughed and thought to himself, "If he only knew how stiff and sore I was, and why, he wouldn't say that."

"First off, that vintage motorcycle you bought from our perpetrator, it turns out it's stolen property so someone will be out tomorrow to collect it. They'll give you a receipt but I'm afraid you're going to be out whatever you paid for it."

Russ was shocked and on top of all the sadness he felt for the young man, this was just all the more disappointing. The money, thankfully, wasn't an issue for him, but his regret at everything to do with the former veterinarian's assistant was overwhelming.

Arnold had once called Russ "Nature's Nobleman." It was a title Arnold had thought up himself, decades earlier when they were in the Navy together, and he believed it captured the character of his strange friend. At his core Russ was a person who loved to see people dream and succeed. He wasn't stupid, and until recently he wouldn't have described himself as naïve. He knew people made bad decisions and the consequences were often inescapable. Nathan's experience with the Blackmailers was just one proof of this sad truth.

He had been happy to think of the young man going off to Veterinary College to fulfill his dream. He hadn't even suspected the 1937 Indian Chief motorcycle could be stolen property and as experienced as he was he would have sworn the story about becoming a Veterinarian was sincere. Of course, people like him wanted to believe the best of others, and this meant they would always give the benefit of the doubt. How and why it had happened, life had taught Russ a disappointing lesson and it was one he wouldn't forget.

"I'll have it ready, Detective."

"Thank you, Russ, I'm sorry."

"Not your fault, these things happen, unfortunately" Russ said stoically. And having a mind like his meant he remembered the exact moment he last spoke that line, "these things happen unfortunately." It was nearly a year earlier when he saw Arnold for the first time. Russ had spoken those words about the death of his late wife.

"The other item is more of a problem and I'm sorry I'm only telling you now."

As Detective James paused, Russ said, "don't worry about it," knowing that human nature was such that by saying those words the Detective would probably worry about it all the more. Russ had found that humans were often among the most puzzling of all the animals.

"Well, you won't say that when I tell you that Marcus Thomas escaped from prison over two weeks ago and they only just now called us. He is considered armed and dangerous."

Russ's heart skipped a beat. He'd thought about Dr. Thomas much more in the past couple weeks than he had in all the time since the R. J. Kaiser Murder Case was closed. He looked up at Thorndike, draped gracefully over a thick branch, and thought "You Devil! You knew about his escape and you've been trying to tell me, but I've been distracted, as usual."

"Russ, are you still there."

"Yes, I'm sorry about that. You're right, that takes me

by surprise."

"He could be anywhere Russ. You have to take precautions."

"He's probably over the Canadian border by now if he has half a brain. I know that's where I'd be" Russ said emphatically.

"I hear you, but revenge does strange things to people, and his cellmate has admitted that Dr. Thomas was obsessed with making you pay. Chief Ramsay is in Bennington for Thanksgiving but I updated him and he said one thing, Russ."

Detective James paused at this point and Russ took it that it was for more than effect.

"Okay, what did the Chief say?"

"He said you'd better take this warning far more seriously than you did the last time you were told that Marcus Thomas was on the hunt for you! He said that you survived that first time, you took a bullet the second time, and that the third time would be a charm! Are you listening Russ?"

"I hear you; I hear you, Detective, and I appreciate you and Chief Ramsay. I'll make some arrangements."

What arrangements he might make were still a mystery to Russ, but one thing was certain. Russ Personette had finally had enough close calls to wake him up. He didn't yet know what he'd do, but he knew it better be good!

The first thing he did was to get himself and his little buddy, that big cat Thorndike, down into his "safe room."

After that he called Lara first.

It was a difficult conversation but she agreed that nothing could hurt Russ Personette more than to see Lara Meredith hurt.

"We'll get our things packed and we'll be ready when you get here."

"I'll be there as soon as I can" he said, his voice tinged with a mix of fear, and desperation.

Next, he called Arnold. Like Russ, Arnold and Rhonda

lived far from others and they lived even more remotely than Russ, out on the dead-end of Lone Mountain Road. Arnold called it "The Road Less Traveled" and had put a quote from Robert Frost's poem, "The Road Not Taken" up in the foyer of his modern home.

**Two roads diverged in a wood, and I –**
**I took the one less traveled by,**
**And that has made all the difference.**

While Russ didn't believe Arnold would be a target of Dr. Marcus Thomas's revenge, he wanted him to know what was happening. All of Russ's hopes for a beautiful Thanksgiving were being dashed, but worst of all was the threat Marcus Thomas posed.

Russ meant it when he said the man was probably over the Canadian border by now. He knew if the roles were reversed that's where he'd be. He also knew that Detective James was right, the desire for revenge did strange things to people.

His third and final call was to Dan Garn, codenamed "The Postman." Dan Garn was really an undercover FBI Agent, a spy, and probably one of the finest rifle shots in the Northeastern United States.

"You listen to me" Dan said demandingly, "you don't leave that safe room for one hour, minimum. Swear it!"

Russ paused a moment too long and Dan hollered across the phone, "Swear it!"

"Okay" Russ gave in, "One hour, but what will that do?

"That will give me time to get there" Dan said, knowing what that would convey to Russ. Dan was taking on the role of Russ's protector.

# CHAPTER NINE
## Mayhem Aplenty

He had chafed at his promise but he'd waited the hour. Now, carrying two large canvas totes filled with clothes, canned foods, and other necessities, and one big cat in a harness, Russ hurried as fast as his aching muscles would move. His large, orange-brick garage was to have been 3 bays with a storage area but one of the last-minute changes that Russ had become famous for, meant that Garn Construction had to design in a fourth bay. Like most new buildings there was lots of empty space in the garage in the early days. Now it held a variety of boxes, both empty and full, the old Indian motorcycle, which would soon be taken away, the Mercury Grand Marquis, sitting out the winter under a car cover thanks to Russ's mechanic, and the huge Lincoln Mark LT Crew Cab pickup truck.

He sat the bags on the concrete floor and carefully strapped Thorndike into the center of the backseat. Even in the stress of the moment Russ noticed that Thorndike always looked like a dignitary arriving at Camp David for a chat with the President, as he sat high in the middle of the seat.

"Time to go, Buddy" Russ said, then he closed the door.

Russ froze. He didn't even have to turn around. He could see the reflection of the tall, young man in the shiny window of the Lincoln, and it wasn't Dan Garn. It was Marcus Thomas and he was holding a pistol.

"You should've moved" he said coldly. He sounded different than Russ remembered. His voice had once sounded almost musical, alive and vibrant. Now it was flat and one dimensional, cold and bitter.

"You should've left" he said again. "You had to know I'd get out. You're smarter than anyone gives you credit for and you knew I'd get out. For such a smart man, you sure were stupid."

This gave him cause to laugh and in that sound Russ recognized some of the former Marcus Thomas' joviality.

"Before I take my revenge I want you to turn around and look at your handiwork, Professor P."

These last words were almost hurled out of Marcus Thomas's mouth and every word was full of bitterness.

Russ turned slowly, holding his arms up.

"Listen Marcus" he said as he turned, but when he saw the young man the words caught in his throat.

"Hideous isn't it? This is what you did, you and that damned, meddling cat." Then the young man screamed, "You ruined my life!"

Russ tried to speak but Marcus yelled, "SHUT UP" and the reverberations echoed around the garage.

Russ was horrified. Marcus had been a handsome man when they first met. The women were attracted to his good looks as much as they were to his beguiling charm. Russ had liked the young man and saw a bright and happy future for him. Now, he didn't even recognize him. A mass of scarring on the throat and face had left a grotesque mask with sneering lips. It had changed his voice as well as his articulation of individual words. Marcus Thomas was painful to look at.

"That's right" he bellowed, "you did this. I had a life, a future, I was happy, rich, and loved. We were going to Saint Kitts, in the Caribbean. We had everything taken care of but you couldn't leave us alone. You had to destroy our happiness, and for what?" he screamed again, shaking his head wildly as he did so but keeping a Glock™ 9mm pointed straight at Russ.

"For what?" he screamed again. "For R. J. Kaiser? The man was a parasite."

Russ couldn't see a way out. Marcus didn't want to hear anything he had to say. He just wanted to explain why he hated Russ, and Thorndike, so much, then he wanted to kill them.

"Listen Marcus" he said again, and again Marcus screamed, "SHUT UP."

"You have nothing to say to me. I thought you were incredible. I thought you were brilliant and you'd make Charbonneau famous. I thought you were my friend."

"I was your friend" Russ said, surprised that Marcus let him get the words out. "I'm still your friend."

"Enough" Marcus screamed, lifting the Glock into firing position. Russ was going to say something when he heard the loud explosion of the pistol and he was thrown back against his big truck.

He tried to clutch at his chest, even through the thick winter coat, but he couldn't. That was when he opened his eyes and saw what had happened.

Marcus Thomas was on the floor of the garage, moaning in agony, his entire body trembling in pain, and blood around` his right knee.

In the door of the garage stood a shadow, darkly silhouetted against a backdrop of bright, white snow.

The shadow in the doorway wore what looked like a fedora and, with arm bent, it held the pistol pointing upward. Russ couldn't make out the face but he knew the shape of a hammerless Ruger™ LCR .38 Special when he saw one.

Over the moans of Marcus Thomas, Russ heard a familiar and reassuring voice.

"Agent 36 never misses."

It was Bernadette, and she wore a wide-brimmed,

waterproof hat shaped very much like the traditional fedora.

"Agent 36" Russ whispered, still in shock, slowly realizing that it had been Marcus who'd been shot, and not him. Then he noticed a tiny hole, smaller than a dime, its edges smooth and round, in the window of the Lincoln.

Even with Bernadette's rescue, Marcus had only missed Russ's head by a fraction of an inch.

Thorndike looked unhurt and Russ stared long and hard at the cat.

"You alright, Buddy?" Russ stammered.

"Yip" was Thorndike's unperturbed answer.

Bernadette retrieved the Glock™ 9mm with her gloved hand and placed it inside the Lincoln. It had fallen a dozen feet from the wounded man.

"You certainly live a charmed life, M."

Ever since he had initiated her as "Agent 36" Russ had found her insistence on calling him by the codename "M", just like in the James Bond movies, to be endearing.

"Why Russ, I feel like your 'Miss Moneypenny'."

She was a unique woman. One of the best cooks anyone had ever known. She could look at a recipe and tell you what ingredients to add to make it better. A notoriously bad shot when hunting animals, Bernadette was the best free-hand pistol shot the State Trooper, who ran the conceal-carry class, had ever seen, ever.

"She's a natural with that pistol, it's like it's just an extension of her hand" he'd said in disbelief.

The quiet Vermont homemaker had been the only person with the instincts and insight to see through Russ's mask and identify him as a spy, years before she'd even met him.

The irony of it all was incredible. Yet, somehow, the unique, 5' 4" woman had showed up in the nick of time to save both him and Thorndike. Now she stood in his garage, gun in hand, in command of the situation. She looked down at the moaning, would-be assassin without mercy and was unmoved by his pleading and moaning.

"I was taking an apple pie out to Lindy Taal's place, for Thanksgiving" she said as casually as if she and Russ were sitting at her kitchen table drinking tea.

"Lindy fell at a seniors' dance in Underhill and sprained her ankle" Bernadette explained.

"I saw this guy's little car on the shoulder of the road, up by the corner of your property" she said pointing to the North. "When I saw the Glock™ holster and the box of 9mm shells in the passenger seat I called the Police and came straight down here, as quiet as you like."

"What is it with these bad guys?" she asked rhetorically. "My grandsons always say the villains in their computer games have to 'monologue' before they do their bad deeds. Why is that I wonder?"

"I think they just really want to be understood" Russ laughed nervously. He was regaining his composure. He'd always been cool under pressure and he hated to admit that after taking an assassin's bullet in the shoulder during the summer, he was more easily shaken.

Seeing that her victim was completely incapacitated Bernadette pulled her coat aside and slid the Ruger 5-shot polymer revolver into her All-American Girl™ Thigh Holster.

"Never leave home without it" she said firmly, happily quoting the slogan for American Express.[21]

Russ's garage looked more like the scene in a Hollywood crime drama than anything from real life. The scarred and disfigured Dr. Marcus Thomas, a former History Professor, lay writhing on the concrete floor, clearly in agony, while his diminutive conqueror, a Vermont Puree-Maker with her own line of foods, stood boldly in the middle of the room, the very picture of calm. It was all seemed so surreal and staged to Russ. Even after

---

[21] "Don't leave home without it" business slogan for American Express created by Ally & Gargano Advertising Agency.

surviving the moment he couldn't help but feel it was something he was dreaming, and he'd wake up soon.

A moment later a breathless Dan Garn ran in and surveyed the scene.

"I got caught behind a snowplow" he said, pointing South, "and a hundred cars, can you believe it?"

"No problem Dan, Agent 36 here saw to it."

Dan Garn, the lean, fit Postman-Poet of the North, handsome in what Eileen had blushingly called "a rugged, Great White North sort of way," looked from Bernadette to Marcus Thomas and back again.

The scene reminded Russ of a historic parallel. The Sioux Chief, Sitting Bull, toured with "The Buffalo Bill Cody Wild West Show™" in the late 1800's and upon watching the petite Annie Oakley shooting her rifle, the famed Chief gave her the name, "Little Sure Shot".

He wasn't surprised when Dan turned to Bernadette.

"Pistol Packin' Mama!" he said in a hushed, reverential tone.

To Russ she'd always be "Agent 36" but when Dan Garn's account of events were read in the Burlington "Free Press", the Jericho "Clarion", and the Pinesburg "Daily Gristmill", the next morning, Bernadette Langlois became irrevocably known as the "Pistol Packin' Mama" to thousands throughout the community.

Dan took control of the garage while Bernadette took Russ and Thorndike back inside and treated them to Hot Chocolate and her famous hot apple pie.

"Poor Lindy won't be getting any of this pie" she said as she served Russ.

"Her loss is my gain, literally" Russ smiled, knowing that the delicious, calorie-packed pie was the last thing his figure needed.

By that evening the Police were gone and Marcus Thomas was back in custody and under guard at the hospital. A barricade of yellow crime tape sealing off the garage was the only evidence that anything out of the norm had happened at Wildrose. Yet, the fact that two men had assailed Russ & Thorndike in two days was a chilling reality. One had paid with his life, the other, as Detective James had assured him, would walk with a painful limp for the rest of his life. It would be a constant reminder, as if the image in the mirror wasn't enough, of Russ Personette and Thorndike.

Russ's Thanksgiving had been spent with Police and in an investigation far from where he'd planned on being. Lara, as well, had canceled her plans and stayed at home.

"I'm just thankful I won't be visiting you in the hospital" she said quietly. "You do worry a girl sometimes."

This last admission had to be the understatement of the year and Russ knew his life had been quite unusual since coming to Vermont. He was still sobered by how close Marcus Thomas' bullet had come to his head and his instant death. He was truly indebted to Agent 36.

On a bright, clear Friday morning, with ice crystals glimmering in the cold air, the front-page Newspaper stories came out with their "Pistol Packin' Mama" headlines. They reported the "nobbling," "hobbling," and capture of the escaped murderer of late RJ Kaiser, "Dr. Marcus Thomas, former Professor of History at Charbonneau College." Bernadette Langlois was identified as the person who'd singlehandedly brought in the dangerous, armed escapee, and the national press couldn't get enough. They picked up the story and by evening Eileen and ten million others were reading about her in New York City. Folks from the Bay of Fundy to Imbler, Oregon, to Hale'iwa, Hawaii, were reading about "The Pistol Packin' Mama" of Vermont. Russ was thankful that the reporter gracefully said the event had taken place somewhere "in the upper Starbuck Valley."

The same reporter had described "the accidental death" of "an as yet unidentified young man" during an attempted break-in at "a residence on Hunters Lane."

Russ thought the reporter deserved a PEN/Faulkner

Award™ for Creative Fiction, but in truth he knew that the care and circumspection that were shown were due to the involvement of his two friends in Law Enforcement, Chief Ramsay and Detective August James. They couldn't keep the news from being reported but they could try to keep Russ's name off the front page of the Free Press.

Russ had a fitful night's sleep, filled with stressful, shadowy dreams, and aimless, impossible struggles. When he awoke and threw his pajamaed legs over the side of his bed, he felt like he hadn't slept at all. His eyes were dry and blinking was painful. His throat hurt so much he wondered if he'd picked up a cold or flu from one of the many people who had been investigating at Wildrose the two previous days. His muscles, especially in his back, were still sore from his treasure-hunting activities on Wednesday, which seemed a lifetime ago. In other words, Russ Personette didn't want to get up.

Two of the Garn Construction men showed up at 9 AM sharp to repair the window that had been broken.

Virginia and Gracie called at 9:30 to thank him again for his beautiful gifts and to tell him they'd been admired by everyone who attended Vivian's annual Thanksgiving Dinner.

Chief Ramsay drove in at 11:30.

"Boy, I can't leave you alone for a minute" the Chief said, with the air of a martyr. Two guys in two days, what's going on here?" He shook his head in disbelief, then he grew suddenly serious.

"I've been on the phone with the state commissioner and you have our sincere apologies that Dr. Thomas's escape was not communicated in real time." Then holding his hand up to stop Russ from speaking, he said, "and before you say it's no big deal I have to say it's a miracle you're alive. Thank God for Bernadette Langlois, although I would never have believed she was such a great shot. I want you to know I filled out the paperwork and nominated her for the Congressional Medal of Honor

Citizens Honor Award.[22] They give out a handful of awards for courage and service every year and I think Bernadette deserves one."

At 12:30 Griff Langlois called to see if Russ had heard anything on the sale of the treasure yet. Russ's Attorney, Alexis Stonecipher of Stonecipher-at-Law, was overseeing the state and federal legalities surrounding the sale of the Morning Star salvage-treasure as there were a long line of buyers ready to bid on the treasure. Russ told him he hadn't yet heard but that was expected because of the Holiday and promised to call first thing.

When Alexis called not five minutes later he was shocked.

"What's the good news?" Russ asked eagerly. Like Griff, news could never come soon enough for Russ.

"Russ, I'm afraid I'm not calling about the treasure. I'm sorry" she said as sweetly as she could. "I'm calling about Vivian Delashmett."

Russ froze. It couldn't be. Vivian had said as much but it couldn't have happened so soon.

"Russ I'm afraid that Vivian passed away in her sleep last night. She was suffering from an inoperable condition."

Silence followed her words and to her credit she remained silent as well. Although she was still quite young Alexis, sadly, had already had a great deal of experience dealing with death in her life.

"Thank you for telling me" Russ finally stammered out the words. "What comes next?" he asked awkwardly.

"Her personal attorney is in New York and she will call us at 2 PM our time. We can meet at your place or here at the office, whichever you are more comfortable with."

"Your phone system will be better, so I'll come in."

"I'm glad" she said, "we can take care of the paperwork while you're here as well."

---

[22] For more information about the Congressional Medal of Honor Society, see: http://www.cmohs.org/.

After ending the call, Russ ran his fingers through his hair and moaned out loud.

"Oh Vivian" was all he could say. "Oh Vivian." A remarkable woman and a dear friend was now gone and the world was an emptier place. The world was poorer for the loss of such people.

Thorndike seemed to sense his loss and he laid quietly on Russ's lap as the man watched the flames in a state as close to a trance as he'd experienced in many years. He'd known death and the most profound loss in his life and unlike the comforting sayings so many shared, Russ found nothing beneficial from the experience. It had taken years for him to come out of a dark depression and those days remained something he never spoke of.

He'd seen the strength in Daphne and Lara and he was honest enough to admit he didn't possess the same. In many ways Russ believed women somehow possessed a deeper inner strength. He'd heard the jokes all his life, mainly from men, but unlike the joke-tellers he believed fortitude of the fair-sex was underestimated. He'd seen it time and again. Like the telepathy he felt growing between him and Thorndike, he didn't understand it. Yet, it was his belief.

Even as he watched the flames he sensed Thorndike's gaze and then, out of the blue he said one word.

"Duncanson."

He brought both hands to his head again, realizing what the word meant, and he said it out loud, "Duncanson, Duncan...son!"

"I'm sorry to bother you Detective, but I've been a blind fool. I know I told you and Chief Ramsay I believed Dr. Charles Duncan was the murderer of John MacKean."

"Yeah, Russ, about that. There's a little problem with that theory because the airport surveillance tape shows Dr. Duncan getting on the plane."

"I know" Russ said, "I mean, I figured that out. What I'm trying to say is Major Robert Duncanson was the man who wrote the Glencoe order and took part in the last stages of the massacre. His name was Duncanson. I don't think it was Dr. Duncan anymore, Detective, I believe it was his son, 'Duncan's Son' or Duncanson."

A long silence followed from the other end of the phone before Detective James spoke.

"This is one of those moments, Russ, when I would give a million dollars to have Chief Ramsay standing right beside me, hearing you talk. I mean, you know what he'd say, right? The stuff you and that Crime-Cat come up with is some of the cockamamiest stuff I've ever heard, but my instincts tell me you two will be proven right again. I don't know how, but I think you've got me on the right track at last. At least, I hope."

Russ shook his head after the call ended.

"Duncanson" he said looking straight at Thorndike. Then he said, "I can't believe I didn't understand what you were trying to say Thorndike." The big cat continued to stare at him.

As Russ dressed for his visit with Alexis he was talking to Thorndike, who had seated himself regally in the center of the large bed.

"Maybe Eileen was right, maybe I'm the problem" he said as he pulled on one of his new suit coats.

"Yeeoww" said Thorndike loudly.

"Yeeoww what?" Russ said, "Eileen was right that I'm the problem or you don't like my jacket?"

Thorndike shook his head, as if trying to communicate with the human was just too much hard work, then he sneezed, then he went to licking his paw and smoothing his silky fur.

Eileen's words wouldn't go away though, they floated through his mind, unbidden and, honestly, unwanted.

"Unfortunately, you are the greatest obstacle to the communication between you and young Thorndike. You are the weak-link Russ."

"Okay" Russ said in a sudden and uncharacteristic flash

of anger, "so I'm the obstacle, the problem, the weak-link."

Thorndike stopped, mid-lick, with his paw still suspended in space and looked at Russ, who sat down in one of the two Danish Modern Teak Lounge Chairs in the bedroom.[23]

He sat staring directly at Thorndike, without moving.

The handsome cat stared back, paw still suspended motionless in space, tongue half-extended to lick.

Russ didn't move. The cat didn't move.

Russ was determined to focus on the cat and nothing else. The cat was determined to go on with his "preening," as Russ often called it, despite knowing full well that preening involved birds and feathers, not cats and fur.

Russ would show Eileen once and for all, with no distractions, that he wasn't the "weak-link."

"This is ridiculous" he thought, and then he rebuked himself and redoubled his efforts to block out all other thoughts.

Thorndike finished his licking his paw, looking back at Russ several times before lowering his leg and sitting up straight.

The cat and the man considered each other in silence for one minute, then for a second. It almost seemed like they were playing a staring game, to see who'd blink first, when Thorndike suddenly yawned.

The long rows of sharp, talon-like teeth were shocking reminders that cats were a top-tier predator. Humans may have tried to domesticate them as beloved pets, but the fact of their position at the unchallenged pinnacle of predators was attested to everyday, with the phrase "King of Beasts." Dogs might be "man's best friend" but the cat held a different position. The feline relationship with their human counterparts bore a degree of independence and sovereignty unknown by their canine equivalents. In fact, Russ knew several men who lamented "Why can't a cat be

---

[23] Danish Modern Teak Lounge Chairs by Komfort Denmark™, Etsy.

more like a dog."

Whenever Russ heard such hilarity, he was reminded of a song from "My Fair Lady," that Rex Harrison sang. Russ remembered it from his misty youth and the lines, as close as he could recall, went something like this:

**Why can't a woman be more like a man?**
**Men are so honest, so thoroughly square;**
**Eternally noble, historically fair.**
**Who, when you win, will always give your back a pat.**
**Why can't a woman be more like that?**[24]

Again and again Russ's mind wandered. He couldn't believe how difficult it was simply to focus his attention on receiving a signal from Thorndike. He viewed himself as an intelligent man, after all, hadn't he accurately deduced the location of the sloop, Morning Star, and that after only an hour or so of studying the evidence, and still, he was unable to focus his thoughts. In fact, he was on the verge of admitting a humiliating defeat when something truly extraordinary happened.

Russ considered the human mind supreme and incredible. Eileen had been correct about him when she said most people viewed humanity as the apex species on the planet.

Now, while focusing his mind on Thorndike, even as flawed as his attempt had been, three words finally presented themselves.

"Drummond," "Wrong," and "Again."

Was it purely his imagination or was it really telepathy? Was his entire 'telepathy theory' just a bunch of hogwash? Russ was beginning to doubt himself.

He'd read a wonderful, rollicking adventure book to Thorndike in the Spring. The big cat had enjoyed that book more than any other Russ had read to him, even

---

[24] "Why Can't a Woman Be More Like a Man?" from the musical, "My Fair Lady," starring Rex Harrison and Audrey Hepburn, 1964.

more than Shakespeare's Macbeth©, Thorndike's clear runner-up. There was no feigning sleep when Russ read either of those books, no-siree!

"What was that book called? Oh, yes, 'Swashbuckler – The Incredible Adventures of Clarence Drummond'."[25]

That had been the last time Russ had thought of the name "Drummond."

"So why are you giving me that name, now?" Russ asked Thorndike out loud. Did the cat want to hear his favorite book again?

To Russ's disgust, Thorndike, the handsome cat who always made sure his catly hygiene was taken care of, lifted a back leg in a pose that would have pained a gymnast, and went to cleaning what Russ had once heard delicately called the "Nether-Regions."[26]

Russ grimaced.

He had coined the phrase "Cleanliness is next to Catliness" when he observed Thorndike's ablutions, but now he looked away, involuntarily.

He thought again of the name.

"Drummond"

Was it the cat's reference to the adventure book? Really? Surely not.

"Drummond, Drummond, Drummond."

Earlier Russ had thought of name Duncanson, out of the blue. Duncanson had been the man who wrote the infamous "Massacre Order" for Glencoe and he took part in the last stages of the massacre.

Then the words "Wrong" and "Again" came quickly to his troubled mind.

Duncanson had NOT taken part in the last stages of the massacre. That was "wrong"! Russ was "wrong again"!

---

[25] "Swashbuckler – The Incredible Adventures of Clarence Drummond," KDP Publishing, ©2020, amazon.com.

[26] Lillian Jackson Braun, author of the "Cat Who" Mystery Series, used the term "nether regions."

"Duncanson didn't kill anyone!" Russ said firmly, looking directly at Thorndike. Duncanson had given the order but he hadn't killed anyone.

"Yip" said the beautiful animal, who was still in his "Painful Gymnast's Pose."

"Duncanson only wrote the order" Russ said. "He only wrote it!"

It was Duncanson's trusted subordinate, Captain Thomas Drummond, "Drummond," who, on the evening of February the 12th, 1692, delivered Duncanson's infamous order to Captain Robert Campbell, who was called "Campbell of Glenlyon".

"It was Captain Thomas Drummond who participated in the last stages of the massacre, not Duncanson."

"In fact" Russ said thoughtfully, "he killed two people."

"Two people."

Russ lifted his hand to his head and ran his fingers through his graying temple.

"Drummond" he said out loud.

"Yeeoww-Yaa-ree-baa," Thorndike said in a long, lyrical, drawn-out call. Russ had never heard the sound before and, whatever it meant, the meaning it conveyed to his mind was powerful.

"Finally, you got it!"

Russ hated to call Detective James again. He knew he had to but he didn't want to. Then, when he did, the young man insisted he wait on hold while he called Chief Ramsay who was still in Bennington with his extended family.

After Russ explained everything via conference call the Chief was beside himself.

"Glencoe, MacDonald, MacIain, MacKean, Campbell, Duncanson, Drummond, come on Russ, what's next? Abergavenny or Hogmanay?[27] You've got to be kidding me?"

---

[27] Abergavenny is a town in Wales. Hogmanay is the Scottish celebration of New Years.

"We've also confirmed that Dr. Duncan, who is still in Mobile, Alabama, by the way, doesn't have a son. He only has a daughter, Margaret, who we've yet to track down" the young Detective said. "She and her father are estranged and he doesn't know where she is living currently."

After a moment while the "gears" in his head were working overtime Russ said, "And I'll bet she's the mother of Ryan Drummond, that would make him Duncan's grandson. He's the young man who sold me the stolen 1937 Indian Chief motorcycle, told me he wanted to be a Veterinarian, and tried to catnap Thorndike!"

"You have got to be kidding me?" Chief Ramsay said again. "Russ" he said in a pleading voice, "we haven't been able to locate the kid's next of kin. Don't you think that this time you might just be clutching at straws?"

"She lives in Vergennes, the oldest city in Vermont" Russ said confidently. "I think she's remarried so she won't have her son's last name, but he told me where she lived."

"Yeah, just like he told you he was going to be a Veterinarian right, that he'd rebuilt the motorcycle himself, and that he was the inventor of tin foil?" Chief Ramsay said facetiously, in obvious frustration.

"We'll look into it, Russ" Detective James said in an even, controlled voice."

After the call ended Russ turned apologetically to Thorndike. The glorious Maine Coon Cat, and winner of a blue ribbon at the local cat show, was now sitting "Adonis-Like" on the back of his favorite leather club chair, in the Ramsay Rosewood Setting.

"I don't blame the Chief" Russ said, "He has the patience of a Saint to deal with me. I've sent them on a merry chase, really."

"Yip" was all Thorndike would commit to.

"And thank you for that vote of confidence" Russ answered humorlessly, shaking his head so that Thorndike couldn't miss the gesture.

Later, the man and the cat walked up the bare, dry

sidewalk with a rare dignity. Russ wore his new Pronto Uomo™ Platinum Executive Fit Sport Coat in taupe check. Thorndike wore his yellow and black, Dean & Tyler™ "Cats Rock" harness for big cats.

"We look pretty good" Russ said as he looked down at Thorndike.

"What?" he said, "A blink is all I get? What do cats know about fashion anyway?" The latter phrase was one of Russ's favorite insults to throw at Thorndike and every time he said it he felt powerful. "This must be how Eileen feels when she insults me" the thought. "Except that what I'm saying is true, what do cats know about fashion anyway?"

"Weak-Link, indeed" Russ huffed.

As they passed the "Stonecipher At-Law" sign that Russ and Dan Garn had put up in the middle of the night some months earlier, Thorndike jumped from the sidewalk and sat down as-pretty-as-you-like in front of it.

The greatest benefit Russ derived from his smart phone, at least in his opinion, was the ease in using it as a camera. He clicked several shots of the big cat as he basked in a rare, warm winter sun, in front of the sign. What was more, Russ was shocked when he lifted the phone and Thorndike did NOT go automatically into his now-famous "Road-Kill Pose." Then he noticed the warning on his phone's screen.

"Insufficient memory to save data."

"Aagh!" Russ exclaimed, "and that darned cat knew it!"

Russ was beside himself. He'd never gotten a good shot of his little buddy, and the moment he'd gotten one this had happened. He shook his head and a thought occurred to him.

"What do humans know about photography!"

Russ spun his head to look at the guilty cat, who judiciously looked away.

"You scoundrel!"

"Yip, yip, yip" Thorndike said, but the cadence of his Feline speech sounded much more like, "ha, ha, ha."

Alexis and her assistant, Mindy Underhill, were talking at the reception desk when Russ & Thorndike, in their Sunday Best, walked in.

Mindy, short for Melinda, and her sister, Mandy, short for Miranda, were the twin-daughters of Claude and Carol Jantzen Underhill. They were the owner/operators of "Underhill Plumbing," which was, ironically, not located in Underhill, Vermont, but in Jericho. Russ had gotten this interesting history from the young woman on one of his first visits to the law firm.

Mindy's eldest sister was named Mariah. Mariah was married to one of the Scrimshaw boys, Rupert perhaps. The Scrimshaws were second-generation "immigrants" from Maine. Mariah was an interior designer and business partner with Samantha Uptheroad. For the purposes of her business Mariah, who went by the nickname "Mars," had kept the recognized Vermont name of Underhill rather than go with the "immigrant" name of Scrimshaw.

So the name of their interior decorating company was "Uptheroad & Underhill," or "U & U," as the young women referred to it, instead of "Uptheroad & Scrimshaw."

"Uptheroad & Underhill" had done the decorating at Wildrose and Russ had gotten to know Mars and Sam well. He enjoyed family names and their stories and he found the Uptheroad & Underhill names fascinating.

"I actually knew an Uptheroad in Washington Court House, Ohio" he'd once said to Samantha, and then he'd had the gall to ask, "any relation?"

The look he'd received was priceless and definitely worth much more than a thousand words.

"If you meet an Uptheroad, I guarantee we'll be related!" He had tried her patience and he recognized the signs of "Name-Fatigue." His name had generated a constant flow of commentary and questioning from the general public and, for once, he wondered what it must feel like to go through life as Bob Smith or Arnold Williams.

On another note, no one had been able to tell him how long the Scrimshaw name would be identified by long-time Chittendenders as an "immigrant" name. This was even more perplexing as one of the ancient mountains was called "Scrimshaw Mountain."

Harley Shaw was only able to tell him that "during the first generation a name is called a 'Refugee Name,' and in the second generation it becomes an 'Immigrant Name'."

"Welcome to Stonecipher At-Law, Mr. Personette" Mindy Underhill said formally, her training coming out. Then, looking at Thorndike she said, "What a magnificent fellow."

"Thank you for coming Russ" Alexis said personably, adding, "Please accept our condolences on your loss, Vivian will be missed."

"Yes" Russ nodded, "I will be lost without her, in many ways."

Alexis showed them into a conference room, saying before they went in, "Vivian's personal attorney is already on screen and ready to meet with us."

Russ had held dozens of meetings using the same method but he still found it impressive to be able to feel so close to someone who might be on the other side of the world.

"Mr. Personette, thank you for meeting with me. I'm Mrs. Delashmett's legal representative in the matter of her last will and testament. Do you understand?"

"I do."

"My name is Ernestine D'Boisvert of Chadwick, Smutz & Hoadley, Attorneys-at-Law, and I would like to offer you my deepest and most sincere sympathies on your loss."

"Thank you" Russ said, even as he translated the woman's last name "D'Boisvert." In English it would have been, "of the Green Wood." Russ knew enough history to know that the Boisvert name came early to Quebec and went back to some of the earliest French Settlers.

"Am I to understand that Ms. Stonecipher is your legal

representative?"

"That is correct" Russ answered.

"Very well, are you ready to begin?"

Alexis had poured out two crystal glasses of water and put some in a crystal bowl on the table in front of the chair where Thorndike sat upright and attentive.

"May I just say" Ms. D'Boisvert said, "what a gorgeous Cat he is?"

"Yeeoww" said Thorndike emphatically.

"He is most appreciative" Russ added.

"Very well" the New York Attorney said, "matters will now proceed according to Ms. Delashmett's own predetermined order. First I will read you a letter from her. Then I will follow up with a summation of Ms. Delashmett's Estate. First of all however, there are two formalities. Do you understand?"

Russ understood, he also knew that for specific legal reasons he was being asked "do you understand."

"Thank you. Is your name Ruskin Makepeace Personette?"

Russ winced at the pronunciation of his full, legal name, just as if someone had punched him in the ribs, and Thorndike looked suddenly at him. Russ got the peculiar notion that the cat was laughing, not outwardly of course, as he had earlier, but inside and uproariously.

"For reasons known only to my parents, yes, that is my full, legal name. They always said they preferred Ruskin Ichabod Personette, but they drew the line at saddling me with initials that spelled RIP." The attorney said nothing and continued.

"And what is your birth 'day'? I do not need the year. Just the month and day."

"I was born on February 29th, so I'll be 15 on my next birthday."

"Yes, quite so" she said nonplused, then added, "thank you."

So far Russ's humor had not been appreciated by Ms.

D'Boisvert, but he could tell Alexis had valued it.

"Now I will read you Ms. Delashmett's letter, but before I begin, would you allow me to say something personal."

"Yes, of course" Russ's voice quavered as he answered and he found himself recalling his many visits and adventures with Vivian. He had tried to use humor to keep his emotions in check but, frankly, it wasn't working.

"I've never done this before" the lady said stiffly, "but as I knew, and served Vivian for the last 20 years of her life I feel her loss as well. What I want to say is, that in all the time I knew that wonderful woman, I never saw her happier than I did after she met you. I want you to know that during our last conversation Vivian referred to you as 'the son she wished she'd had'."

Alexis had wisely stocked the table with a box of tissue and Russ dabbed at his eyes.

Thorndike rose up on his hind legs and in a movement that was incredibly human he reached out a forepaw and put it on top of Russ's hand. After a moment he sat back down in his own seat.

"What a remarkable thing" Alexis said, in surprise.

"Yes" agreed Ernestine D'Boisvert, "very."

"Now for the letter" Ms. D'Boisvert began after a moment.

"Dear, Dear Russ, God certainly saved the best for last with regard to you. You came along at just the right time for us and I don't know what I would have done had you not arrived when you did. Not only were you a man who could be trusted, but, as you will see, you were the man to entrust with my most important possessions. You know very well that I refer to Winston Churchill and Benjamin Disraeli. I know you will honor me by loving my precious little friends just as you love your very special Thorndike.

I also entrust to your care something that has been important to me, and which I have looked after as a faithful steward would, the Estate and fortune of my dear, late husband's people, the Delashmett's.

I cannot burden you with the many demanding business enterprises I oversaw. So, in the last six months I've overseen the quiet sale of every business and property other than Caledonia itself.

I ask you not to concern yourself with any further attempt to expand the Delashmett Fortune. This was the heavy burden I carried over the last 78 years and this responsibility has been fulfilled.

Beyond my two sweet friends, I burden and entrust you as my faithful steward only in caring for the Estate and the fortune.

With the first, I ask you to move to Caledonia permanently and care for Winston and Benjamin there. Caledonia is the only home they've ever known and losing me will be shock enough for them to deal with. They both adore you and you spoil them so, that I know they will find happiness with you and Thorndike at Caledonia.

With the second, I ask that you use the fortune to do as much good as you can. You have a rare and noble heart; one which money will empower but not corrupt or command. This is one of the reasons I said you were the perfect man to entrust.

I supported many causes in my time and have made plans for those I cared for to be taken care of into the future. You will have no one to call upon your charity at my behest. You were a blessing to me, to Bernadette and Lou, to Arnold and Rhonda, Virginia and Gracie, Dear Daphne, Nathan and Ben, Beautiful Lara, and so many more in this community. I ask you to freely find your own way forward in being a blessing in our world.

If you do good with what I leave you, then that will be enough for me. I cherished your friendship more, I think, than you will ever know and your visits lifted all our spirits. You are the one and only person I have had the pleasure of never saying "goodbye" too and I look forward to seeing you again, someday, someplace, for such is my firm, fixed, and sincere belief. I remain very truly your friend, Vivian

Q. Delashmett, Caledonia Estate, The Pine Valley."

Russ had wiped his eyes many times during the reading of Vivian's letter and he had sobbed a time or two as well. He wondered how the attorney had gotten through the reading but when he looked up he saw that she too had been wiping her eyes, and so had Alexis.

"I must say, Mr. Personette, I've never seen another letter like this in my career."

The rest of the meeting was somewhat a blur to Russ. His emotions were raw and more than once he had to get hold of himself. What was clear from the presentation was that the Delashmett Fortune, which had been almost immeasurable before, had been doubled by Vivian's sale of the businesses and other properties which she had managed for so long. The Fortune, as Vivian had referred to it, was in the hundreds of billions of dollars, and shook Russ to the soles of his feet. More than ever before he understood why the Chandler Gang had targeted the energetic little woman.

"Vivian sat up her own cremation and I have seen that her wishes are being carried out. She also prepared an obituary, not wanting to force that duty upon you, and it will run in the Free Press newspaper tomorrow. She wants no funeral or service at this time. She would like you to scatter her ashes in Innisfree Brook on the Estate, at the location of the large Pavilion, on the first day of Spring in the coming year. She said this was her favorite spot. She has made a list of the guests she would like invited and gives you the liberty of adding any others you'd like.

"Vivian's accounts have been transferred to your name, Mr. Personette, and your credit and account cards and documents have been sent express for delivery to you at Caledonia tomorrow. Lastly, let me say that I, and Chadwick, Smutz & Hoadley, will continue to serve you in the function we served Vivian, for as long as you desire or until you name new representation."

# CHAPTER TEN
## New Beginnings

Russ parked in the spot he used on his first visit to Caledonia and as he and Thorndike exited the big Lincoln he looked around him, remembering that first meeting with Vivian and Benjamin. He remembered her Shillelagh, which she had purchased on a trip to its namesake village in Ireland when she was "young," by which she meant when she was 70. Russ admired walking staves of all kinds and none more than the Shillelagh. Vivian's had been the traditional Blackthorn, a hardwood, and it had the shine of years of loving wear. He wondered now, where it might be.

Russ's mind came back to the present. The parking lot and roads of the Estate had been maintained well during winter and despite nearly two feet of snow all around they were bare and dry. The Manor House, as Vivian referred to it, was still glorious, but it no longer seemed as vast and mysterious as it had during his early visits. He knew his way around the old place well enough now that he wouldn't get lost. At least this was the case on the ground floor and the second floor. Beyond that, on the "Family Floors" he had never ventured.

"Welcome to your new home, Mr. Personette, and is this young master Thorndike?" the Head of Household asked as Russ entered the cavernous and magnificent, two-story high Main Hall.

Edward Bright, "Edward-Arthur William Bright," to be exact, was the 40-something "Head of Household" in charge of the Manor House. He had joined Vivian as a young man and had worked his way up the ladder to manage a staff of 28 "Domestics".

"Yes, this is my buddy Thorndike" Russ said, surprised at how shaken his nerves still were.

"Sir" Edward said, noticing Russ's ashen complexion, "may we serve you tea in the Little MacIntosh?"

The Little MacIntosh was a cozy, Black Walnut paneled sitting room on the ground floor, just off the Main Hall.

"That would be wonderful, and if you could have Benjamin and Winston brought to me there, I would like to introduce them to Thorndike."

Edward hesitated, uneasily, then apologetically said, "I'm afraid master Winston has been out-of-sorts, of late, and remains at large in the Delashmett Library, Sir."

"I understand" Russ said casually, well aware he was not playing the part of the new "Laird" as formally as Mr. Bright would have liked. "Bring us tea in the Library and I'll see what we can do."

"Right away, Sir."

Russ made his way to the Library on his own. It was the first time a member of staff had not escorted him directly to the "Mistress," as Vivian was called by her employees. Her mother-in-law had been called the "Mistress" as well and Vivian respected the traditions put in place by those who had gone before her, those who had established Caledonia. She had been the Mistress of Caledonia for almost 80 years and Caledonia was over 80 years old when she had first come to it, "a young, windblown thing, out of the rough west".

Thorndike walked into the vast and awe-inspiring, two-story Delashmett Library without pause, and then he sat down to take in its entirety.

Russ removed his harness and remembered his first visit to the library, which was always referred to as "The Delashmett Library," and he couldn't forget that this was the room where Vivian had chosen to take her final leave of him.

As the man and the cat surveyed the great space, "Master Winston," as the staff referred to him, watched from high above on the shiny brass banister of the second level bookshelves. While Winston was called "Master Winston," Benjamin was "Young Master Benjamin." Just as with "immigrant names," Russ wondered how old Benjamin would have to be before he too became just "Master Benjamin."

The cat and the bird beheld each other with what appeared to be a mutual respect, silently, then, if Russ didn't imagine it, a slight nod. Both were among the top predators of their species, huge by comparison to their own peers, and, truth be told, fearless. Winston had once stood his ground and warded off a snake, if the $5^{th}$ Chapter of Vivian's autobiography could be trusted. This, their first meeting, was a momentous occasion fraught with unforeseen possibilities.

Russ just wanted them to be friends.

Without warning the great bird let go of the railing and in a series of descending spirals, he glided effortlessly down onto Russ's broad shoulder. During his descent the sound of the wind in his feathers was impressive.

"Hello Winston" Russ said, "with a smile in his voice," as Bernadette had often described it.

"This fine example of the Feline Species, of which there are at present 37 sub-groups, is Thorndike."

"Thorndike, this grand Patriarch is a member of the Classification Aves and the Species "Psittacus Erithacus," isn't that right Winston?"

"Hello, Hello, brrrrinnngggg, brrrrinnngggg" Winston said authoritatively.

"Yeeoww-Yaa-ree-baa," Thorndike said with equal resonance, if not fluent English.

With that, the familiar sound of a running dog's well-filed claws digging into the carpet could be heard.

"Here comes Young Master Benjamin" Russ said with unusual formality, acknowledging that "the proprieties must be observed," just as was stated in one of his favorite movies of all time, "The Quiet Man."

Benjamin came tearing excitedly around one of the half-dozen large, Stickley Brothers™ Settle-Sofa's that populated the library. When the little Westie saw the big Maine Coon Cat for the first time he jumped two feet in the air, spun, and vanished around the Settle-Sofa once more.

Only when Russ called to him did he reappear, timidly.

"Benji" he said, tempting the muscular little dog with a Rocco & Roxie's™ Jerky Stick treat, "this is Thorndike, he's going to be a new friend."

Almost as if the little dog understood English he came around the sofa once more, his entire body shaking from the powerful wagging of his tail.

"There, Russ said as he knelt down and delivered a well-earned treat simultaneously to both Thorndike and Benjamin. Both animals were grateful and took their treats where they felt they could enjoy them most comfortably. Thorndike went to a cushioned window-seat in front of one of the tall library windows looking out on the beautiful grounds of Caledonia Estate and across the Pine Valley.

Meanwhile, Benjamin gnawed noisily on his R & R treat on a Persian carpet beneath one of the four exquisite

Charles Rennie MacIntosh™ library tables.

Edward Bright and a maid with a nametag that said "Calpurnia" came in with a tea cart. Russ was sitting quietly in one of the Chippendale™ wingback chairs he and Vivian had used during their final visit and Winston was once again enjoying his own Caitec® Oven-Fresh Bites Mixed Berry Cookie Parrot Treats on a brass near Russ.

"I see you brought the John Hancock tea set" Russ said, showing himself to be one of "Vivian's Veteran Visitors." Caledonia had an entire room displaying dozens of tea services from across time and around the world. The deep burgundy and rich gold of the John Hancock Tea Service had been one of Russ's favorites when he saw the display, but he had never had the honor of using it. The rule was that certain services were used only on certain days or occasions.

"Yes, Sir" Edward said respectfully. "The Mistress took care to remind me that this set had always been the tea service 'of New Beginnings' and superseded all others. I was ordered to make sure your first tea at Caledonia was served using the John Hancock Tea Service."

Some sets were reserved for a certain holiday and some might be used only once a year. This last scenario was the case with the "New Year's Eve Set," the Reed & Barton® Hampton Court™ Tea Service, which, by Caledonian Tradition, could only be used on that one occasion each year.

"And Mrs. Dale's Blueberry Scones, my favorite" Russ said happily.

"Yes Sir" Edward Bright said, "She made them especially for you, for today, Sir."

"If there is nothing else, Sir?" Edward asked before dismissing Calpurnia.

"Actually" Russ said, "I keep a litter-box in my vehicle."

"There will be no need, Sir" Edward said quickly. "The Mistress saw to everything, ahead of time, as it were. Considering Young Master Thorndike's size we have several large, deep litterboxes in discreet locations on every floor. Including here in the Delashmett Library."

"Excellent" Russ said, surprised at Vivian's foresight and then realizing that he shouldn't be surprised at all, as she had always minded the details.

"In that case" Russ said, I only have one other thing.

"How may I be of service, Sir."

"I've asked a guest over for dinner" he said.

Russ had invited Lara to dine with him once he left Alexis Stonecipher's office. Having missed their long-awaited plans for Thanksgiving with the Williams he thought it would be nice to spend a quiet evening with his fiancé.

"Very well, Sir, do you have a particular meal in mind? Or, as you may know, Mrs. Dale has been preparing the Mistress's menu for today. That would be Sesame-Teriyaki Top Sirloin, lobster tail, and flame-grilled lemon-garlic prawns, served with Garlic-Pepper Zucchini, and the Mistress's favorite cucumber dip, and Garlic Bread. The wine would be Willamette Valley Vineyards™ Estate Pinot Noir. Dessert would be Mrs. Dale's own German Apple Strudel recipe, served hot, and topped with Ben & Jerry's™ Vanilla ice cream. The Mistress liked to support Ben & Jerry's™ since they are just down the road in Burlington and she found their products quite tasty."

"Mr. Bright" Russ said in his most pleased voice. "Let's stay the course and enjoy the meal Mrs. Dale had scheduled, and until further notice, let's maintain the Mistress's menu schedules."

"Very well, Sir, if that is all?"

"Yes, thank you" Russ said, quickly mastering his new role as "Laird of the Manor." The truth was Russ had been a leader in business for many years and was comfortable giving directions in a respectful way and also in showing sincere appreciation. These twin strengths had served him well over the years.

Mr. Bright dismissed Calpurnia with instructions for

Mrs. Dale then he turned back to Russ.

"If I may, Sir."

"Yes, of course" Russ said curiously.

"The Mistress gave me instructions on certain matters she wanted you to know about and, if this is an acceptable time?"

Mr. Bright had the habit of ending a sentence prematurely by turning it into a question. Vivian had told Russ about it on one occasion and wondered if it had been a part of his training.

"Please" Russ said, motioning to the adjacent Chippendale wingback.

Mr. Bright looked at the chair with a mix of suspicion and fear, as if it would bite him. Russ understood his "Head of Household's" discomfort and simply said, "Please, Continue."

Thus freed of the threatening Chippendale, Mr. Bright took up his assignment.

"First then, the Mistress's quarters have been cleared, cleaned, and prepared for you. Per her orders a new mattress and pillows were delivered this morning and new linens and blankets, in Jade-Green, have been washed and placed. New drapes, also in the same color, have replaced the former drapes on all windows and a complimentary-colored Persian carpet has been placed."

"Vivian thought of everything didn't she?" Russ said solemnly.

"The Mistress was the master of detail" Mr. Bright said with open admiration.

"Yes" Russ said meditatively, "I remember that the Devil is in the details." It was something Vivian had said to a young maid.

"Second then" Edward Bright continued, "beyond the many litter boxes we've placed, Young Master Thorndike has three sets of the JW Pet Skid Stop™ Heavyweight Pet Bowls located throughout the manor. One is in your Master Suite, another here in the Delashmett Library, and in your personal sitting room, known as the Quilloran Room. Each set will be cleaned daily just as we do for Winston and Benji. Three Mila™ cat beds identical to those he has at your residence at Wildrose, are in the same three areas and more can be placed if you wish. We've also laid up a small reserve of the same Smalls™ pet food in the flavors he prefers."

"Very good" said Russ, thoroughly impressed.

"The Mistress has a moving company arriving at Wildrose tomorrow, Saturday, at 9 AM to gather all your personal possessions, wardrobe, and any additional items you would like moved."

"Also, the Mistress wanted you to meet with her Head of Security and with her Head of Grounds, Fields, and Forests. I've tentatively arranged those for meetings for here, tomorrow afternoon, if that is acceptable."

Russ thought for a moment and approved.

"Finally" Edward said in a quavering voice that showed how hard the words were for him to speak, "the Mistress identified a Ming Meiping Vase adorned with a Phoenix, from the Delashmett Collection, to serve as her crematory urn. The funeral home will bring you the urn when the cremation is complete. She would appreciate it if you would keep it on the mantle in the Quilloran Room. That room was her special place and unlike other rooms throughout the Manor it takes the name of the Mistress or Laird."

"Really?" Russ said, "Do you mean it will be called 'The Personette Room'?"

"Yes, Sir, once the Mistress's remains are laid to rest, in the Spring, the name will change."

"I see, it seems Caledonia has a rule for everything."

"As is fitting for a noble family residence approaching its 180th anniversary, it has traditions for many things, Sir."

Russ stayed in the library after his Head of Household left. He sipped Caledonia's rich Oolong Tea while the animals all rested quietly. Benjamin slept with his head on

Russ's foot and Thorndike napped on Russ's lap. Winston sat atop the wingback chair above Russ's right shoulder.

For himself, Russ felt as if he were still in shock. Vivian was gone. Thorndike had nearly been taken from him by force. Marcus Thomas had escaped from prison and come to kill him and Thorndike both. Marcus was seriously injured and in the hospital and Ryan Drummond was now dead. Both these events happened on the grounds of Wildrose, and, with virtually no notice, he was leaving the home he'd made for himself and Thorndike. He was now "Laird" of Caledonia Estate and owner of one of the largest private fortunes in America.

Around him the only sounds were the crackle of the fire in the beautiful fireplace, and the ticking of the Michael Bird™ "Fine Marquetry Longcase Grandfather Clock" from London, circa 1683.

Russ woke an hour later to the vibration of the phone in his pocket.

"Hey there, you old scallywag." Arnold called over the phone. "Are you alright? You sure had us scared when you warned us about Marcus. Can you believe that Bernadette singlehandedly captured him. She saw his car along the road and stopped to help. They're calling her the 'Pistol Packin' Mama' now."

Russ feigned ignorance of the part Bernadette had played and said nothing about the death at Wildrose. This latter oversight was made possible by the reporter who had only said, "the Starbuck Valley" as the scene of the crime.

Instead, he explained to Arnold about the shock of Vivian's passing and how he was working to help organize her affairs.

"Of course, of course" Arnold said thoughtfully. "I should have known, I'm sorry, Russ, I know you were good friends."

"Yes" Russ admitted, "we met under strange circumstances but it led to a wonderful friendship." Russ didn't mention that he was her sole beneficiary or the fact that he was moving to Caledonia. All those things could come out in time.

"We'll have to get together for dinner before Christmas, to make up for Thanksgiving." Arnold said.

"Sure thing" Russ agreed, "Maybe the Old Homestead Pub could put up with us one more time!"

After ending the call Russ put his hand out for Winston to climb on, then he transferred the bird to his shoulder.

"One moment please, brrrrinnngggg" Winston said.

Then Russ picked up his taupe checked sports coat and called to Thorndike and Benjamin. The menagerie made their way back to the main hall and took the elevator to the third floor. Once there Russ simply followed Benjamin and hoped the little dog would take him to what was now called, "The Laird's Suite." Black Walnut paneling in the wide halls throughout the Manor House was magnificent and Russ soon found the bedroom suite, which had only recently been Vivian's for almost 80 years, to be even more glorious.

It had been redecorated to accommodate a man's tastes more comfortably and a new mattress lay on the original 1870's, Elmwood Burl, Victorian bed.

"Wow" Russ said when he saw the room. He had stayed at the Drake Hotel in Chicago and the Plaza in New York, and his new master bedroom could have been among those hotels' finest rooms. Large windows looked out over the beautiful grounds and the heavily wooded backdrop of Berryman Ridge and its highest peak, Mount Emily, rising up 2,000 feet in the background. Russ saw one of Thorndike's Mila™ cat beds on a large footstool, perhaps 16 inches above the floor and located in the corner nearest the bed.

"You'll like that, Thorndike, they're already spoiling you."

In another corner a large double doorway opened into one of the tower turrets. The light-filled room was surrounded by windows. It had been Vivian's private office and a large, custom-made cherrywood desk with a replica of Thomas Jefferson's rotating bookstand at one end, holding five books, sat empty except for a photograph of Vivian, Benjamin, and Winston that must have been taken recently. In the lower right hand corner Vivian's characteristic round-script said, "To Russ, Warmest Wishes. V."

It seemed like the room and Vivian were inviting him to come in and make it his.

At the other end of the bedroom double doors led to a private setting room with its own fireplace. Edward Bright had called this the "Quilloran Room." A half-dozen new red leather club chairs, similar to his Wildrose chairs, sat around the room. Together with deep burgundy Persian rugs, the dark wood paneling, and small, natural-stone fireplace and gave the room an intimate feel.

Caledonia was a wonder, even after visiting it so many times, and when Russ hurried out to the parking lot to open the door of Lara's new SUV she was spellbound by its majesty.

"I've only heard about this place" she said quietly, "and seen it in passing, of course, but I loved the book Nathan and Daphne put together. They really captured the splendor of the place, didn't they?"

"Yes, they did" Russ agreed.

The night was dark and the windows of Caledonia shined with a warm, welcoming yellow glow that was magnified by a thousand lights from the giant Christmas Tree that stood in the nearly 3-story tall Main Hall.

"It's breathtaking" she said sincerely. Then she noticed that Russ was only looking at her and seemed even more spellbound.

He suddenly took her in his arms in the middle of the parking lot, and under a Vermont winter sky filled with millions of stars, he began to dance with her and sing quietly.

"Are the stars out tonight? I don't know if it's cloudy or

bright, 'cause I only have eyes for you, dear." He hummed as they spun under the stars for another minute and then he finished his serenade with "I don't know if we're in a garden, or on a crowded avenue, You are here, so am I, Maybe millions of people pass by, But they all disappear from view, because I only have eyes for you."[28]

"Oh Russ" she said when they finished. "You know how to take a girl's breath away."

"I think you are the most beautiful thing I've ever seen" he said sincerely.

When they came in the main entry, through two-sets of double-doors of oak, brass, and thick glass windows, a young woman with a name tag that said, "Eugenie," pronounced "ooh-jhen-ee," took Lara's winter coat and gloves and welcomed her to Caledonia.

Lara thanked her and turned toward Russ. Her thoroughly bewitched fiancé was clearly smitten and did nothing to hide his admiration.

"Will you forgive me? My winter boots are in the Telluride, but I just had to wear my high heels for tonight."

Pointing to a little bundle of Mistletoe that hung above them, Russ kissed her.

"There" he said, "I forgive you now."

"By Caledonian Tradition" Russ said proudly, "the Mistletoe is to be hung on the morning of the day after Thanksgiving and taken down on the morning following New Year's Day."

"What a sweet tradition and what a glorious Christmas Tree."

"Douglas Fir" Russ said proudly. Vivian had one hundred of them planted 75 years ago. They're a beautiful grove today, and she has some planted each year to keep Caledonia and its friends in Christmas Trees. We have six of them in the Manor House alone" Russ said, sounding much more like a proud owner than he realized.

---

[28] "I Only Have Eyes For You," by the Flamingo's, 1958.

"Of course, this is the largest of them."

"What a dear woman she was" Lara said, her eyes shining under a thousand bright lights on the twenty-foot-tall tree.

"I'll never forget her" Russ said, then at an approaching sound that was now familiar to him he said, "Here come the Troops!"

Benji was the first of the bunch to notice Russ had snuck out of the library. He tore around the corner and slid on the marble flooring. Wiggling and wagging as he came to a happy stop at Russ's feet. Next came the swoosh of wings and Winston glided effortlessly to Russ's shoulder. Lastly, came the stately Thorndike, making his Grand Entrance.

Lara's "Oohhs and Aahhs" let each of the animals know they were admired and adored.

"I started reading them one of Vivian's favorite adventure books tonight. It's a well-worn, leatherbound First Edition from who knows when. They love it, either that or they like the sound of my voice. It's called 'The King's Buccaneer,' and it's about a Privateer in the 1700's who has been talked into helping put the secret son of France's late King on the throne. There are lots of pirates, which Parrots like Winston just love, and aliases, which satisfies Thorndike's lurid fascination with undercover activities, and long, hard-to-pronounce French names, which, because he's Scottish, always makes Benji happy. So far so good."[29]

"You are the funniest man I've ever loved" Lara said with a bewitching smile.

"Well, as they say, a Pirate by any other name would smell just as sweet!"

"Maybe not" Lara insisted.

They laughed together as Russ showed his beautiful fiancé to a warm fireside in the cozy, wood paneled Little

---

[29] "The King's Buccaneer – The Story of Captain Robert Osborne," KDP Publishing, ©2020, amazon.com.

MacIntosh sitting room, which had its own, much smaller Christmas tree, not far from the Main Hall.

"Supper will be served in 30 minutes, Sir." It was the young woman who'd taken Lara's coat, Eugenie. Russ couldn't help but smile at the irony. At Caledonia the evening meal was called "supper" while in all of Chittenden County everyone but him, and the stalwart Eston Phillips, called it dinner.

"Would you like a glass of wine, apfelschorle or mineral water, or perhaps tea? Our wine tonight is the Willamette Valley Vineyards™ Estate Pinot Noir, or I can get you a list of the Caledonian Cellar."

The word "apfelschorle" had sparked Russ's interest and he asked what it was.

"It's an apple spritzer, Sir, a mixture of juice from select Caledonian Farms apples and highly carbonated water. It is quite refreshing and bottled in glass under the Mistress's own label. It also has the added benefit of being isotonic" she added conspiratorially.

"Isotonic?" Lara asked curiously.

"That means it is easily absorbed and digested by the body, basically" Russ said matter-of-factly.

Two apfelschorle were ordered and Russ asked for the bottle to be brought as well.

"I want to see 'the Mistress's own label' Russ said after Eugenie left.

Russ and Lara lingered in the Little MacIntosh Room, talking quietly in front of the fire while Thorndike chose Lara's lap, Winston selected Russ's right shoulder, which Edward Bright had earlier provided with a gray terrycloth hand towel, and "Young Master Benjamin" laid his head on Russ's Rockport® Saxxen Wingtip Dress Shoes, in Cognac Brown.

"I'm still shaken by what happened at Wildrose" Lara said quietly.

"I am too" Russ admitted, "but I'll tell you something, if you promise to keep it a secret."

He was trying to lighten the mood but Lara took him seriously.

"I promise."

"Well, you know I love Wildrose."

"Yes, of course. It's perfect for you and Thorndike and you saved it from inevitable ruin."

"Yes" Russ agreed, "and I would have been naturally troubled by Vivian's wish that I move here, but the truth is, with all that's happened at Wildrose in the short time since we moved there, I'm actually ready to leave."

"I don't blame you" Lara said sympathetically. "You barely survived the Chandler Gang's assassination attempt during the summer and now, and with Marcus, and...the young man."

Lara didn't want to be more specific about what had happened at Wildrose in the last 72 hours, and Russ didn't blame her.

"Everything together" Russ said, "I actually feel relieved to be moving, and though it's supposed to be a 'state secret' I happen to know that Caledonia has extraordinary security. I won't say what happened to us at Wildrose couldn't happen here, but I will say our odds here are much better."

"I'm so pleased to hear that, Russ. I knew how much you and Thorndike loved Wildrose, and it's in a beautiful spot too. I was afraid you'd be very disappointed to be leaving there."

"On the contrary" Russ smiled, "but my new situation has gotten the gears in my thick, Scottish skull going 'round, and I want to ask you something."

"Why Mr. Personette, you've already asked 'The Question,' whatever else could you be thinking about?"

Lara was a reserved person, although she enjoyed family and friends immensely, but those who knew her best knew that she had a surprising secret.

Lara had true thespian or theatrical talents. She had a repertoire of dozens of accents from Darth Vader™ and

Princess Leia™ of Star Wars® fame, to Darby O'Gill, from the Disney movie, "Darby O'Gill and the Little People," to the Welsh of Eliza Doolittle's father, Alfred P. Doolittle, in the musical, "My Fair Lady."

"I'm wishin' ta tell ya, I'm wantin' ta tell ya, I'm waitin' ta tell ya."

Lara had also mastered regional accents such as Cockney, and the Antebellum South. The words she'd just spoken were in the classical Southern accent, just as Scarlett O'Hara might have delivered them in "Gone With the Wind."

"Why Mr. Personette, you've already asked 'The Question,' whatever else could you be thinking about?"

"Frankly, Scarlett" he began, "I told you that Vivian wanted me to do as much good as I could, so let me tell you about a few of my plans, and you tell me what you think."

"Very well, Mr. Personette, you have the floor."

"When I was young I heard, or read the quote, "money is like manure, it works best when it's spread around helping young things grow.[30] Now, not only do I have virtually limitless funds, but I also have Vivian's simple command, 'Go forth and spread manure'!"

Lara laughed at her handsome, sincere, sometimes hilarious fiancé.

"It's so hard to believe, Russ."

"What is?" he asked sincerely.

"Everything that's happened since you came to Vermont" Lara answered, "it is all so unbelievable."

Russ nodded in agreement.

"You're right about that, Lara. The truth here in Vermont really is stranger than fiction!"

Russ couldn't help but think back over the past year. Both his books had been written in Ohio but were about historical figures from this very area of Vermont. His best

[30] Quote by Thornton Wilder

friend from the Navy not only happened to live here, as Lara had pointed out, but he was also a Professor at the same college and was using one of the same classrooms. Russ had helped get Professor Dudley's unpublished manuscript to his editor, Eileen, and the story of that "best-seller" was now history, so to speak. He'd gotten to know two women who were the closest relatives of the two people involved in the Eton Falls Bank Robbery, whom he had subsequently cleared, and one of those women was an artist who just happened to paint the places where Russ had lived and knew so well.

A "Big Name" in Hollywood decided to turn both his books into blockbuster movies. Then there was Thorndike himself. The relationship that had developed between the man and the cat never ceased to remind Russ of one of his favorite movies, "Casablanca," and Humphrey Bogart's line about "of all the gin joints in all the world..." and "I think this is the beginning of a beautiful friendship." In fact, a vintage poster for "Casablanca," with Bogart in his Fedora and trenchcoat, holding the pistol, and with the beautiful Ingrid Bergman next to him, with a backdrop of the other cast-members, had hung in a prominent place in his bedroom at Wildrose.

Even the naming of "Thorndike" was a tale worthy of a great fiction story. It was so hard to believe it had to be true, yet no one would ever believe it was anything but pure fiction. The theories of Edward Lee Thorndike, regarding the telepathic "connectionism" between humans and cats, of all animals, still amazed Russ!

Russ's eclectic and eccentric collection of interests and skills, such as his knowledge of handwriting, shoes, knots, and Scottish History, had stunned the local Chief of Police, a courageous man in his own right. Chief Ramsay had been willing to make use of Russ's "cockamamie soup" ideas from the very beginning.

Russ had uncovered the secret of the forged "Kaiser Suicide Letter" when there was still time to catch the fleeing murderers, all because Thorndike had decided to knock a book off the shelf. His realization that the Germanic and Latin names of his boss, Reginald Julius Kaiser, meant that he had been assassinated by conspirators named Marcus and Cassia, had come almost too late, but their decision to murder Russ had been their undoing. Again and again it had been Thorndike who had been the key factor in the equations.

The fact that his commissioning of the Vermont Puree-Maker, with her own line of foods, as the dauntless "Agent 36", and his fast-friendship with Dane VanWert, had led both of those admirable people to subsequently save his life, still amazed him.

The bond that had grown between "That Darned Dan Garn," the Postman – Builder – Spy – Poet Laureate – Alternative Energy Expert – Triathlete with his own bronze statue and an Alaska-Sized personality, had created a pretty good team.

And who could have foreseen Russ possessing a secret channel into the heart of the FBI's regional hierarchy, through Special Agent-in-Charge, Claymont Awmiller?

Russ was never ignorant of the irony that without Thorndike he would never have been involved in any of the mysteries which had surrounded him since arriving in Vermont, and would, therefore, never have been in danger from the villains who needed him silenced.

He'd only ever felt such a connection once before, with a big Black Labrador Retriever, and the dog had ended up saving his life, too.

"It's incredible!" Lara said in her gentle voice. "And now you begin a new chapter, as Vivian's heir and 'chief manure spreader,' is that what you're saying."

"And I want to start by helping your Great-Aunt Virginia, Gracie, Charlie, Veronica, and Daphne."

Eugenie returned with two glasses and a deep, ruby red bottle with an elegant label, "Quilloran's Crest."

"Here you are, Sir, the Mistress's own label!"

# CHAPTER ELEVEN
## "Codename Iudas"

Saturday was a surprisingly balmy 32° and, as usual, there was no wind in the Starbuck Valley. The sky was bright blue and the hills and fields were covered in their winter blanket of thick, white snow, but the roads were clear and dry. Lara had volunteered to help Russ with his movers and at Wildrose they were nearly done after several hours of boxing and loading. It was at that moment a silver car pulled slowly into the crowded parking lot and maneuvered around the moving truck and several vehicles, including Russ's big Lincoln Mark LT.

"Russ, there's someone out here to see you." Lara hollered from the front door.

He was in the back bedroom boxing valuables, pictures, and items he'd take back to Caledonia in the Lincoln.

"Harley, what on earth you doing here, and in the Aston Martin of all things?"

"I couldn't resist taking the old girl out for a lope on the dry pavement, say, but what are you doing Russ? Are you moving to Hawaii with your share of the sunken treasure? You know, that's what I'm thinking of doing, myself."

"Don't tempt me" Russ said, remembering the time he'd been stationed there in the Navy. He remembered "The Sapphire Seas" and repeated, "Don't tempt me."

He put the box he was carrying in the big pickup and when he turned around the diminutive treasure-hunter/local folklorist was standing beside him.

"The Caribbean is it, then?" the little man pressed.

"Well, I guess it'll get around soon enough" Russ said as he leaned down and looked at the sporty interior of the 1963 Aston Martin DB5.

"Beautiful machine" he said to Harley."

"Yeah, she is" Harley agreed, "but you were saying something."

"Yes" Russ admitted reluctantly. "I'm moving into Vivian Delashmett's old place."

This statement, in Chittenden County, was like being in England and saying, "I'm moving into the Queen's 'Old Place' at Windsor."

Harley was stunned by the news and he stood there with his mouth hanging open for a good minute before he said anything.

"I heard the sad news, too bad" he said, hanging his head and taking his winter cap with earmuffs off. "She was one of a kind, I can tell you, one of a kind. Her husband was my classmate you know, great at math" Harley said, shaking his head, "but terrible in history."

"Really" Russ said, surprised that Harley had such a close connection. "I'll miss her" he admitted.

"So you inherited Caledonia, huh? Or you buying it with your share of the golden doubloons?" Harley snooped unashamedly.

Russ did the little man no favors though.

"Something like that" he said mysteriously, but Harley wasn't so easily thrown off the track.

"Nah, even with your share of the Morning Star's gold it wouldn't even make a down payment on Caledonia. Did you know they were offered 15 million dollars for one of their Chinese vases?" Harley rubbed his chin and looked at Russ, then he said, "So the old gal willed it all to you, huh? We'll, she couldn't have chosen better, says I, and as they had no children of their own, that's how it should be!"

Having worked all this out in his mind Harley seemed ready to get the Chittenden County Grapevine humming.

Russ tried to counter the little man's snooping with his own. "What are you really doing out today, and in your James Bond Car?"

"Russ, you know me better'n most, and I just can't take it anymore."

Harley hung his head and seemed so troubled at that moment that Russ was honestly worried for his friend.

"What is it, Harley, what can I do to help?"

"Are you serious, Russ, would you be willing to help me?"

"Of course, I'd do anything."

"I know you to be a man of your word, Mr. Personette, and I'll hold you to it, you can be sure of that" he said. Brightening instantly, he pulled his car keys from his pocket and handed them to Russ.

"What's this?" Russ asked in confusion.

"Them's the keys to the old car with the steering wheel on the wrong side" Harley said with satisfaction, as he pointed to the Aston Martin. "You gave me your word, remember. You see, I'm a laughingstock, Russ, I won't beat about the bush. Wherever I take it they say 'hey Marge, look over there, it's that little farmer-man from up Starbuck Way! You remember, we heard about him through the Grapevine, he's the guy who needed a cat to fix his car. Hahaha!' I can't take it anymore, Russ."

Harley was smiling as he said all this, but he was serious about being a laughingstock. Once the story had leaked, ironically through Harley's own retelling of it, it gained a popularity that was rare, even by Chittenden County Standards. Soon enough, the joke was on Harley.

"You loved the car when you saw it" Harley said bluntly,

"and Thorndike fixed it, so I thought it made sense to bring it up here to you, and you said you'd do anything to help me, and now you've got the keys."

With that Harley headed briskly up the gravel driveway toward Hunters Lane, with an energy unheard of in a "90-some" year old man. At the head of the drive another car waited to take him home.

As everything sunk in, it was Russ's turn to be stunned.

"Harley wait" he shouted after his friend.

"The papers are in the Jockey-Box, I've taken care of everything, all you have to do is sign em' and turn em' in."

Harley got into the other car and Russ watched him disappear down the road waving his winter cap wildly from an open passenger window for a good half mile.

"What's that, Russ?" Lara asked as she came out with a box of framed photographs. "Oh, is that Harley's lovely James Bond Car, the one Thorndike fixed? I heard about that one" Lara laughed out loud.

"Yes" Russ said in a whisper, "James Bond. Harley just gave it to me, title and all."

"I told you, he's a little dear, and a snoop too. I do hope you didn't tell him anything, otherwise the whole county will know you're the 'New Laird of Caledonia' before lunch."

"What?" Russ said, snapping out of his trance at last.

"Isn't that interesting" Lara said sweetly, giving him a kiss on the cheek, "you lose a motorcycle but gain a car!

Russ laughed but it was interesting that the unexpected loss of one of his favorite motorcycles of all time was followed so quickly by the gift of one of his favorite classic cars?"

He ran his hand over the highly polished body of the foreign sportscar and shook his head. What kind of world was it where some people begrudged the smallest act of kindness while others were the very sole of generosity? Here Russ was, a stranger to Chittenden County not so long ago, and in the past four days two people had tried to harm him, seriously, while two people had showered him with unbelievable kindness.

He was still standing beside the car when Lara came out again and called to him.

"Hey Handsome" she said, "We need to be getting back to Caledonia for your meetings, right?"

Lara bravely drove the big Lincoln 4-wheel drive and Russ followed happily in his new Aston Martin, loving every minute in the powerful, throaty, iconic British sportscar.

He couldn't believe what Harley Shaw had done, or what Vivian had done, for that matter. For a man as generous and kind as Russ Personette, nothing ever shocked him more than to be the recipient of the same kindness and generosity he gave. Something Vivian had written in her final letter had touched on this characteristic of Russ's.

"You have a rare and noble heart; one which money will empower but not corrupt or command. This is one of the reasons I said you were the perfect man to entrust."

"Excuse me, Sir" said a young woman standing in the doorway of his office. She had red hair, tucked up in a bun in back, and a name tag that said "Delphine."

Russ had several piles of graded papers arranged on the desk in his "public office." It had been "The Mistress's Study" for almost 80 years and now it was officially called "The Laird's Study". Some of the papers were essays and some were tests, and all were graded, recorded, and ready to be handed out to his students on Monday. His trusted English-made "Hanshaws® Briefcase Satchel" sat beside him.

"Yes" he said, looking up.

"Mr. Cunningham is here for your 2 PM appointment. I'll show him up if you like."

"Thank you, Delphine, that would be very nice."

Vivian had expressed a great deal of faith in James Cunningham, her Head of Security, during one of Russ's visits and it hadn't been easy for him to hold his tongue. Russ had been a leader in business for three decades and he'd solved more problems than he cared to think about. He had serious questions about how the Chandler Gang had infiltrated Caledonia and Vivian's life. If Cunningham was half as good as Vivian said he was, then he should have at least uncovered the bugging that had taken place, and he hadn't.

In fact, although Russ hadn't said anything to anyone, not even to Lara, he had plenty of suspicion for everyone working on the estate. It didn't matter what their job title was either and having seen the size of the Delashmett Fortune he understood what a tempting target Vivian had been, and what a target he was now.

He'd shared his thoughts with Special Agent Awmiller months before and had "called in" some of the favors after the Chandler Gang had been scooped up. While the entire enterprise had been "highly irregular" the Agent wasn't averse to sharing information on the staff members at Caledonia or with looking further into their histories.

Beyond the "official" avenues among the many "irons" Russ had put in his Attorney's "fire," was arranging for private investigators to look into every employee working at Caledonia Estate. It wasn't easy for the young woman and her staff to juggle all Russ's demands. After all, some of the other "irons in the fire" was the "retirement" of the beloved Donald Frobisher and the creation of "Ronald Fernsby," the purchase of the historic Sacajawea Hotel, several financial and property transfers, the processing and sale of the sunken treasure of the British Sloop, HMS Morning Star, and, after the reading of Vivian's will, a review of accounts and spending.

Russ was a wonderful, thoughtful, appreciative man, but he was also a demanding boss who expected employees to earn the wage he paid them. This was true of contractors as well as attorneys, and Dan Garn would be the first to attest to the heavy workload Russ was willing to put on him and his team. All this work was great for job security but it could also be a real challenge, especially since, for people like Dan Garn and Alexis Stonecipher, Russ Personette was not their only customer or client.

The red-headed Delphine knocked and the Head of Security was shown in.

"Mr. Personette."

James DeWitt Cunningham was in his middle-50's, like Russ, but shorter, with small, dark brown eyes and advanced balding that had been managed with the popular method, a completely shaven head. Like Russ he was also carrying a few extra pounds.

The two men shared a firm handshake and Russ said, "we'll be retiring to the Quilloran Room, Delphine, and I'd like coffee and some of Mrs. Daly's delicious scones brought up. What would you like, Mr. Cunningham?"

"A coffee will be fine" he said flatly, "cream, two sugars" he finished. Russ noticed there was neither a "please" nor a "thank you."

"Thank you, Delphine" Russ made a point of saying.

The two men made their way to a nearby stairwell and were soon on the third floor, the Family Area, as it was called.

The "Quilloran Room" was Russ's private setting room and he had chosen the room particularly for this meeting because it was the only one he had personally swept for bugs. At least here he knew he wasn't taped or observed. Because of this he knew this was the only room he could securely bug himself. Mr. Cunningham had no clue he was being recorded and listened to, even as they spoke, and by many more people than just Russ Personette."

The men chose red leather club chairs and sat on either side of the small, natural-stone fireplace, facing each other.

As Russ seemed in no hurry to speak Mr. Cunningham said, "I should offer you a welcome to Caledonia."

Unlike Edward Bright, the Head of Household, and everyone else he'd met so far, there was no "Sir" in James

Cunningham's speech.

"Can you tell me a little about your work history?" Russ said, cordially but directly.

"My career was spent with the FBI, and after retirement I was recruited by Vivian to modernize security here at Caledonia."

"Did you know Desmond MacKay, at the FBI?" Russ asked with obvious excitement.

"I did not" James Cunningham said bluntly, "and as my work with the Agency was classified, I'm unable to say more."

"Oh, that is too bad" Russ said with obvious disappointment. "I was hoping to get an idea of your skillset and strengths."

"And weaknesses" the Head of Security said confrontationally.

"Not necessarily" Russ replied in a friendly manner, "but you must admit, as your employer that is my right."

"I have nothing to prove" Cunningham said.

"On the contrary, Mr. Cunningham, you have everything to prove" Russ said directly, "since you were in charge of security while a conspiracy was carried out freely and boldly right here in this very home and against your former employer, Ms. Vivian Delashmett."

The Head of Security glared at Russ openly, threateningly. Russ had seen the same technique so many times before that it was now "old hat" and predictable to him. Yet Russ Personette, for all his kindness and nobility of character, was not a man to be intimidated.

"This meeting is over" James Cunningham said authoritatively. "If you want to speak to me again you can come to my office during working hours, otherwise, I have nothing to say to you."

With that, Caledonia's Head of Security rose and walked to the door.

"If you open that door, Mr. Cunningham, I'll walk you to your car and see you off this property forever."

Russ took a sip of his favorite coffee, Folgers Classic Roast™, which Edward Bright had quickly purchased and stocked on Caledonia's shelves.

"You wouldn't dare" the man hissed, "you need me."

"Why would I need someone so inept at their job, or so complicit with the criminals, that he would have let his last employer be killed without even warning her what was happening? Why would I even want someone like that around?"

Russ said these words calmly and with an air of cordiality that shocked Mr. Cunningham.

"Why would I need someone who was nothing more than a paper-pusher at the FBI, someone so mediocre that the Agency even 'invited' him to take early retirement?"

James Cunningham froze. He had no way of knowing how Russ could have known his internal history with the FBI and he certainly would never have guessed that Special Agent-in-Charge, Claymont Awmiller, had been more than happy to investigate Cunningham for Russ. After all, neither Russ Personette nor Thorndike's names ever appeared in any of the open reports regarding the case against the Chandler Gang. The glory for that huge success went all to the Special Agent and his team. It was only in one sealed and classified report that Awmiller had felt safe enough to identify his true source in breaking the case, Russ Personette.

"How did you say it, 'your work with the Agency was classified.' That's laughable isn't it?"

Russ left these insulting words hanging out there in air for his Head of Security to consider.

"What do you want from me?"

"I would have thought that my desires would be obvious to you, Mr. Cunningham. After all, we both know you didn't fail Vivian out of ineptness, don't we. No Head of Security could possibly have been that bad. Even a routine sweep for bugs, standard protocol, would have uncovered the danger to her. So you aren't stupid or inept, that only leaves one option doesn't it. You're guilty! You were one of 'the fish that got away,' they missed you when they gathered up the net, but I didn't miss you, did I?."

"I don't know what you're talking about" the man said with a shaky voice.

"Very well" Russ said emphatically. "Never say I didn't give you the chance. Let me say this though, before we pass the point of no return. There are a lot of people in prison and in the docks right now, because of me Mr. Cunningham, and while you think yourself clever, you're really just 'my next guy'."

"How much do you want?" he asked quickly.

"Well, it isn't cheap to run a place like Caledonia, you have to admit that, right? Your annual salary alone puts a big hole in a million dollars."

"You mean, you want me to work for free?"

"Why would I want that? As I've already said, you were happy to profit from the murder of your last boss, I mean, honestly, what would I have to look forward to if I kept you around? Really? I'd be lucky to have 3 to 6 months, right?"

"Then you want me to resign?"

James Cunningham had turned and come back to the middle of the room, where he stood looking at Russ like a young boy in the Principal's office.

"Well, that's a beginning, and that would minimize the scandal, but that wouldn't help me pay my bills now would it?"

"You're blackmailing me, then?" the Head of Security stuttered.

"Oh, come now" Russ said, as if he were losing his patience. "You conspired to kill your last employer and you want me to blush over blackmailing you? Don't be so childish, Mr. Cunningham, you insult my intelligence and I don't like to be insulted."

"How much do you want?" he asked quietly.

"I want 2 billion dollars" Russ said seriously, then he laughed and said, "but I can't get that, can I? So I'll settle for 10 million."

"10 Million!" exclaimed Cunningham. "I could never get that much."

"Just like you said, 'your work with the Agency was classified' right? You have 10.2 million dollars in your combined accounts, including the secret, offshore deposits, right? So let's dispense with the theatrics, Mr. Cunningham. Frankly, I'm losing my patience with you and your lies, and I promise you, you won't like me if I lose my patience."

Russ looked at the man eye-to-eye for the first time since they sat down and whatever James Cunningham saw, it terrified him.

He staggered back to his chair and fell into it.

"So I resign quietly, pay you 10 million dollars, and then you forget what you know?"

"No, James" Russ said with a smile. "Where's the justice in that? Where's my enjoyment? You see, Vivian was important to me and you were helping to murder her. And where's my safety. If you're roaming around Eton Falls, penniless, I'll have plenty to worry about. So, here's what we're going to do. You resign immediately, empty out your pockets and your ankle holster, walk directly to your car and leave. You pay me the money within 72 hours, and then you move to Southeast Asia. I want you as far away from me as I can get you, and then, and only then, I forget I ever heard the name James Cunningham. That gets us a little closer to justice and safety, wouldn't you agree?"

James Cunningham scratched his forehead so hard it began to bleed, then he wrang his hands together and looked at the fire.

Two knocks on the door followed by a 10 second pause was the protocol at Caledonia. It had been that way with the "Domestics" even before Vivian had joined the Delashmett Family, and so it had remained.

After the standard knocks and the pause Delphine entered pushing the tea cart.

"The scones are just from the oven, Sir, Mrs. Daly made me wait so that you could have them fresh."

"Thank you, Delphine, that was very thoughtful" Russ said with a sincere smile.

The young woman smiled in return but made an obvious effort not to look at Mr. James Cunningham who, bent forward in his chair with his elbows on his knees and his head hanging low, looked like the embodiment of dejection.

As the young "Domestic," as the maids at Caledonia were called, walked toward the door, all Russ's attention was focused on the right hand of Mr. James Cunningham.

"No, no" Russ said suddenly, after the door had closed, "let's have none of that foolishness."

The long-time Head of Security had begun reaching for the pistol in his ankle holster when Russ interrupted him. Looking up, James Cunningham saw the tip of a pistol just protruding from under a pillow on Russ's lap. He could tell it was a large caliber, 9mm at least, with a silencer tip pointed straight at him.

"Don't tempt me, Mr. Cunningham, believe me when I say there is nothing I would like more than to give you your just desserts. Your betrayal of my friend, Vivian Delashmett, after all she had done for you and all the trust she placed in you, has earned you every bullet in my clip, twice over."

The smile on Russ's lips was just as broad and just as sincere as when he'd told Delphine, "Thank you, that was very thoughtful."

"Now, with the index finger and thumb on your left-hand reach around and pull your pistol out backwards, then lay it on the rug and sit up straight, and do it all very slowly, or they will be referring to you as 'the late Mr. Cunningham'."

"That's it" Russ said, as the man obeyed his instructions.

With his left foot Russ slid the gun smoothly under his

own chair and said, "What did they offer you anyway, what was the price for betraying Vivian? 30 pieces of Silver!"

"William Chandler" James Cunningham began, then he stopped. "First tell me how you knew about me?" he demanded.

Russ looked at the bald-headed man and shook his head.

"It was purely an elementary deduction in the beginning, Mr. Cunningham, after all, they couldn't have done it without you, could they? Pure logic. Your position made you of critical importance. If they were going to kill Vivian Delashmett, they needed her Head of Security." Then Russ added, "And who was in a better place to purchase the bugs and trackers than you?"

Cunningham immediately stared at Russ; fear written in his eyes.

"That's right" Russ said without explaining, "there was a certain irony in buying those items with Caledonia's own money, but you never should have done it. Sloppy, careless, unprofessional" Russ said, again shaking his head in disappointment.

"How do you know all of this?" the desperate man asked.

"I am who I am, James. This is what I do. This is what I've always done. You aren't my first rodeo, heck, you aren't even my hundredth rodeo!"

The man stared at Russ in utter disbelief.

"Now" Russ said calmly, "Chandler's computer implicated all of his fellow conspirators except one, a person known only by a codename, 'Iudas.' You insisted on anonymity from the beginning, that much you learned from the Agency, and no one could ever have proven who 'Iudas' was, definitively. So you thought you were safe. That was where you made your biggest mistake though."

At this point James Cunningham hung his head again, the gesture of a defeated man.

"You could have chosen a million codenames and

walked free, but you couldn't help yourself. You felt so clever and so proud, 'the FBI paper-pusher-who-made-good,' and since none of your fellow conspirators had a clue what 'Iudas' was, you thought 'where's the harm.' No one knew that in Archaic and Classical Latin there was no letter 'J,' and it wouldn't appear for hundreds of years after the fall of the Empire. The letter 'I' was used instead. So Jesus was spelled 'I E S V S' and, your codename, 'I U D A S' meant 'Judas,' the man who betrayed his master. Only, in your case, you betrayed your Mistress, didn't you?"

James Cunningham began to shake and then to weep. He had broken. As Russ had rightly said, he'd never been anything more than a low-level administrator at the Agency, and when he was given even a little power he abused it, so a low-level paper-pusher he'd remained. Now, his world was collapsing all around him and he broke.

"Back to my question" Russ demanded mercilessly. "What did Chandler offer you to betray Vivian?"

"William Chandler told me I'd get 10%, and Caledonia, for my part."

James Cunningham couldn't look at Russ. He continued to stare at the floor and wiped his face with his hands.

"Where do you want me to bring the money?" he said passively.

"Not here" Russ said emphatically. "I never want you here again. We'll meet at my place, at Wildrose, and don't be late."

As Russ stood at the front door of Caledonia and watched James Cunningham get into his expensive BMW 8-Series sportscar, the door of the Little MacIntosh sitting room opened and Claymont Awmiller, the FBI's handsome Special Agent-in-Charge, came out slowly.

"We got everything, Russ. My people are waiting for him at the gate. You sure made great use of the information I got you."

Russ smiled at his friend.

Earlier in the year Claymont had acted on Russ's hunch about William Chandler, aka William Chaloner, the diabolical head of the Chandler Gang, and the man had been apprehended a short distance over the Canadian border.

"Your one tough cookie, Professor. If you ever want a job 'back in the Family,' let me know. I'll make it happen. I really owe you."

Russ looked at the FBI man who'd become a good friend over the preceding months.

"You don't owe me anything, Claymont" he said, putting his hand on the Agent's shoulder.

"Everything you just saw was for Vivian. Wherever she is I hope she can see justice being done."

Russ's name didn't appear in the Sunday Free Press regarding the arrest of Mr. James Cunningham, formerly the Head of Security at Caledonia Estate in the Pine Valley. However, a succinct paragraph in the bottom, right-hand corner of the front page, entitled "Sunken Schooner Located," identified "Ross Personetti" as one of the search team members.

"Ross Personetti" Lou roared with laughter as he read the Sunday edition of the paper in his recliner at "Nut Run Farm."

"Oh Bernadette, you've got to hear this. That poor guy never gets a break! Next time I see him, remind me to call him 'Ross Personetti'!"

"I'll do no such thing Louis Noel Langlois" Bernadette's voice boomed from the kitchen, "and neither will you."

Lou chuckled to himself and said, "We'll see."

"I heard that!"

# CHAPTER TWELVE
## "Personette, Russ Personette"

"Is Leticia her real name?"

"I beg your pardon, Sir."

"Is Leticia that young ladies real name?"

"No, Sir, it isn't." Edward Bright admitted honestly.

The young woman in question had just brought the two men their drinks, a Quilloran's Crest™ Apfelschorle Apple-Spritzer, for Russ and a Perrier™ carbonated mineral water with natural orange flavor, for Mr. Bright. Russ had discovered that he had a weakness for the Quilloran's Crest™ Apfelschorle, which had been made with "select Caledonian Farms™ apples since 1952".

Although it was Saturday, Russ had called the Head of Household in for an emergency update on Mr. James Cunningham.

"Is Calpurnia the other woman's real name?"

"I'm afraid not, Sir, no, it isn't. If I may explain?"

Russ nodded and said, "Please do."

"The only staff who are called by their legal names are the Senior Cook, Mrs. Dale, and the Heads of each Department."

"And would I be right that this is another Caledonian Tradition?"

"Yes, actually, Sir, of longstanding. There has been a Calpurnia, a Florence, a Delphine, and a Leticia in this house since 1908. When the former Mistress's Mother-in-Law, Mrs. Delashmett, Senior, took over Caledonia and created the list of approved names."

"Tell me Edward, what are their real names?"

Russ was surprised when his Head of Household, who investigations had shown to be both conscientious and committed to the good of Caledonia, said that Leticia's "legal name" was Annette VanWert. He thought to himself that she was surely she's related to his friend, Dane VanWert.

"Leticia is Annette VanWert. Calpurnia is Cassandra Killoran. Eugenie is Hester Van Winkle. Delphine is Roxy Arbuckle. Lloyd is Ricky Perkins. Florence is Lexy Tunstall, Annalise is Kelly Hoffman, and Thorpe is Rudy Sunkel.

"I'm sure that Mrs. Delashmett, Senior, saw good reason for this in 1908" Russ said positively, then he continued, "but this is one tradition I would like to end immediately."

Edward Bright almost choked on his Perrier water.

"I beg pardon, Sir, I'm afraid I choked."

The idea of changing such an old tradition so suddenly shocked the Head of Household and it was only with difficulty that he was able to maintain his composure.

"I understand your wishes, Sir. I will order new name tags immediately, however, with your leave I would like to continue with the current names and name tags until the new ones are received."

"As long as the change is implemented within two weeks. I don't like the idea of people being forced by their employer to use a false name and, as you get to know me, you'll find I like to move quickly once a decision is reached."

"I understand, Sir, and I assure you" Mr. Bright continued speaking for some time but he was mainly trying to reconcile his mind to the change.

"Don't let this change throw you, Edward, I assure you there will be more to come."

This statement had a chilling effect on Caledonia's Head of Household and his imagination seemed to be envisioning a kind of Vermont equivalent to Edgar Allan Poe's "The Fall of the House of Usher."[31]

With that Russ launched into a summarization of the resignation and arrest of James Cunningham. When he was finished, Mr. Bright fidgeted in his chair and Thorndike raised his head from Russ's lap and stared at the man.

"You may speak freely, Mr. Bright."

"Well, Sir, if I may, the door being closed and Mr. Cunningham being truly finished here, I would."

Again Russ found himself saying, "Please do."

"The Mistress likened her three Department Heads to the Christmas carol, 'We Three Kings of Orient Are', which was written in 1857. We were to show unity and support for each other just as the Three Kings had done. There was never to be any criticism among us or below-stairs, as it were. Her one exception was the case of ignoble or illegal behavior, in which case we were to report promptly to the Mistress." Edward Bright said honestly.

"And did you" Russ asked encouragingly, "report promptly?"

"I must tell you yes, Sir, I did. Mr. Cunningham's unfortunate manner with members of staff was not such as to reach the level of ignoble, but his habit of roaming the residence when the Mistress was away, which was not supposed to be allowed to those outside the household without accompaniment, and his turning up in the most unexpected places at unusual times, well, right or wrong, I

---

[31] "The Fall of the House of Usher," Edgar Allan Poe, 1839.

took to be akin to spying, Sir, and I reported it."

"What did Vivian do?"

"She said she would take it under advisement and thanked me for my concern."

"Well, Edward" Russ said kindly, "as I know how seriously you take your job, I feel that you can be told you were right to be concerned. I should also tell you that a thorough investigation of all staff members has been aggressively conducted. My one goal now is to make sure those I surround myself with are trustworthy. If you have any further concerns about anyone on staff I would welcome your insights."

"I understand, Sir."

Russ apologized for bringing him in on his Saturday off and his Head of Household assured him it was no trouble.

"I was coming in to oversee the supper anyway, Sir" Edward Bright said with a smile, and then a paroxysm seized the man and he nearly collapsed back into his chair. He stood staring, half bent over, his blue eyes bulging.

"What is it?" Russ said with such concern that he rushed to Mr. Bright's side, sending Thorndike flying from his lap.

"A thousand pardons, Sir."

The man was in agony.

"I was sworn to secrecy regarding tonight's supper and I've failed my trust."

Russ had wondered what Mr. Bright had meant when he said, "I was coming in to oversee the supper anyway, Sir," but the man's apoplectic fit came over him so suddenly that Russ didn't pursue an answer. Now Edward Bright said, "I'm sorry, Sir."

Russ had him sit back down and explain himself.

"Well, Ms. Meredith approached me in secret, to plan a surprise party for you, and I agreed to see to it without your knowing, Sir. I didn't mean to break my pledge, Sir."

"Rest easy, Edward" Russ said graciously. "I promise to act so suitably surprised that no one will guess I knew."

"Thank you, Sir" said the shaken Head of Household. "I would have hated to disappoint Ms. Meredith and the party goers."

After Mr. Bright departed Russ turned to Thorndike with a stern expression.

"Did you know about this, this Shindig?"

Thorndike looked innocent enough and Russ didn't know Winston and Benjamin well enough yet, in his opinion, to cross-examine them, so he let the matter drop with a shrug of his shoulders.

"What could she be up to, that's what I'm wondering."

Russ was a curious creature, quite similar to a feline.

It was the Saturday before the last 3 weeks of the school term and Christmas-New Year's Break. He couldn't think of anything significant to do with the Saturday following Thanksgiving. The Friday following was "Black Friday," everyone knew that, but they hadn't come up with a name for Saturday yet, had they? Had he been that out of touch?

Was it "Mauve Saturday"? He laughed at the thought and remembered "Maundy Thursday." That was the name for the sacred celebrations that took place on the Thursday before Easter. Russ had always liked the sound of it, "Maundy Thursday," and thought the only thing that could have sounded better was "Maundy Tuesday."

He'd heard of "Cyber Monday", the Monday after Thanksgiving, and probably the year's most profitable shopping day online.

Still, he had no idea why the Saturday following Thanksgiving would be a celebration day.

Russ's curiosity was what his editor, Eileen, had once described as "one of his defining characteristics" and Lara would agree with her. Eileen was elegant, chic, comfortable in every social situation, intelligent, and knowledgeable in a number of surprising fields, including psychology and "Feline Studies." She loved to speak of things like "defining characteristics."

"Impatience must be another one of my 'defining

characteristics' too" he said to Thorndike, Benji, & Winston, what Russ sometimes called "The Menagerie," "Because it's sure is hard to wait to find out what she has planned."

As he and "The Three Amigos" headed to his bedroom to shower and dress more formally, he wondered what life would be like after he and Lara were married, in February.

Princess Charlotte was Lara's fun-loving kitten and he would often say, "je suis Carlotta," which meant, "I am Carlotta," simply because he loved the way the words sounded.

For her part, Charlotte adored Russ, although he felt he was loved merely for his shoelaces!

Lara also had a noisy little Cockatiel named, quite appropriately, "Sunshine," and she seemed to love Russ too. Whenever he visited she would land on his shoulder and snuggle right up to his neck. It was a cute gesture but if she made her piercing squawk in that position, Russ found himself nearly paralyzed by the deafening noise. For such a small bird it was amazing how loud she could be at times. Usually though, her little chirps and cheeps were adorable.

Russ was told that Sunshine would not do "The Cockatiel Serenade," an intricate whistle-song that only male Cockatiels performed, but he enjoyed her company and her softer sounds.

Once Princess Charlotte and Sunshine joined "The Three Amigos" what would Russ call them? There was, of course, "The Menagerie," but that didn't have quite the ring to it Russ enjoyed in his words.

This was a perplexing puzzle for him until he saw his lavender "Thorndike & Company™" sweatshirt in the top of one of the mover's boxes.

"Of course" he said out loud, "Thorndike & Company™." That would be perfect. "I wonder why I didn't think of that before?"

Only then did Russ notice that Thorndike had been staring at him with a particularly focused gaze. The cat simply shook his head and jumped up to his Mila™ cat bed.

"Cats" Russ said, "can't live with 'em, can't live without 'em!" Then he thought, "That should be on a T-Shirt too!"

An hour later, as he dutifully tied his shoes, he heard a quiet knock on his bedroom door.

"Mr. Gorgeous, are you decent?"

It was the love of his life who, as his fiancé, had been given "The Freedom of the Castle" and could roam when and where she liked without worrying the staff.

"Come in, Mrs. Gorgeous" he hollered back.

"Oh my, don't you clean up nicely" she said as she bent and gave him a loving kiss.

"Me?" questioned Russ sincerely. "What are you doing here?" he said with a smile, "isn't there a fashion-runway in Paris missing you?"

Lara gave him that half-smile that made him go weak-at-the-knees and said, "I was hoping you'd notice."

Lara wore stylish ivory high heels and an exquisite, Knee-Length, pearl-pink Chiffon Column Dress, by JJ's House of Fashion™, with Cowl Neck and Ruffled shoulder.

"Notice?" Russ exclaimed, "you shine brighter than the stars."

Lara turned and kissed her spellbound fiancé and then, while he caught his breath, she handed him his Ralph Lauren® Blue Check Executive Fit™ Sport Coat.

"You'll need this" she said mysteriously, "and a nice tie to go with it."

While Russ feigned surprise and asked all the predictable questions, which she ignored, Lara went and picked out the perfect tie, then helped him put it on.

Once she was finished she moved gracefully to his side and said, "Now don't you look handsome."

Russ looked into the full-length mirror with Lara on his arm and couldn't help but say that she was the most beautiful and wonderful woman in the whole world.

"You are a shameless flatterer, Russ Personette."

"Me?" he questioned, "I just tell the truth."

As he buttoned his sport coat Lara asked, "By the way, what is that on the toes of your shoes?"

"Yeah" Russ said facetiously, "as if you didn't know. Those, m'Lady, are sweet Princess Charlotte's sharp little claw marks."

Russ had no more than said these words when he remembered a time, nearly a year earlier, when someone else said the same thing.

Dr. Dudley had said, "I knew this cat when he was just a kitten and he was so playful." Then pointing to the tip of his left shoe he'd said, "Those tiny scratch marks came from his teeth when he was just a wee, small thing."

Now Russ had said the same thing about Lara's little "Princess Charlotte" and he had the strangest sensation.

"Does that mean Charlotte will grow into a second Thorndike, a telepathic crime-solver with a cruel sense of humor?"

"Yeeoww!" said Thorndike, unexpectedly.

"I thought so" Russ said in an accusatory voice, staring at his little buddy, "I thought so."

"Okay Boys, time to go." Lara held the bedroom door open as Russ, Benjamin, and Thorndike trailed obediently through.

"What about you? Winston, do you really plan to sit this one out?" Lara smiled at the beautiful African Gray Parrot sitting on his brass stand like some ancient potentate upon his throne. Then, suddenly, the big bird let go, flew gracefully out the door and down the hallway, to light on Russ's shoulder.

The elevator looked like a petting zoo as the 2 humans and 3 friends descended from the $3^{rd}$ floor. Despite expecting some kind of surprise, and, as Edward Bright had confessed, some "party-goers," when the elevator opened Russ found himself utterly shocked.

At least a hundred people filled the cavernous, Main

Hall of Caledonia. A hundred noisy people, at that, and even though he had been accidentally warned, Russ was almost afraid to come out of the elevator.

Young Master Benjamin fearlessly led the way, running happily out to greet what he took to be his adoring fans. To his great delight many people stooped down to adore the cute little Westie. Lara and Russ went next and as soon as they stepped out of the elevator, Winston took to the sky and found a quiet perch on the second floor, overlooking the Hall. Thorndike, like an iconic Hollywood Star, followed last, making the grand entrance much to the joy of the guests.

The giant Christmas tree ablaze with lights, the elegant surroundings, the sound of Bing Crosby singing holiday songs in the background and a hundred friendly faces all near and dear to Russ Personette created a moment in time that he would never forget. Happiness, over his last years, had been an elusive thing. The death of his beloved wife and daughter in a winter car accident had inaugurated a dark time in his life. It was a time he never believed he'd escape, but in Vermont, and of all places, Chittenden County, he had found a haven.

It wasn't that the place was immune to the vicissitudes of life, in fact, Vivian's passing was a case in point. Rather it was the love and acceptance that he'd found there that began to break the spell that sadness had cast over his soft heart. Russ Personette could be tough. Special Agent-in-Charge Claymont Awmiller had made that clear.

"Your one tough cookie, Professor."

The truth surrounding Professor P was more complex. Eileen would have said that kindness and empathy for others were among his most fundamental "defining characteristics."

He looked from smiling, happy face to smiling, happy face and was reminded of their engagement "shindig" at the Old Homestead Pub.

Bernadette and Lou were there, looking happier than

Russ had ever seen them.

"Oh, Russ, you look so stately" Bernadette said, giving her "spy-boss" a peck on the cheek.

"I brought my Scottish Shortbread Cookies for a light dessert; I know you can't resist them."

Russ beamed a boyish smile.

"Resist them, who wants to resist Bernadette's World-Famous Light & Fluffy Scottish Shortbread Cookies®." Then he whispered to her, "They're Agent 36's Secret Weapon, you know?"

"And did you know they're selling like hotcakes?" her husband Lou added, shaking Russ firmly by the hand.

"Pancakes, Dear" Bernadette corrected.

"Pancakes, flapjacks, hotcakes, griddle-cakes, silver-dollars, jonnycakes, buckwheat cakes, call 'em what you will, her Scottish Shortbread Cookies are flying off the shelves."

Russ laughed at Lou's colorful explanation and said, "I'd swear to the House Committee on Flapjacks that they're just plain addictive."

"Me too!" said Lou emphatically, adding with a cruel smile, "thanks for inviting us, Mr. Personetti!"

Russ, ever sensitive about his names, flinched at Lou's joke and gave him a sidelong glare to think about.

Then it was Lara's Great-Aunt Virginia and Gracie. They seemed somehow smaller to Russ, but both wore their gifts proudly. Virginia wore her Biddy Murphy® Irish Ruana with a Celtic-Knot design and Gracie had her Tiffany™ Peacock Feather Shawl.

"Bless you for the beautiful shawl" Gracie said, "I've never had a more beautiful gift."

Virginia pulled him down and kissed him sweetly, her eyes glistening.

"We're so proud of you, dear Russ."

Russ saw Charlie, Veronica, and Ben across the sea of faces. The young people waved, smiled, and lifted their glasses to him, as if in a toast to something, but they didn't dare try to cross the room.

"It would have been easier to part the Red Sea than get through that bunch, Uncle Russ" Ben said later on in the evening.

Chief Ramsay and his kind and longsuffering wife, Sharon, caught him by the arm. He and Sharon had met before and he could see she was used to her husband's long and irregular work hours, called out day and night, weekend and holiday, without fail, but the danger of his job, she'd confided in Russ, was something she truly disliked and she hoped desperately for an early retirement. Russ remembered his late wife and the long hours and stressful work he'd been committed to for so many years in manufacturing. If only he could have had a "normal" 9 to 5 job, how different things might have been.

"Ross Personetti, is that you?"

Russ shrugged his shoulders. There was going to be no way to escape it, now he had to admit it. Fate was a cruel thing and regarding Russ's names it seemed he was doomed to go on suffering from "Taxation with Misrepresentation," as he'd long referred to the phenomenon.

Shortly after, Russ got pulled aside again and ran into Nathan and Dr. Mariell Thompson, and he wasn't completely surprised to see them holding hands.

"Congratulations Professor P" she said as she hugged him.

Russ smiled and nodded but he wondered why people were offering him congratulations.

Dan Garn was there with his lovely wife, Gretchen. His star was still shining brightly and he was quite the celebrity with several guests buzzing around him. The recent public unveiling of his life-sized bronze statue in front of the Jericho City Hall, "The Dan Garn Postman-Poet of the North Country Statue," had been carried in all the local papers and brought a new wave of hero worship his way.

"Just what he needs" Russ thought as the two men

smiled and nodded at each other over the crowd. Then Russ mumbled, "That darned Dan Garn!"

Harley and Fiona Shaw greeted him warmly.

"Did you get the old girl home safely?" the little man asked with a handsome smile, showing his perfect teeth.

"She's resting safely in Caledonia's heated garage!" Russ said proudly.

"Heated garage!" Harley exclaimed, "you're gonna spoil her for sure."

"I'll never be able to thank you enough."

"P'shaw" Harley exclaimed, "after all you and that darned mechanically-inclined cat have done for me, I keep expectin' a bill in the mail."

They laughed like men who understood each other well and Russ was pulled away suddenly, only to see two more dear souls. He beamed with joy when he saw Eston & Greta Phillips, and hugs were shared all around.

"Oh sweet Russ" was all Greta could say as she patted his cheek.

"We call it 'supper' here at Caledonia, Eston."

The news of this shocked the amazing mechanic and disappointed his dear wife.

"Then this is the only place in the whole County where it isn't mistakenly called it dinner."

The two men nodded in agreement, they were brothers in a lonely cause, doomed in the end to be overwhelmed by the millions who, through no particular fault of their own, called the evening meal by the "wrong name." Russ said, "It's a lonely path, Eston, but we're committed to stay the course."

"Aye, we are" Eston agreed wholeheartedly, "to the bitter end, Russ, to the bitter end."

Russ could see the tall form of Detective August James moving through the crowd, apparently unaware that he was moving directly toward Russ and Lara.

"Russ, there you are, I couldn't see you down there in the crowd."

"Hahaha" Russ said sarcastically, "I get that all the time." Then Russ saw a stunningly attractive, petite woman next to the tall Detective. She wore cardinal red Clio Square™ Midi-length sheath dress by Bardot® with matching high heels.

"Russ this is my wife" the handsome Detective said proudly, "Mallory."

"My Great-Grandmother's name was also Mallory" Russ said sincerely as he shook her hand, then he introduced Lara.

"We've known your husband so long" Lara said sweetly, "it's a privilege to finally meet his wife."

"Thank you Lara" she said, "I feel like I know you, Russ, and Thorndike, too, I've heard so much." Then she turned to Russ and said, "And thank you Russ, for encouraging August to do that screentest, we're so excited about his opportunity. Did you know they start shooting in February? I shouldn't say 'shooting' like that should I, everyone will panic and it will be all my fault."

She was a personable young woman and the perfect complement to the Detective who had become a good and trusted friend.

"You are a beautiful couple" Lara said before she and Russ were pulled away by another wave of humanity.

Griff Langlois and his wife, Christy, were there, as was David Gaertner and his wife, Cindy. Dane VanWert and his daughter, Taylor, in a lovely dress, greeted him as old friends. They were all beaming the smiles of co-conspirators who knew they'd all soon be rich from the gold doubloons from the Sloop "Morning Star."

"Good to see you Ross" Taylor said with a broad smile.

"Hahaha" Russ said again, "thanks a million, young lady!"

Russ truly felt love from everyone in the room.

A dashing Dr. Roger Dudley and his fiancé, Suzanne, managed to pull him in another direction, congratulating him even as they reunited him with Lara.

"Congratulations to you two, as well." Russ said with sincerity, before another turn of the masses moved them on again.

"We're always being separated by the crowd" she said to him, and he whispered into her ear, "Why is everyone congratulating me?"

She laughed happily without answering his question.

He pulled her close suddenly and whispered into her lovely ear, "You are a little troublemaker!"

Lara agreed with him happily, her smile illuminating the entire room.

"Hey Professor P" came the voice of Special Agent Awmiller.

"You again" Russ said with a laugh, "you're like the proverbial bad penny, you just keep showing up!"

The men laughed for a moment until Russ was pulled away again.

Drinks and hors d'oeuvres were being served in the Mountain Lounge, as the first-floor room in the northeast tower was called, and everyone was in a celebratory mood.

Arnold threw his arms around his old friend and Rhonda and Lara embraced delicately.

"You old Sea Lawyer, what am I going to do with you?"

Russ always felt a little better when Arnold and Rhonda were around. When he first came to Vermont it had been them who'd adopted him, "off the street," as he put it, and made him feel like an important part of their family.

"What do you mean?" Russ asked sincerely.

"What do you mean, what do I mean?" Arnold said, gesturing around at the incredible Manor House.

"I turn my back on you for a minute and then I find out you've inherited the finest estate in the upper Northeast of America, and I hear congratulations are in order on another front too" he said with an air of amazement.

Russ tried to get more information out of his old Navy buddy but Arnold wasn't about to spill the beans.

"Looking forward to it" Arnold said just before Rhonda

pulled him away and they disappeared into the hors d'oeuvres line.

Lara had pulled off a tremendous coup and Russ found he didn't have to pretend to be surprised.

"Mr. Bright" Russ said, cornering the man near the room that housed the Delashmett Collection of Art and Artifacts.

"How are you managing" he asked with concern.

"Good Evening, Sir" he said, appearing a little frazzled Russ thought. "We're managing, Sir. This is larger than most of the Mistresses gatherings, but we're managing."

"Excellent" Russ said, then he added, "I'm certainly surprised by all this."

"Thank you for saying so, Sir" said a relieved Head of Household.

Most of the Domestics were on hand and Russ recognized Delphine, Leticia, and Calpurnia, but he didn't see Eugenie, and he'd never met Angharad before. The servers were going to and fro, keeping guests and the Mountain Lounge supplied.

After thirty minutes of mingling and visiting the soft sound of the supper gong on the second floor sounded three times and an announcement over the state-of-the-art PA System told the guests to make their way to the Green Mountain Dining Room. This was Caledonia's immense, formal dining room and was used only for the most special occasions.

Name tags at each setting around the table and a map, handed out when guests arrived, got the guests to their correct seats. It showed them not only the general location of their seats at the table, but also the location of bathrooms, and other areas open to them on the first floor. One such room housed the Delashmett Collection. This museum quality room held several paintings by famous artists, valuable porcelains and pottery, bronze sculptures, a single service of all of Caledonia's dinner sets, tapestries, and fine crystal from around the world. Many of the guests were enjoying their first visit to Caledonia and having heard of the exhibit all their lives, they made sure to spend time enjoying The Collection.

The Three Amigos were deftly and quietly scooped up and taken to their fates. A surprised Thorndike and a resigned Winston went back to Russ's bedroom and their respective boudoirs, while a gangly Domestic with freckles and red hair, and a nametag that said "Lloyd," took an excited Benjamin on his "nightly promenade," as Vivian had named it, down the lamplit paths of Caledonia.

Russ was seated at the head of a magnificently laid table easily 75 feet long and 6 feet wide. To his right side sat Lara, and next to her was Lara's beautiful mother, Audra. To his left sat Special Agent Claymont Awmiller and next to him was his boss, Thomas Martin.

Russ looked around the table, taking in each face for a few seconds, and a line from "It's a Wonderful Life," with Jimmy Stewart, floated gently through his memory.

"Remember, George: no man is a failure who has friends."

The supper was an unforgettable occasion not only for the feast, of which Russ selected the prime rib and red russet potato and Lara chose the Chicken Cordon Bleu with Rice Pilaf, but also for its service, which was flawless.

The beauty of the Green Mountain Dining Room was difficult to describe. A dark wood wainscotting lined the bottom four feet of the walls while a light green William Morris™ wallpaper, printed in 1872 and called "Larkspur", covered the walls. Chandeliers of intricate crystals cut in Ireland in 1868 by Waterford™, specifically for Caledonia, hung over the table.

Epic landscape paintings showing mountains and wilderness, from Hudson River School painters with names like Frederic Church, John Kensett, Sanford Gifford, Albert Bierstadt, and Susan Barstow, hung under brass display lamps. Some of them had hung in the formal dining room since the 1860's.

Everyone considered it one of their most memorable evenings and shortly into the meal Edward Bright entered through the end door behind Russ and explained that two guests had arrived late and should he show them in.

Russ, of course, said "yes" and shortly the door at the far end of the room, closest to the front doors of Caledonia opened and Eileen and Daphne were shown in.

Russ, overjoyed to see two of the most special ladies in his life, rose and went to embrace them.

"I'm so sorry we're late, Russ" Eileen said, "our plane got a late start due to snow and one thing led to another."

Daphne gave Russ a giant hug, leaving him in no doubt of her affection, and kissed him on the cheek.

Russ assured them he was just glad to have them there and Mr. Bright helped them to their seats and saw to their orders.

At one point Russ leaned over and asked Lara how many guests were there and she whispered back, "120".

Russ still hadn't been able to figure out the reason for the supper although he knew it was to congratulate him for something. He couldn't imagine Lara would have hosted such an event to celebrate his inheriting Caledonia, yet this was the only notable event he knew of recently.

The discovery of the Morning Star had made the news but Russ discounted this on two counts. First, while the discovery had been reported, the discovery of 10,000 Golden Sovereigns, his "Operation Golden Doubloon", had not. The public remained ignorant of the great treasure, at least for now. Second, the reporter had named the members of the search team and, as Lou Langlois had been so happy to remind him, his name was spelled as "Ross Personetti." He believed few readers would pause long enough to connect Ross Personetti with the well-known Professor P.

Matters remained the same throughout dessert when Special Agent Claymont Awmiller leaned over and whispered to him.

"Mr. Martin wants me to make the speech and then he'll be the one who presents you with the medal, alright?"

Russ nodded. It was neither the time nor the place to cross examine Claymont Awmiller but the gears in Russ's mind were certainly spinning at high speed.

After dinner the guests made their ways quietly, and as directed, back to the main hall. Russ thought, after a meal like that, most people would have been glad to settle in for a long winter's nap.

In the Main Hall they found a veritable mass of comfortable, padded chairs set up in rows with a center aisle. A carpeted platform and Walnut podium in the area in front of the elevator showed that, while Russ had told Mr. Cunningham this wasn't his first rodeo, this banquet wasn't the staff of Caledonia's first rodeo either.

There was even a photographer set up near the platform, with her camera on a tripod and two large cloth light reflectors off to the side.

The lights on the Christmas tree had been turned off, the general lighting had been turned down, and extra lights on the ceiling high above focused on the podium. Mr. Bright tested the microphone and welcomed the FBI Agents to come to the podium.

Mr. Martin sat down in one of seats, while Claymont Awmiller, more dashing than ever, adjusted the microphone.

Lara had steered Russ to reserved seats in the front row and he watched with curiosity. After everyone was seated and silence descended on the hall, the Special Agent began speaking.

"As you all know" he began confidently, "we have gathered together here in this beautiful place, to honor one of our fellow citizens and a dear friend to all of us, Mr. Russ Personette."

The audience erupted with unrestrained clapping, happy to have been included for the special occasion.

Russ was uncomfortable as the center of public

attention and he felt his cheeks flush. He was still ignorant of the specific reason he was being honored and, for the life of him, he couldn't piece any of it together.

With his boss sitting behind him, Claymont Awmiller was constrained in how humorous he could be on such a formal occasion and when he continued it was with an appropriate degree of seriousness.

"Today we are all well aware of the crimes carried out by the Chandler Gang but few know the critical role Russ Personette played in uncovering and stopping their reign of corruption and murder."

Now Russ finally knew why everyone had been congratulating him and why Lara had arranged the evening's banquet, but he honestly wished his participation in the events had remained a secret.

"Now I'm going to read the description of the award we are presenting to Russ this evening." Claymont looked out on all the eager faces in the audience. Not only were they all friends of the eccentric History Professor, but they also seemed to sense they were watching a significant moment in history.

"The FBI Medal for Meritorious Achievement is awarded for extraordinary and exceptional meritorious service in a duty of extreme challenge and great responsibility, extraordinary and exceptional achievements in connection with criminal or national security cases or projects, or a decisive, exemplary act that results in the protection or the direct saving of life in severe jeopardy in the line of duty."

Russ was speechless. He had been in the intelligence community for decades and he knew the FBI presented only a handful of such awards each year. To have been selected as one of those recipients was humbling and, in fact, shocking. He sat in silence as Claymont took a large plaque from one of the seats and began reading.

"Mr. Russ Personette's decisive, courageous, and exemplary actions resulted in the direct saving of life in severe jeopardy and aided in identifying criminal conspirators for prosecution, all while exposing himself to extreme danger. For his exceptional meritorious service to his fellow citizens, his community, and Nation, the Federal Bureau of Investigation proudly presents him with this Medal for Meritorious Achievement." The Special Agent finished speaking then looked directly at Russ and said, "Russ, would you please join us on the platform for the presentation of your medal by FBI Assistant Director Thomas Martin?"

Russ stood uneasily and quietly made his way forward into the bright light. The shock of the entire event was hard for his mind to comprehend and later he realized that he remembered little of what took place after this point.

As Special Agent Awmiller turned Russ to face the audience, Assistant Director Thomas Martin stepped to the podium and gave a short speech.

"It is with deep appreciation and gratitude that I, Thomas Martin, on behalf of the Federal Bureau of Investigation, proudly award Russ Personette with the Medal of Meritorious Achievement." With this the Assistant Director stepped behind Russ and lowered the magnificent indigo blue enamel and gold medal down on his chest and clasped the ribbon band closed behind his neck. Both FBI men shook his hand while his 120 friends and loved ones and a dozen Caledonia staff members stood and clapped their approval. The photographer's camera flashed incessantly.

Lara, Eileen, and Daphne were all given guest rooms for the night and as Russ kissed Lara "good night" outside "The Rose Room" she looked at him proudly.

"Now you'll really have to introduce yourself as 'Personette, Russ Personette' wherever you go. Just like 'Bond, James Bond'."

As a tired Russ walked to his bedroom he realized that Lara was right about one thing, his days of anonymity in the broader community were over for good.

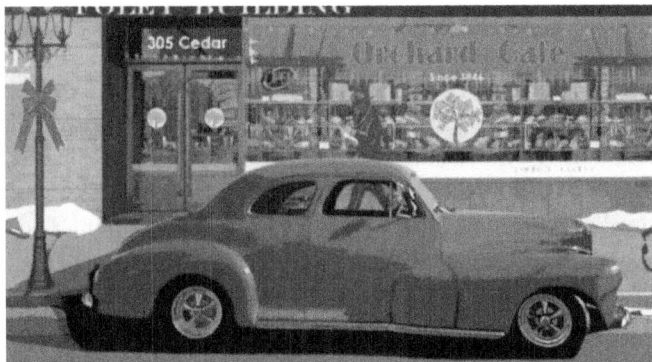

# CHAPTER FOURTEEN
## "The Caledonia Project"

"Hey, sorry to wake your Lordship!"

Chief Ramsay was sitting in a wingback chair beside the large fireplace in the Main Hall, directly across the wide room from the giant Douglas Fir Christmas Tree, and he was clearly enjoying himself.

It was early on the Sunday before Christmas and all through the Manor House, not a creature was stirring except for that darned cat, Thorndike. The big cat had mastered his environment completely and now he thought the grand old building was there just for his entertainment. He knew where every pet door, food and water bowl, pet bed, and every good view was on every floor. No doubt Young Master Benjamin had shown him around. He knew where to go when the gong sounded mealtime and now he sat in front of the majestic Christmas Tree, ignoring Chief Ramsay and looking longingly upon the growing mountain of presents.

"They told me I had a visitor" Russ said bluntly. "It's hard to believe that Caledonia will celebrate its 180$^{th}$ anniversary in June, and still the riffraff won't leave us alone.

Russ flashed a broad smile. He had identified with the Chief from the first instant they met and he considered him one of his best friends.

"I ordered us some tea, but tell me what brings you out this way, good news I hope?"

"That depends on how good a memory you have, Mr. Personetti, or is it Professor P today? Or Mr. Gorgeous?"

Russ sat down in his Baturina™ Navy Blue Paisley Silk Pajamas and matching Dressing Gown, his slippered feet pointing toward the small fire in the huge fireplace. He did look like the Laird of some Scottish Castle.

"I have a pretty good memory" he said honestly.

"Then perhaps you can tell me what the late Ryan Drummond was wearing on his feet when you found him lying in the snow at Wildrose."

Russ thought back to that day. That was the terrible moment he'd seen Thorndike out in the snow, sitting in the middle of a wide blood trail. Russ's mind had been focused on Thorndike, exclusively, and his memory was a blank.

"I don't" he said thoughtfully.

"No, I didn't think you would" the Chief said smugly.

"Whys that?"

"Well, take a look at this."

Chief Ramsay pulled several photographs out of a battered manila envelope and handed Russ two of the photos of the young man's body, each from a different angle. The pictures brought that horrible day vividly back to life. In both photos the young man's shoes were covered by snow.

"You can't remember what you've never seen" the Chief said.

Then he handed Russ another photograph.

"Blundstone® 500 Chelsea Boots" Russ said in surprise.

"I know I gave you a hard time about that Cock-a-leekie Soup story about the Rhodesian Moccasin Company that was founded in 1066 by Alexander Graham Bell" Chief Ramsay admitted guiltily, with a laugh, "but it looks like you were on the right trail after all."

Russ laughed heartily at the Chief's roundabout apology and Thorndike looked over his shoulder to see what was going on. The cat walked over nonchalantly and jumped up into Russ's lap and a moment later Benji came scurrying around the corner, followed by Annette VanWert with her tea cart.

"I brought the Irish Breakfast Tea, Sir."

Russ was very appreciative with his staff and Annette, for her part, curtsied and hurried away. Three weeks earlier most of the house staff had gone by "traditional names," chosen for them by the Head of Household from a list that was made by a woman born in the 1800's. Russ had changed that and now, for the first time in over 110 years, Caledonia's employees went by the own names. It was considered a "radical change" by those "below stairs."

"Great tea" the Chief said.

"One of my two favorite breakfast teas."

"I'll have to get then name of it" the Chief said sincerely.

Russ couldn't forget that just a short year before he'd come to Vermont with all his worldly possessions in his 1998 Mercury Grand Marquis and always bought the least expensive, generic tea on the store shelf. Now a maid was delivering him Twining's® Irish Breakfast Tea in a set of china that was valued at more than the most expensive home he'd ever owned. It had been an indescribable change and was accompanied by more adventure than either of the two men seated there would have liked to admit.

"Founded in 1066 by Alexander Graham Bell, right? That's great Chief." Russ laughed at the humor of his longsuffering friend and marveled at Chief Ramsay's ability to handle the most nightmarish situations with composure.

"Well, you have to admit, sometimes your stories seem pretty wild."

"Yeeoww" Thorndike said in a drawn-out wail of agreement.

"See" the Chief said, "even Thorndike admits it."

"So, is Ryan related to Dr. Charles Duncan?" Russ asked openly.

"Yes, he was his grandson. And you were correct that Dr. Duncan's estranged daughter, Mrs. Margaret Merridew, was the boy's mother. She's had a lot of her own problems too and when Dr. Duncan returned from his Thanksgiving holiday he found his home broken in to. Among other things taken, his winter boots were missing. He called us in but admitted he suspected his own grandson of the theft. He said Ryan had a troubled childhood and had made a lot of mistakes. As his Grandfather he'd tried to help, but nothing he did made any lasting improvements and, as with his daughter, there was a point where he just had to let the young man go his way."

Russ had seen Dr. Duncan in passing over the past three weeks, ever since the end of Thanksgiving break and the death of the man's Grandson. He'd noticed he was quieter and more distant than usual and Russ hadn't seen the boots again. He was sure of that, but he hadn't pried and he hadn't revealed the part that he and Thorndike had played in the life and death of Ryan Drummond.

"A sad story" Russ said soberly.

"And more common than you'd imagine."

"I'm sorry to hear that" Russ mused.

"Yeah, but that's why I'm here at 7:30 AM on a Sunday morning, when I should be up at my shop working on my wonderful wife's Christmas present."

"Whys that?" Russ asked.

"Well, I've already sent the evidence to your buddies at the FBI, but it seems your former employee, James Cunningham, was acquainted with the deceased."

Russ was a literary man, a writer, and he knew there were two ways of communicating. The first, everyone recognized, was by saying what you meant. The second was in what the speaker or writer chose not to say.

"Acquainted with Ryan Drummond?" Russ asked, wondering what the Chief hadn't said.

"Employer then" Chief Ramsay said, "Detective James found a string of texts on Ryan Drummond's phone."

Russ was suddenly paralyzed by a horrible realization, and one that froze his blood.

"Wait a minute, Chief, if Ryan Drummond was wearing those boots."

"That's right, Russ, he killed John MacKean. A Drummond killed a MacKean, or a MacIain, right here in Chittenden County, Vermont, just like it happened in Glencoe, Scotland, in 1692. You see, Professor, you're teaching me History too, as we go along."

"But why?" Russ stammered, "did it have anything to do with Cunningham?"

"MacKean owned a big parcel of land in the Pine Valley, bordering Caledonia on the north. He'd never sell, but his heirs would. I don't know how Cunningham found out about it but he knew. He sent Ryan Drummond the kill order in a text. Can you believe it? And if you hadn't been able to identify the boot tread from that Armenian Goloshes Company founded in 1492 by Nicole Kidman, we probably never would have put two and two together."

Chief Ramsay was a good man, but like Detective James, Dan Garn, Claymont Awmiller, and Thomas Martin, he had routinely blurred the boundaries of the law with regard to Russ Personette. Now he handed his friend the transcripts of some other texts between Caledonia's former Head of Security and the 19-year-old, former Veterinarian's Assistant, Ryan Drummond.

Russ read through the pages quickly, shocked by all he saw there. Thorndike stared at Russ the entire time.

"This means the catnapping of Thorndike was the plan of James Cunningham all along. Ryan Drummond was just his foot-soldier."

"Yes, his assassin really" the Chief said soberly.

"And he planned to have Thorndike killed immediately, he was never going to return him for the ransom."

"That's right" the Chief admitted.

"But why?" Russ asked sincerely. "Why?"

"Revenge, maybe" the Chief said, "and power. We see it all the time, when someone without ethics and honor gains the power to do evil, they are virtually always corrupted by it. They don't stop themselves; they force us to stop them."

"Revenge" Russ said flatly, and then he remembered what Detective James had said weeks earlier, about Marcus Thomas.

"Revenge does strange things to people. Dr. Thomas was obsessed with making you pay."

"Revenge" he said again.

"Well, think about it. Cunningham told you he'd get 10% of the Delashmett Fortune and Caledonia Estate in its entirety. That's a lot to play for and you, and Thorndike here, foiled him. Not only that, but you swept up all of the other members of the Chandler Gang too, so that dog wasn't going to hunt anymore. He was never going to be the filthy rich Laird of Caledonia." Then Chief Ramsay added, "No offense."

"None taken" Russ said, still deep in his thoughts.

"Then, to top it all off, who inherits Caledonia? The very man, and cat, who had been his downfall. It must have been real tough for him to report to you and see you as his boss and the new Laird of Caledonia. Who knows how long he'd been counting on that title for himself."

"I can see your point" Russ said suddenly, a chill running up his spine. He had instantly recalled the feeling he'd had when Dr. Marcus Thomas had been convicted, "Case Closed." But the case hadn't remained closed and just a few weeks earlier Marcus had come back into his life. Once James Cunningham was put away Russ would've had the same thought, but now he wondered. How far would revenge go? He thought of both men and wondered if he would now have them in the back of his mind for the rest of his life. Would he forever be looking over his shoulder and wondering, worrying about two men obsessed by thoughts of revenge against him, and Thorndike.

"Are you okay, Russ?"

"Just thinking" Russ said mysteriously.

"Well, I wanted you to know that you and Thorndike were right about everything and to let you know about the unexpected connection between the two men, and MacKean. And now, since my wife thinks I'm working on her Black Walnut jewelry cabinet for Christmas, I suppose I should get going."

"Thank you" Russ said without getting up, not wanting to disturb Thorndike on his lap or Benji, who laid with his head on Russ's slipper.

"Speaking of your wife" Russ asked, "did she enjoy the banquet?"

"Oh, yes, she did" Chief Ramsay said with a wide grin. "It was the grandest Cèilidh we've enjoyed in years and she loves any excuse to force me into a suit."[32] Then the Chief confessed a secret.

"All our lives we've heard about Caledonia but to actually be here, and to see it in its Christmas glory, that was special too."

"I don't know how you all kept that a secret but I sure had no clue what was coming."

"That was all Lara" the Policeman said, "You've got a real keeper there."

As Chief Ramsay left he called over his shoulder, "Thanks for the tea. Twining's® Irish Breakfast Tea, got it."

Russ sighed in relief. Since first hearing the nickname

---

[32] A "Cèilidh," pronounced "Kay-Lee," is a traditional gathering in Scottish and Irish communities.

Lara had given Russ, Chief Ramsay had not failed to call him "Mr. Gorgeous" every chance he got. So today was a first.

"Names" Russ said as he looked into the flickering flames and sipped on his tea, "who needs them?"

He was supposed to meet Lara at the Orchard Café for breakfast at 9 AM so he made his way back upstairs to his "Master Suite", complete with its own private office, massive walk-in closet, which was really a series of closets and drawers wrapped around its own large room, exquisite master bath in white marble, and a private sitting room, the "Quilloran Room".

As the roads were still clear and dry he texted for the Aston Martin to be brought to the side-door, where a long glass roof covered the drive for guest pick-up and drop off.

He had to admit, he loved driving the classic car and as he slid into the nicely warmed-up Aston Martin that morning, Lara's whispered words fluttered playfully through his mind.

"Now you'll have to introduce yourself as 'Personette, Russ Personette'."

A few months earlier he had reproached Dan Garn for "looking like James Bond" and not blending in and "disappearing in plain view" like he was supposed to do. Now, here he was, driving the exact car James Bond used in several movies, a silver Aston Martin DB5, and loving it.

In fact, he'd been so surprised he'd called Lara and told her to leave her Kia® Telluride™ in her garage.

"I'll pick you up, beautiful."

The Aston Martin wasn't just an iconic car, as it prowled slowly down the avenue the rough-edged "throatiness" of the motor absolutely called for attention. It was as if the designers and builders had set out to build a car that would say, "Look at Me!"

"I feel like Eve Moneypenny, riding alongside my own spy in his Aston Martin" Lara said playfully.

Miss Moneypenny had been a recurring character in the

James Bond books and movies. Some of the women in his life had begun referring to themselves as his "Miss Moneypenny" since Harley Shaw had "deeded him the rights" to the 1963 Aston Martin.

Russ pulled up to the Café and saw Dr. Debbie's beautifully restored, 1948 cherry red Ford "Businessman Coupe", parked among the flock of nondescript, modern automobiles.

"What a pleasure to see the classics taken care of" Russ said, almost to himself.

"Yes, it looks like you weren't the only one who couldn't resist bringing them out on a beautiful day."

Dr. Debbie was a small animal and bird veterinarian and her clinic, "The Purple Parrot™" had taken care of Winston for almost a decade. Seeing the popular Veterinarian's car out front reminded him of Ryan Drummond and Russ wondered if Debbie had heard anything yet about her former assistant.

Lara's Aunt Agnes owned the Orchard Café, which had been started by Lara's grandparents in 1946. Lara's mother, Audra, and Aunt, Agnes, were their only children.

Agnes only "worked the counter" on Sunday's anymore and that was just to have the chance to visit with "Her Regulars."

Harley Shaw, community "folklorist," historian, wind-surfer extraordinaire, ice sailor, member of the Polar Bear Club, nonagenarian, and sunken treasure hunter, was one of the charter members in the "Regulars" and he had his own "reserved" stool at the far end of the café's counter.

His lovely wife, Fiona, was one of the sisterhood of wives, sisters, and widows, who inhabited the tables nearer the front windows.

"Hello Russ" Agnes called, "The usual?" she asked with a broad smile.

"You bet; a wise man never messes with perfection!"

"You remember that" Fiona said firmly, "after you're married!"

The "Old Timers" who filled the café roared with laughter at Fiona's sound defense of women in general and of Lara in particular.

"That's right, Mr. Gorgeous, a wise man never messes with perfection." Harley said from his stool, enjoying the chance to rub it in.

"Oh yes, Mr. Shaw" Fiona said, clearly in the ascendancy, "like you practice what you preach!"

Once again everyone laughed.

Many of the regulars offered their congratulations on his "FBI Award," others congratulated him on inheriting "The Old Delashmett Place," which was their misleading name for Vivian's magnificent Caledonia Estate, and others just enjoyed hooting out "Mr. Gorgeous" for a minute or two.

"Hi Russ, how are the Three Amigos doing?" Dr. Debbie asked as she invited them to sit in her booth. She was speaking of Russ's nickname for Winston, Benjamin, and Thorndike, "The Three Amigos."

Before Russ could answer, someone in the next booth said, "You'll have to find a new name soon enough. Once you're married there will be three more mouths to feed."

It was Viola Longbranch-Snodgrass. Her parents had run the Longbranch Saloon in Underhill for the better part of 60-odd years, and though it was called a "saloon" it was really a restaurant. She and her husband, Herb Snodgrass, had owned the Snodgrass Feed and Seed in Cozy Corner until he died of congestive heart failure and she sold out.

Everyone laughed at Viola's comment.

Aunt Agnes's "Sunday Regulars" were a rowdy, raucous bunch. Taken as a group they represented 2,000 years of life-experience and they had the sharp minds and sharp tongues to go along with it. They were opinionated, generally well-set in their ways, and surprisingly stubborn.

One of them, a tall, thin woman called "Marty" MacCracken, stubbornly maintained that they weren't stubborn. She insisted that they were, rather, "Fiercely

Independent" and Russ, true Scot that he was, had taken this up almost like the battle cry of a Highland Clan. "Fiercely Independent" became his way of celebrating their irascible natures and good, old-fashioned stubbornness.

Russ found them fascinating and had taken to calling them the "Orchard Café Irregulars™," much to their enjoyment.

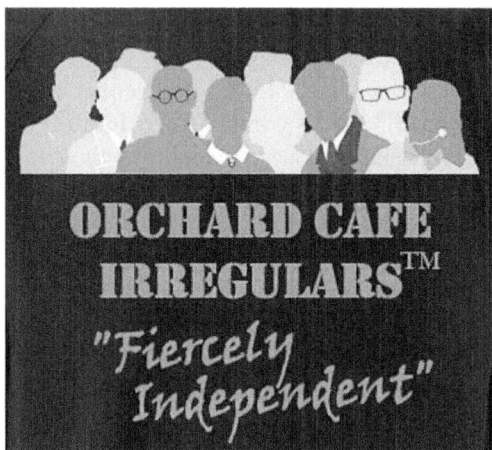

Russ had picked up the idea from the "Baker Street Irregulars", a group of "street urchins" who worked as an unorthodox spy network for Sherlock Holmes on the gritty streets of London.[33] Holmes's creator, author Sir Arthur Conan Doyle, wrote that the "Irregulars" could "go everywhere and hear everything".

He'd even had special navy blue and gold sweatshirts designed and printed for the group. It was a handsome logo peopled with the silhouettes of many of the "Irregulars" taken from high school graduation pictures, in some cases almost 70 years old themselves, wedding pictures, military

---

[33] "The Baker Street Irregulars" appear in three of Sir Arthur Conan Doyle's "Sherlock Holmes Mysteries": "A Study in Scarlet", © 1887, "The Sign of the Four" ©1890, and "The Adventure of the Crooked Man" ©1893.

portraits, and in one case, of a couple taken just the day before in front of their home. Emblazoned boldly on the logo, under "Orchard Café Irregulars™" was the group motto, "Fiercely Independent."

The "Sunday Regulars" loved it and every Sunday since they wore their "Irregulars" sweatshirts with pride.

"Viola's right" Debbie said, "I'll have to add Princess Charlotte and darling Sunshine to the Caledonia Gang's Roster! There will be 5 of them then."

"Yeah" Hap Elmer said, "It'll be like Doris Day and Cary Grant in the old movie, 'Yours, Mine, and Ours'."

Somebody said, "I think you're a little confused, Hap, it was Lucille Ball and Jimmy Stewart who were in 'Yours, Mine, and Ours'."

"No, it was Deborah Kerr and Stewart Granger" a high voice in the booths declared with authority. "And it was made in 1968. I remember it was the same year my first grandchild was born."

"Did you know Stewart Granger's real name was Jimmy Stewart?"

"Jimmy Stewart was in 'It's a Wonderful Life.' I loved that movie and the Angel" yet another person chimed in.

"Cary Grant's real name is Archibald Leach" a quavering voice added happily, "or maybe it was Oswald Leach."

"Deborah Kerr and Stewart Granger starred in 'The Prisoner of Zenda,' in 1955, not in 'Yours, Mine, and Ours'."

"I heard that Bob Denver and John Denver were brothers, twins, separated at birth and raised by different families, sad story, but they always had the same kind of haircuts."

"Jimmy Stewart's best movie was 'Mr. Deeds goes to Washington'."

"Deborah Kerr and Stewart Granger starred in 'King Solomon's Mines' in 1950, not in 'Yours, Mine, and Ours'."

"Well, I knew it had a 'mine' in it!"

"Did you know Jimmy Stewart's real name was Gerry Maitland?"

"It was Gary Cooper who starred in the 'Mr. Deeds' movie in 1936, only it wasn't called, 'Mr. Deeds goes to Washington'."

"Well, if it wasn't Doris Day and Gary Cooper who played in 'Yours, Mine, and Ours,' who was it?"

"Jimmy Stewart starred in 'Mr. Smith Goes to Washington' in 1939. Gary Cooper starred in "Mr. Deeds Goes to Town' in 1936."

"Well no wonder I'm confused."

"Lucille Ball and Henry Fonda played in 'Yours, Mine, and Ours' in 1968."

"I don't remember them being in that movie."

It was just a typical 5 minutes at the Orchard Café and Russ, Lara, and Dr. Debbie couldn't keep from smiling.

"I see you brought out the Old Red Ford" Russ said quietly as the ebb and flow of old movie conversations continued to buzz around them.

"And I see you brought out a magnificent Aston Martin" Dr. Debbie said happily. Like Russ she loved classic cars. "There's a rumor going around the county that Harley tried to get that car running for 30 years and your Thorndike fixed it in a second, is that true?"

Russ glanced over his shoulder at Harley, who, as Lara once said, acted "like he was deaf as a post but he has excellent hearing and is always on the alert for news." Sure enough, even in the midst of all the talk the little man had been eavesdropping on their conversation from his stool at the bar, and now, dejected by Dr. Debbie's talk of the "rumor" he sat with his head hanging down.

"Well, I know Harley had the car in storage for 30 years" Russ said diplomatically, "but Thorndike did lend a hand in fixing it."

Harley lifted his head, surprised not to be thrown under the bus for the sake of a laugh.

"What an amazing cat" Dr. Debbie said.

"And boy does he know it" Russ added with a laugh, "boy does he know it."

"Here's your usual" Aunt Agnes said, with the clank of heavy plates, "enjoy."

"Aah, perfection, thank you Aunt Agnes" Russ said with a broad grin.

After the first wave of the "early risers" emptied out of the Café, among them Aunt Agnes herself, Harley and Fiona Shaw, Dr. Debbie, Viola Longbranch-Snodgrass, and Hap and Candy Elmer, some of the younger set began to arrive for the "brunch" menu.

Russ had been quietly explaining the connection between James Cunningham and Ryan Drummond to Lara when someone grabbed him by the shoulder.

"Hey Uncle Russ, can we crash your party?"

It was Russ's adopted Nephew, Arnold and Rhonda's son, Nathan, and his date, the lovely Mariell Thompson. Russ and Lara welcomed them happily.

"You must be staying in town for the Christmas Holiday" Russ said to Mariell.

"Yes" the young History Professor said excitedly. When Nathan told me you'd invited him and his family to Caledonia for Christmas Day I decided that sunny old Austin and Mount Bonnell could wait until Spring Break. Besides" she said happily, taking Nathan by the arm, "I can take Nathan with me then and introduce him to my parents and family. They will love him."

Mariell's excitement was met with a fearful expression on Nathan's face and they all laughed.

"So, did I hear you talking about Cunningham and Drummond when we came in?" Mariell asked frankly, without any thought of whether or not Russ would want to share the topic with others.

"Yes" Russ said hesitantly, unsure of what she might have heard.

"Project Caledonia, huh? I didn't know you were a

history buff, Lara."

"Well, I have been the department's secretary for many years but it's really Russ whose made history more exciting for me."

Russ's mind was spinning at the words Mariell had just spoken, "Project Caledonia."

"What were you referring to?" Lara asked Mariell, "what's Project Caledonia?"

"So" Mariell started out, "you were talking about James Cunningham and Thomas Drummond. They lived in the 1600's and were two of the most important leaders in what historians for two centuries called the 'The Darién Scheme'. Now it's usually called the 'Caledonia Project' or, sometimes just 'New Caledonia'."

Mariell was intelligent, articulate, and highly educated in American and European History. Russ had once felt out of place for his lack of a doctorate. With people like Mariell Thompson around he could have felt even more outdistanced. Mariell was, after all, a summa cum laude graduate of Dartmouth College.

"She's right" Russ said, "200 years before the Panama Canal came into existence, a group of mostly independent minded Scots decided to start an overland trade route and colony on the Isthmus of Panama. Late 1690's if I recall correctly."

"That's right" Mariell happily agreed, "New Caledonia. Major James Cunningham of Aiket Castle, in Ayrshire, Scotland, was in charge of the ships going over. Aiket Castle still stands today in Scotland. Captain Thomas Drummond, who played an infamous role in the massacre of MacIains at Glencoe, was an effective leader once they arrived in Panama. 'We will call this country Caledonia; and ourselves, Caledonians' he said. It failed in the end, but mainly because of English opposition."

Russ was impressed with Mariell's knowledge but there was something else overriding that thought. Russ was troubled. Even as the conversation turned away from history to the upcoming festivities they would enjoy at Caledonia Estate, Russ's mind wandered back to that day that now felt so long ago. It was the day he saw the book on the floor in his office. As he pulled "Glencoe – Story of the Massacre," by John Ross Prebble, out from under his office table he knew it was one of "Thorndike's books." When he saw the mass of claw marks in the middle of the page he knew there was a cat to blame, but he had failed. From beginning to end he now felt that he had failed to focus. Yes, Mariell was impressive and her knowledge of the facts was sound, but Russ had known full well about the Caledonia Project, he knew about Major James Cunningham and Captain Thomas Drummond. He knew about Drummond's involvement in both the Glencoe Massacre and the colonization of New Caledonia. He should have put two-and-two together. If he had he would have looked for a connection between the modern-day James Cunningham, the Head of Security at Caledonia, and Ryan Drummond.

Thorndike had tried. He'd done just about everything a cat could do to communicate the facts to Russ.

As the silver Aston Martin pulled slowly out of its parking place in front of the Orchard Café, Lara turned to Russ.

"Is something bothering you, Darling. Ever since Mariell brought up Project Caledonia you've been quiet."

It was a 5-minute drive to Lara's home on Orchard Terrace, 15 to 20 minutes out Hunters Lane to Wildrose, and 20 to 30 minutes to Caledonia Estate on Whistling Duck Road. Yet Russ drove out through the countryside for more than an hour as he explained how he was feeling about his failure.

"I didn't want that book to be one of 'Thorndike's books' and I never focused on it like I should have. I didn't think about the development of names and stayed stuck on MacIains to long. Then I got stuck on Campbells next and didn't put the puzzle pieces together with Duncanson and

Drummond for the longest time. I had the police chasing after Dr. Duncan instead of his grandson. I knew about Project Caledonia, probably since before Mariell's birth, and I didn't put Cunningham and Drummond together. It was Chief Ramsay who told me about their connection after the fact, when, if I'd just thought clearly, I could have put him onto the possibility long before. Thorndike does all he can and then I fail him."

"Russ" Lara said kindly, "I love you."

"I love you, too." Russ said sheepishly.

"You are a brilliant man and you've accomplished so much in the year I've known you. You and Thorndike have cleared up things I never thought I'd understand, you've solved crimes, and, most wonderfully, you've even helped save lives. You've even squeezed in a little time to court the girl you love. You've survived assassination attempts, taken one bullet, and barely dodged another. Thorndike has been drugged and barely escaped a catnapping. You've moved 3 times in one year, started a new job, retired, and then re-entered the workplace. You've dealt with so much violence and death in that amount of time, and even after you saved Vivian what you really did was give her the time she needed to put her affairs in order. Like she said, if the Chandler Gang would have waited another six months she would have gone out on her own. You can write upside-down, decipher handwriting, footprints in the snow, fix heating systems, and even tell whether the person tying a complicated knot in a rope is right or left-handed. Whether anyone else knows it or not, Russ, you really are a real-life, modern-day Sherlock Holmes. I guess what I'm trying to say is, don't be too hard on yourself."

Russ wouldn't have believed anything could have changed his mind about his failures yet Lara's words of wisdom had done just that.

"Lara, could I interest you in a strawberry sundae?"

# CHAPTER FIFTEEN
## The Order of the Golden Doubloon

Time waits for no man, woman, dog, or even cat for that matter. So it was for Santa Claus as well. Christmas could not be held back, nor could Russ Personette, for all his cleverness, even slow time down to help him finish his last-minute shopping and wrapping.

So it was that Russ Personette, fulltime Professor of History, one-time recipient of the Federal Bureau of Investigation's Medal for Meritorious Achievement, part-time billionaire philanthropist, and proud owner of a 1963 Aston Martin DB5, spent the week before Christmas running to and fro throughout the land, in search of the right gifts for his many friends.

He had little enough time because, in the strange mind of the man, he felt he needed to be the one to wrap each gift himself. In the end, finding the gift was sometimes the easiest part of his job. In time reason and desperation slowly crept in and he finally accepted the ready help of many of the Caledonian staff with gift wrapping. Imagine his surprise when he discovered that, as with the banquet, this was not their "first rodeo" either.

"For the Mistress" Edward Bright, Head of Household,

told him, "Christmas was the most important Holiday of the year. No effort was spared in making everything perfect, the staff always wrapped her many gifts, every guest was treated like royalty and each meal was the finest feast Caledonia could provide." After a short pause the man said, "The letters of thanks the Mistress received from appreciative guests after the Holidays were a point of pride for her and for each of us."

Russ was touched by these sincere words. Vivian's energy had always impressed him and since arriving at Caledonia he had been constantly surprised by the efficient organization she had created and managed. She'd once confessed to him that she'd "just been slacking off and taking it easy for years."

Yet, with the exception of James Cunningham, Russ had found the staff that ran the estate to be highly skilled and committed professionals. Whether it was the team who oversaw the grounds, security, or the Manor House, they'd impressed him to no end.

Now he was seeing just how deeply his friend and her staff had taken their responsibilities.

Russ loved Vivian as a person and a friend and, still, he was the new Laird of Caledonia and, like it or not, he was different. He was from a different generation and had no connection to the generation of 1908. They had created many of the "traditions" by which Caledonia still operated in the New Millennium and Vivian had been content to maintain those ways. Russ on the other hand, to the shock of his employees, had ended many of those traditions in his first weeks at Caledonia.

For one, all employees now went by their own names and, most challenging of all for his Head of Household, Edward Bright, Russ seemed intent on making Caledonia a place of "first names." The term "Domestics," by which the staff had been known for almost 150 years, had been retired in favor of "Associates". And Russ had overturned the cornerstone rule of Caledonia Holidays, that all staff worked all Holiday's. In place he instituted a "radical" change, requiring that anyone who worked certain Holidays in one year would have those same Holidays off in the coming year. Russ would have loved to allow all of his employees to be home with their families but the realities of a large estate, where entertaining guests was a norm, made that impossible.

"At least some will be home with their families" he told himself and with that he had to be content. Especially as he was intending to have guests and entertain during the Holidays.

The new "Laird's" changes made life more comfortable and flexible for his employees and, in Russ's mind, they brought Caledonia into the modern age as an employer. While creating a new leadership position for Mrs. Daly, whose age was beginning to prove a challenge in her former position, he increased her salary and simultaneously reduced the load on Edward Bright, without reducing his wage.

In his Security Department, instead of replacing James Cunningham, Russ made the equally "radical" decision to hire 3 Security Chiefs, and three Assistants, for each of the shifts. He promoted several from his current team and brought in some from outside. This change would increase his involvement in Security but he felt it would also make it less likely that another "all-powerful" James Cunningham could rise up to threaten Caledonia's future.

Despite his worry over gifts and preparations Russ was more excited about Christmas than he'd been in many years. He now found it painful to think about his darkest times, after the loss of his late wife and daughter, when Christmas had been just another day, or a time to withdraw from all the bustle of the holidays, into a cocoon of isolation and sleep.

Basking in the love of a wonderful woman, surrounded by the incredible Christmas atmosphere of Caledonia, complete with the strong pine scent of Ponderosa Pine wreaths shipped straight from that area of Idaho where Vivian had first met her husband, and buoyed by the warm embrace of hundreds of friends and well-wishers, many of them his students, Russ was experiencing nothing less than a childlike re-discovery of Christmas. His strange and almost inexplicable connection with Thorndike and his unbelievable and truly limitless budget were two additional factors that made this Christmas one of the most novel Holiday experiences of his entire life.

"Nature's Nobleman" had been the title given him by his old friend, Arnold Williams. It had been his two-word summarization of Russ Personette and all those who came to know Russ had found it to be true.

While Russ had once agreed with Dr. Mariell Thompson, saying, "maybe I do sound a little like Ebenezer Scrooge," the truth was the exact opposite. Russ Personette, for all his faults, foibles, and eccentricities, real or imagined, was anything but the cheap, grinding, miserly, greedy character of Scrooge in Charles Dicken's story, "A Christmas Carol."

In fact, it was his genuine kindness and sincere generosity that struck many people first and most powerfully. Christmas had always been his favorite holiday and rightly so. What holiday would be more welcome to anyone than Christmas would be to a generous soul who loved to give to others?

Even on a busy Wednesday morning, two days before Christmas, he was feeling very much like the proverbial "kid in a candy shop" and Thorndike and Benjamin seemed to share his reverie.

Russ woke at 7 AM on Wednesday morning to a thermometer that read, to his absolute disbelief, 40.5° Fahrenheit.

"Is this Vermont? Or Grand Cayman?" he said, as he put Benji's tartan coat and Tam O'Shanter cap on the little animal. Both these items had been custom made in the bright red Quilloran Tartan. The little dog wiggled his entire body so happily it was nearly impossible for Russ to buckle the straps.

Thorndike, on the other hand, was refined in his dignity and waited his turn with the yellow and black, Dean & Tyler™ "Cats Rock" harness for big cats.

Russ had taken up the habit of a pre-breakfast walk along the paths of Caledonia and Benji and Thorndike were his usual companions.

"We've got 23 miles of mostly-flat paved walking trails on the estate and another 4 miles of mountain trails on Berryman Ridge, all the way up to the summit of Mount Emily" the Head of Grounds, Fields, and Forests, Doug Fife had told him during their first meeting.

Russ wanted to discover every inch of the beautiful estate. Vivian had been famous for her walking and claimed that it, and Caledonia's Red Whortleberry Jam, were the two keys to her health. The jam, like the Apfelschorle, was produced under the Quilloran's™ label and advertised as "made with select Caledonian Farms™ Red Whortleberries since 1956".

Benji, at least, was always up for a trek. Although he was still young he'd been raised the right way, and from "puppyhood" he'd accompanied Vivian on her daily pilgrimages into the woods. Thorndike, on the other hand, was more mysterious in his approach to their outings. Sometimes he stopped to sniff at a patch of snow, or an odd leaf left over from the heady days of Autumn. Other times he headed for his favorite target, the locations where the Red Whortleberries grew.

When Russ questioned Doug Fife about the plant he was surprised to learn something about Scotland which he hadn't known.

"They are a member of the Heather family" he'd said, proud to display his knowledge to the new "Laird." "The Mistress had a dozen plants imported from the highlands of Scotland back in the 50's and we've cultivated them in small patches across grounds until we now have about 5 acres of the plants. It's a modest harvest but it was enough to supply the Mistress's personal and gift requirements." Then he said, "And the fact that it was the 'plant badge' of the Mistress's Scottish Clan meant the world to all of us."

Russ was surprised and touched by these words. He knew the clan badges, tartans, and mottoes of dozens of Clans but before meeting Vivian he hadn't studied Clan Quilloran.

The Red Whortleberry, often called Lingonberries in America, were a favorite of Thorndike's. When his stops and detours became too much for his comrades Russ would pick up the big cat and perch him on his broad shoulder.

The odd sight of cat, man, and dog, in this strange pose, had caught the attention of several members of staff. For "The Amazing Thorndike," as Eileen referred to him, with his supernatural sense of balance, the position seemed a comfortable and natural fit. After a morning outing of a mile to a mile and a half all three adventurers returned to the warmth of Caledonia ready for their respective breakfasts. Russ often returned with a sprig of Red Whortleberry, a quaint reminder of his friend Vivian.

Russ was going to have several guests staying with him for Christmas and this too was a part of his excitement. As bachelors living at Wildrose, he and Thorndike didn't require much additional help, and Mrs. Tibbetts had supplied that, but as the Laird of Caledonia he knew far more was expected.

Edward Bright had gently enlightened him, saying that he and his staff were proud of the Estate and the roles they played there. They were also proud to be able to impress guests when they had them, just as they had at Russ's award banquet.

"The Mistress aimed to impress every guest to Caledonia."

Russ asked what he could do to help and he was surprised to be handed a file with questionnaires for each guest. The list of questions included such items as any special needs, allergies, food sensitivities, known preferences, and the like, even favorite colors and candies.

"The Mistress provided us with completed forms for each guest, so that we could prepare rooms, menus, and staff for their stay. We will keep these forms on record so you only need to fill them out once. Then we'll add to them as we get to know each guest personally."

Russ never ceased to be amazed at all the work Vivian, Mr. Bright, Mrs. Daly, and everyone else had done to make Caledonia a success.

The list of guests included an old friend, Dr. Les Teal, Director of Research & Development at Russ's former food manufacturing company in Ohio, and his wonderful wife, Glenda. They were flying up to be with Russ at Caledonia during Christmas and New Year's.

Eileen was flying in from New York City with her reclusive, homebody of a husband, Neville. He had been a jeweler for almost half a century and retired just the year before. She told Russ that it was only her vivid descriptions of Caledonia's glory that had inspired him to pack his little-used traveling bags and head out to "the Great White North." They too would stay at Caledonia during Christmas and New Year's Holidays.

Daphne, as well, had been invited to stay at Caledonia and despite living only 30 minutes away she had jumped at the chance. She loved Eileen's company and had even won the friendship of the usually withdrawn Neville, during her month-long stay with the couple in New York. She also adored Russ and, though he hated to admit it, the young woman was one of Thorndike's favorite friends. Without admitting it, even to himself, Russ had begun to see Daphne as a daughter and this was all the easier since she had so few family left in the world, and they were far away and apparently uninterested in her.

Russ was looking forward to a very special Caledonia Christmas.

After breakfast in the breathtaking little dining room, referred to as the "Van Deusen Dining Room," Russ showered and dressed for a 10 AM meeting "regarding Federal and State of Vermont Salvage Laws impacting sunken vessels" at the offices of Stonecipher at-Law. He expected all of the members of "Operation Golden Doubloon" to be in attendance.

"Salvage Law, sounds fascinating, doesn't it? I hope it's nothing like 'Wake of the Red Witch' with  John Wayne and Gail Russell."[34]

Thorndike was seeing to his post-breakfast ablutions himself but he paused to give Russ a stare.

"Better you than me" came through so vividly that Russ couldn't help but catch his breath. He "knew" he'd imagined everything, but the power of the human mind to create and reinforce an idea simply stunned him.

Even Russ, who believed he shared some sort of telepathic connection with the handsome, brilliant cat, didn't think for a moment that what he'd just imagined was anything more than pure mental gymnastics.

The temperature was 44° when he slid behind the big steering wheel of the idling Aston Martin and Russ wondered what was going on in Vermont. The snow in the Pine Valley was down to a single foot now and the MacIntosh River, which ran through the estate, was full of meltwater as he crossed over the bridge and turned onto a perfectly dry Whistling Duck Road.

Russ parked the silver Aston Martin between Dane Van Wert's huge, metallic green Ford Triton and Griff Langlois' massive, bright yellow, 1956 Dodge Power Wagon™ with shiny black fenders and running boards. The exotic sports car was dwarfed by the two domestic behemoths.

David Gaertner's white Chevrolet Crew Cab was

[34] "Wake of the Red Witch" starring John Wayne, Gail Russell, 1948, based on the novel by Garland Roark, ©1946.

parked near the front of Stonecipher at-Law.

"What happened to Vermont's Winter?" Russ asked, after friendly greetings, as he took his seat in the conference room.

Everyone from "Operation Golden Doubloon" now sat around the long table, looking much cleaner and relaxed than they had the last time Russ had seen them on the ice above the dive site.

"This is the year without a winter" Harley declared confidently. "Happens about every hundred years or so. My grandaddy told me about it happening when he was a boy, around 1900. The ice is melting on the lake."

The sad expression on Harley's face at this last statement was obvious.

"Haven't gone ice sailing once."

"They had a year without summer back in 1815-16" Griff Langlois said matter-of-factly, "a volcano in the Pacific caused it, famine killed a lot of people."[35]

"Got all your Christmas shopping done, Russ?" David asked with a broad smile.

"Almost" Russ said, it wasn't completely true but he justified it with the thought that it was "almost true."

"You can always just get me a lottery ticket" Dane said. Having heard the story of Arnold's winning lottery ticket everyone laughed.

"You don't need that now" Griff said.

"That's a fact" said Harley, "we got ourselves a golden lottery ticket."

"It's called the Morning Star, right?"

"I hope you're right about that" Russ said mysteriously, "depending on state and federal salvage taxes we could

[35] "The Year Without a Summer," considered "a volcanic winter," it was the result of 6 successive volcanic eruptions worldwide, from 1808 and culminating with the massive 1815 eruption of Mount Tambora in today's Indonesia. It caused major food shortages, famine, and death. Source: wikipedia

each get $53.75."

"On that note" Alexis said as she entered and closed the door, "I'm afraid we have much to discuss."

Alexis Stonecipher was an attractive young woman and fourth generation attorney in Eton Falls. Her Great Grandfather, Cyprian Godfrey Stonecipher, had been the first attorney-at-law in Eton Falls.

She looked around the table at her clients and, uncharacteristically, she didn't smile.

"As I've already told you, salvage is at best a shadowy area of maritime law. While you recovered the sunken treasure, you do not own it."

"What do you mean?" Griff asked bluntly. "Of course we own it, we are the 'Salvors'." This was the technical name for those who conducted the "salvaging."

"Actually, not" Alexis said.

The dismay on the faces of everyone but Russ was apparent. For Russ, his comment about getting $53.75 after all the government entities had taken all their slices out of the pie, was an expectation based on experience. His knowledge of History made it impossible for him to overlook the details, like the fact that even just 100 years earlier Americans paid none of the numberless taxes they paid today. In just one century an entire governmental paradigm had been overthrown and it didn't come cheaply.

"Yes" he thought to himself as he looked around the table, "these men gave up years of their lives and we risked life, limb, health, and certainly our comfort, to find and extract 10,000 golden doubloons, lost and forgotten for over 240-some-years, but we don't own the treasure."

"In the case of the sloop, Morning Star, the 4th Circuit Court has recognized the State of Vermont with jurisdictional ownership" Alexis said, bluntly.

Harley wanted to say something but words escaped the little man. For some reason everyone looked at Russ but he remained silent and waited for his Attorney to continue. He could feel the disappointment in his "partners."

"The State of Vermont has granted you an 'award for salvage' equal to 40% of sale value."

Russ could see the shock on his friends faces and then the wheels in their minds began grinding. How much would that be? Would it even cover their expenses?

"That's, that's only $860,000.00 each" Griff said. He had been expecting at least 2 million.

"Yes" Alexis admitted, "it would have been, but for two factors. First, Mr. Personette has opted out of your partnership, 'The Order of the Golden Doubloon,' and is leaving his share to be split evenly among the remaining four partners."

Once again every eye turned on Russ.

"You can't do that, Russ" Harley said, "you were the one who located the treasure."

"Even with that it's just barely over a million" Griff said.

"Half of what we hoped for" David said in little more than a whisper.

"Except for the second factor" Alexis continued. "You see, I questioned your valuation of the treasure at 10 million dollars and sought a revaluation. The appraisal of three European businesses that deal in historic gold pieces settled on an average value of $43,300,000, and a bullion house in London, England, has tendered an offer in this sum to the State of Vermont. This left the state with no recourse other than to accept the valuation and pay you 40% of this sum."

Even as each man struggled to fathom this news and calculate their share Alexis continued.

"I have your checks here. Less my fees, you will each receive 4.25 million dollars."

This was even more than the men had hoped to get when there were only three partners and they were all shocked.

"I don't know another man who would have done what you did, Russ" Griff said later in the parking lot. "Lou was right about you all along."

Dane VanWert looked at Russ and shook his head. "You made sure I was a partner and then you didn't even take your share, it makes me wonder if you had that planned all along."

Russ laughed at his young friend and said, "Well, you did save my life, right?"

As Russ pulled out of the parking lot David Gaertner, one of four of Chittenden County's newest multi-millionaires, and richer than he'd ever really dreamed he'd be, bent down to the open car window and shook Russ's hand.

He didn't say "thank you," but his eyes did, and as he stood up again he said, "the Professor who drove and Aston Martin." Then he added, "You did us one better than a lottery ticket, didn't you?"

# CHAPTER SIXTEEN
## A Very Caledonian Christmas

Russ pulled the Aston Martin through the massive, Vermont granite gate posts of Caledonia. Each was topped with the life-sized bronze statue of a Rocky Mountain Bull Elk, just like those seen around the Caledonia Mine in the far west. As he did so, giant snowflakes began to fall from the darkening sky. The driveway dipped down into what everyone at Caledonia called "the Burn." It was the shallow valley of the MacIntosh River. As Russ crossed the old stone bridge he looked up through the Sugar Maples and Black Walnut trees at the three circular towers and the single square tower of Caledonia, the Manor House as Vivian referred to it.

Sitting in a first-floor window of the square tower that

housed the Delashmett Library, and staring at Russ, was a magnificent cat. Thorndike was waiting for his return.

"I wonder what he's thinking?" Russ said out loud. "That darned cat!"

Three hours later a freshly washed Russ, smelling of cologne, climbed into the snow-white Lincoln® Mark LT Crew Cab 4-wheel drive pickup with a matching white fiberglass canopy and gave thanks for truck. In the hours since he'd returned home in the Aston Martin, temperatures had dropped 20 degrees and almost 3 inches of heavy snow had blanketed all of northern Vermont.

"So much for Harley's 'Year Without a Winter'."

Les and Glenda were scheduled to arrive at Burlington International Airport within an hour of Eileen and Neville and Russ would bring them all home to Caledonia safely and comfortably in the big Lincoln. Daphne would arrive around 6 PM, just in time for a grand welcoming supper in the Van Deusen Dining Room.

"I owe you for this one Eston" Russ said as he turned onto a snow packed Whistling Duck Road and headed for the airport. If he hadn't listened to Eston and Greta he'd be driving his 1998 Mercury Grand Marquise, rear-wheel drive, and he admitted freely now that he wouldn't have felt safe.

Russ had known Les, Glenda, and Eileen for years, but he'd only met Eileen's husband on a couple occasions. Now they'd be together for two weeks and Russ hoped all would be enjoyable.

As matters turned out Ohio was getting hit with the same storm and Les and Glenda's flight would be arriving late. As he waited on a seat that was more like an old-fashioned church pew, a man sat down beside him.

"Waiting for someone?"

Russ recognized the voice and looked up. It was Dr. Charles Duncan, his fellow History Professor at Charbonneau College.

"Hello" Russ said, happy to see a familiar face. "It looks

like you are getting ready to fly out."

"I was" the distinguished looking Professor said, "but they've canceled all outgoing flights until further notice. I guess this storm is due to last several days."

As the conversation lulled into silence Russ felt the discomfort of being tied intimately to the death of Dr. Duncan's Grandson, Ryan Drummond. To his shock the man suddenly opened that exact subject.

"At least he's at peace now" he said solemnly, but without sadness.

Russ expressed his sadness and offered his condolences but Dr. Duncan only replied, "Ryan was never able to find a place of peace, at least his struggle is over."

After a silent pause he said something that shocked Russ again.

"I find it strange that tragedy should strike both my grandson and his father so close to each other."

To Russ's questions Dr. Duncan said, "James Cunningham has been arrested."

"James Cunningham" Russ said, "the Head of Security at Caledonia Estate?" He found it impossible to believe they were talking about the same man.

"Yes" Dr. Duncan said, "Ryan's father."

"Well" the man said, standing up and offering Russ his hand, "I wish you a Merry Christmas and thank you for making me feel welcome at Charbonneau. I should have said it long before now, but I do appreciate it, Professor Personette."

Russ stood and shook hands, offering him a "Happy New Year" despite the circumstances.

With that Dr. Duncan turned and walked with his large roller-suitcase toward the exit and a line of taxis waiting outside.

Suddenly Russ called out his name.

"You aren't going to be able to go home for Christmas and New Year's after all?" Russ asked.

"No, Mother Nature got me this time" he said in a flat

voice.

"Then why don't you join my extended family. You won't even need a taxi, I've got the room, and you've already packed your bags."

"I couldn't intrude" he said quietly, "but thanks for the offer."

"What if I told you I have one of the finest cooks in the Northeast United States and the best Red Whortleberry Jam in the whole world" Russ pressed.

"Wouldn't I put you to a lot of extra work?"

"What's one more person when you already have a dozen or so? And you'd have your own room, in a castle."

Dr. Duncan looked at Russ for a moment. Such a radical change of plans seemed unthinkable, but then he realized his plans had already been radically changed, and without his consent, by Mother Nature, just as he'd said.

"I'd welcome a change of scenery from my four walls and I've heard that Caledonia is beautiful" he admitted, "and I've always had a weakness for good food."

"I'll take that as a 'yes' then" Russ said happily. He knew very well what it was like to spend the Holiday alone and he wished that on no one, especially a man who'd just lost his only Grandson.

"Thank you, Professor Personette" he said as he continued to stare. He'd found such hospitality rare in his life and couldn't believe that his fellow Professor would open his home to him so spontaneously.

Russ texted the addition of Dr. Duncan to Edward Bright and received confirmation that the Rose Suite would be prepared, almost immediately.

"A place shall be added for him in the Van Deusen Dining Room as well."

"Everything is ready for your arrival" Russ said after a moment and almost simultaneously a noisy throng of people came flooding down the hall from the secured terminals.

For a glorious 5 minutes it was like Old-Home Week

for Russ. He greeted old friends and happily introduced them to each other. Everyone was excited and even Eileen's husband and Professor Duncan seemed caught up in the excitement of the moment and the splendor that waited for them at Caledonia.

"What a Christmas Eve-Eve" Les said as they left the airport and drove through the falling snow.

"It's almost mesmerizing" his wife Glenda added.

"It reminds me of my childhood" Neville Shute said with a strange kind of joy in his voice.

"It's hard to believe" Professor Duncan said. "We've had such clement weather of late, then winter returned."

"Thank you for having us, Russ" Eileen added, "this already feels like the most wonderful of vacations, and I have the privilege of knowing what awaits us at Caledonia."

"Yes you do" Russ said, "you were at my surprise party and you never breathed a word of warning to me."

"That's right, I'm a good little conspirator, and besides, Lara swore us all to silence!"

Everyone laughed and Russ couldn't help but feel the same, electric, childlike joy the others were experiencing.

"Even through the snow I can see something looming off to our left, Russ, what is that?" asked Neville, giving in completely to his curiosity. Normally he wouldn't have said a word.

"That's Berryman Ridge, it's part of the Green Mountain National Forest."

"Your estate extends up the ridge doesn't it?" Eileen asked. "I told Neville about all your wonderful trails."

"Yes, it does" Russ said, still finding it strange to have people refer to Caledonia as "his."

"We've got 23 miles of mostly-flat paved walking trails on the estate and another 4 miles of graveled mountain trails on the Ridge" he said, happily plagiarizing his Head of Grounds, Fields, and Forests, Doug Fife.

"It sounds magnificent, Russ" Glenda said.

"It's one of America's finest old family estates from the

1800's" Russ admitted, "and my nephew just had a book about it published. It tells the history of the place."

"And it has the most glorious pictures of the estate too" Eileen added. "Daphne will be there tonight, won't she, Russ?"

"Yes, she will" he said smiling. He remembered the black-haired girl from a year earlier. She rarely smiled in those days. Her transformation had been one of the brightest chapters in Russ's recent life and he felt a strong, almost parental love for the young woman.

"She's the one who took all the pictures for the book. She's an artist with several paintings on display in New York" Eileen said proudly, "and she has a gift for knowing how to create an exquisite picture."

"She really does" agreed Neville with an exuberance Eileen hadn't seen in decades, "we've got the book about Caledonia and the photographs are breathtaking."

"Here we are" Eileen said with enthusiasm. Pointing through the heavy veil of falling snow she said, "You can see the lights of the Manor House, just there."

Russ had slowed to a crawl, his blinker flashing his intention to turn to an empty road void of traffic.

"I see it" Glenda said suddenly. "It's absolutely huge."

"I see the towers" Les said with glee, "it really is a castle."

Russ turned slowly into the drive between the gateposts and Professor Duncan said, "Wow, those are impressive."

When they got to the "castle," as Les had called it, Russ drove past and turned in the covered drive where they could unload out of the falling snow.

The warm, yellow light from inside beckoned to the guests and the profusion of Christmas lights, Ponderosa Pine wreaths, and cardinal red ribbons gave Caledonia a festive air.

Russ ushered everyone in the door where Edward Bright, working late specifically to welcome Caledonia's guests, made them all feel like VIP's. Champagne, the Old

Homestead Orchard Cove Cider™, and Quilloran's Crest
Apfelschorle, with hors d'oeuvres, were being served in the
Main Hall, where "the Yule log" was burning in the giant
fireplace and a thousand lights shimmered on the twenty-
foot-tall Douglas Fir.

Daphne arrived within minutes and a new round of
greetings and introductions took place. She was surprised
to find herself and her photographs and paintings quite the
center of attention. At one point the entire group marched
off around the corner and into the wood paneled Little
MacIntosh Sitting Room where Russ had hung Daphne's
8 x 6-foot painting of the snow-capped Elkhorn Mountains
in Northeast Oregon. Les, who had traveled in the west,
declared the painting exquisite and Professor Duncan said
he would love to see Daphne paint the Matterhorn in
Switzerland in the same style.

"It would be an instant classic. An impressionist's view
of Bierstadt's 'Sunrise on the Matterhorn'."[36]

"It would" said Eileen's husband.

Neville was in a kind of seventh heaven, reveling in the
architecture and grandeur of Caledonia and he'd found a
ready companion in Professor Duncan. To Russ's surprise
he heard his fellow Professor say that he'd gotten his minor
in Historic European Architecture. The two men sipped
their drinks and spoke of banisters, bulwarks, flying-
buttresses, blue-slate roof tiles, and medieval stone
"crenelations" with abandon.

The associates in their crisp dove-gray 3-piece suits with
white shirts and black ties or their matching dresses with
white collars and cuffs, and black bows, kept everyone in a
celebratory mood. Some saw to the luggage which was all
delivered to their respective rooms. Even the beds would
be "turned down" while guests were at supper.

After drinks Edward Bright said in his most formal

---

[36] "Sunrise on the Matterhorn", by Albert Bierstadt, Metropolitan
Museum of Art.

English, "Supper will be served in one hour in the Van Deusen Dining Room," and the associates quietly and efficiently showed guests to their rooms. They would have an hour to freshen up before the evening meal.

Russ joined Thorndike, Benji, and Winston in the Quilloran Room for a few minutes of relaxation before he dressed for supper. Lara was to arrive shortly before supper and Russ, a "wonderful worrier" by nature, was thankful he'd decided to give her the new 4-wheel drive Kia® Telluride™ in his favorite garnet-red.

The evening meal was a treat for the senses with delicious food, a spectacular environment, outstanding service from the associates, and beautifully dressed men and women enjoying each other's company.

The next afternoon, Christmas Eve, Russ left Caledonia in the Lincoln like a Santa Claus in his modern-day sleigh. Daphne agreed to accompany him, as if she were one of his Elves, and they began a circuitous route over the snow packed roads and through the deep woods of Chittenden County.

Gift cards to the tune of several thousand dollars were handed to Lara's Great-Aunt Virginia and to Gracie at the door of the little home they shared on Killoran Drive.

Chief Ramsay was surprised when he opened the door to find Russ Personette standing there with a Christmas card in his hand. Russ had already given the Chief one present. It was a book entitled "Fodor's™ Travel Guide of Scotland." The Chief knew this because he'd opened the gift early, without permission and without confessing.

"What did you give him?" Daphne asked as they drove away, leaving the Chief still waving.

"Two weeks in Scotland" Russ said with a smile. "It's time the Ramsays made a pilgrimage back to their Mother Country."

"You are the sweetest man I know" Daphne said, then she added mysteriously, "well, almost!"

The revelation that she might have a special someone

made Russ happy and he said, "Do tell!"

"You'll see soon enough" she laughed.

Detective & Mrs. James received a sizable gift card to help them with travel expenses back and forth on their trips to Hollywood. Russ assured them that becoming the next Rudolph Valentino/John Wayne wouldn't be an easy or inexpensive endeavor.

Others on Russ's long list continued to be surprised to receive a Christmas Eve visit and the inevitable wonderful gift.

At Dan Garn's place Russ handed over a large bag of beautifully wrapped gifts especially chosen by Russ for "all the little Garn's."

When Dan asked if they'd like to come in, Russ creatively quoted Robert Frost's poem, "Stopping by Woods on a Snowy Evening," saying, "Santa has miles to go before he sleeps."

Russ knew the poem was Dan's personal favorite and he just couldn't resist.

Christmas Day came in with a breakfast feast fit for a King. The morning was bright and clear and three feet of snow covered the Pine Valley from north to south.

Everyone was there. Russ's stay-in guests as well as Arnold, Rhonda, Lou, Bernadette and Lara. Lou and Bernadette loved seeing Les again. He had launched the "Bernadette's World Famous™" line of foods and given them the grand tour and "Royal Treatment" in Ohio.

Nathan brought Dr. Mariell Thompson, as expected, but she was surprised and happy to see Professor Duncan there as well.

"We've almost gotten the whole team together" she exclaimed. Only Dr. Roger Dudley was missing but he was with Suzanne and his soon-to-be in-laws for the Holidays.

Ben showed up with his date, which to Russ's amazement was Lara's daughter, Veronica.

When Lara's son, Charlie, arrived Russ got another shock.

Daphne pulled the young man over to Russ and pointedly said, "I want you to meet the sweetest guy in the whole world."

By mid-morning everyone was gathered in the Main Hall and filled with anticipation.

The first gift opened was a Pendleton™ Saddle Mountain Blanket, "in warm hues inspired by sunrise on a mountain range, with a row of morning stars heralding a new day."[37]

Everyone said it was beautiful and Bernadette clung to it like a little girl with her first doll.

"I always wanted a Pendleton™ blanket, Russ."

Russ had remembered her saying that shortly after they met and there one thing about Russ Personette, he didn't forget much.

The next gift was huge and oddly shaped. Russ had been intrigued by it since it arrived at Caledonia in the ugliest wrapping paper he had ever seen, about 43 acres of the stuff. It was from Arnold and Rhonda, "to Ross Personetti."

"What do you mean 'the ugliest wrapping paper you've ever seen?" Arnold demanded.

"The Santa Claus looks like the Wicked Witch of the West, or the North, or the East" Russ said to a dozen laughing people.

"You're looking at it upside-down, silly!" Rhonda said as she shook her head. "Of all the people who should have known, a guy who writes upside-down, after all, should have realized that."

The laughter around the room was deafening and Benji darted from person to person in a state of unbridled excitement. Thorndike looked on from Eileen's lap with what could only be called a stoic grin of approval for Rhonda's comment. If anyone knew how difficult it was to

[37] As advertised, 64" x 80", pure virgin wool, uncombed for sharper pattern, made in in Pendleton, Oregon, USA.

communicate with Russ, after all, it was the handsome cat.

Russ bent his head as far as he could to get the perspective and, as if by magic, the Wicked Witch vanished and the sweetest, plump-cheeked Santa came into sharp focus. In fact, Russ confessed he'd rarely seen a more cheery Santa Claus in all his years. The laughter continued unabated for almost a minute after that.

Russ pulled off the "Wicked Witch-Cheery Santa" wrapping paper like a little boy and revealed the strangest looking contraption he'd ever seen, and that was saying something.

"Oh boy" Russ said facetiously, "A Time Machine!"

"It's a bike" Arnold said in a humorless voice.

"Actually" Rhonda corrected, "it's a 3-wheeled bike known as a 'recumbent'. It's called a Performer JC-26X Rear-Suspension Recumbent Trike in Sunrise Orange."

"Now you'll be able to see all 867 miles of Caledonia's trails" Arnold said glibly.

"We even put a rear basket on for Thorndike and Benji to travel in style" Rhonda said sweetly.

In all honesty it was probably the strangest gift Russ had ever received, but in its own awkward, surprising way, it was glorious, and it had been given in kindness by dear friends.

After a moment of silence Russ honestly said, "I love it!"

Cheers celebrated his comment and Neville even gave voice to the traditional calls of early Americans, saying, "Huzzah! Huzzah! Huzzah!"

The next gift went to Professor Duncan, to his surprise. Edward Bright had been better than his word. The truth was that Vivian had a long tradition of giving gift baskets filled with a variety of Caledonian and Vermont products including the Quilloran's Crest™ Red Whortleberry Jam and Apfelschorle Apple Spritzer, Sidehill Farms™ Strawberry-Rhubarb Jam, the Old Homestead Orchard Cove Cider™, Green Mountain Sugar House™ 100% Pure Maple Syrup, and a variety of Sugarbush Farm™

Cheeses.

The baskets themselves were works of art and the custom-made products of well-known Vermont "Master Basket Maker," Linda "Deeda" Lomasney, of "Deeda's Baskets."[38]

The baskets made for Caledonia Estate were called "Shay's Baskets™" and carried a wide band of Black Walnut-stained weaving with two thin, bordering bands of Cherrywood-stained weave, called "Caledonia Banding."

Professor Duncan was full of appreciation for the beautiful and thoughtful gift.

Nathan handed Russ a five foot long, tubular shaped present next. It just said "to Russ" but as it was perfectly wrapped Russ knew it wasn't from Arnold or Chief Ramsay.

He rattled it and at the sound Ben gave his guess.

"A top-of-the-line Garcia™ fishing rod" and Nathan quickly added his own guess.

"With a Mitchell™ ball-bearing reel!"

Lou said, "Those are my Grandsons, raised 'em right!"

When Russ got the end open he found, to his shock, Vivian's Irish Shillelagh. He had wondered where it had gone and no doubt she had instructed Mr. Bright to wrap it for Russ. He loved it and held it tightly as he explained that it had been Vivian's.

"What a dear woman she was" Bernadette said, as she dabbed her eyes.

Winston was the next happy recipient of an exquisitely wrapped gift which turned out to be his favorite treats, Caitec® Oven-Fresh Bites Mixed Berry Cookie Parrot Treats.

Nathan had been handing out the gifts randomly and the next lucky winner was Eileen and Neville.

"A framed portrait of Thorndike and his blue ribbon" guessed Neville as he tried to feel through the gift wrap.

---

[38] https://deedasbaskets.com

"We already have one of those" Eileen said crisply.

When they jointly tore the paper off, their ensuing silence shocked everyone.

"Well, whad'ya get" Lou asked, "an autographed picture of Russ?"

"Yeah" said Ben, "inquiring minds want to know!"[39]

When Eileen covered her face and began crying and Neville remained silent and looking downward at the framed gift, no one knew what to say.

Lara got a box of tissues for Eileen, and Daphne looked over at Russ in concern.

Finally Neville stood up, shakily, and handed the gift to Bernadette, who was sitting nearest them. As he crossed the room to where Russ was sitting, Bernadette gasped and handed the frame to her husband.

Neville didn't trust himself to say anything but he reached out and shook Russ's hand, then returned to the sofa where he hugged his wife.

"Well I'll be a Jacobite's Grand-Nephew" Lou said with a long, low whistle.

Slowly the framed gift made its way partly around the room and it was often followed by a whistle or an exclamation of some sort.

Lara was the only person who knew what the gift was beforehand, and she just smiled at Eileen and Neville.

Eileen finally stood up and Russ did also. They hugged in the middle of the room and she turned to the group.

"Russ gave us Wildrose" she said breathlessly. "This is the title to Wildrose."

All those who hadn't seen the framed document yet gasped in shock.

"She has been talking about retiring lately" Neville said with a smile, barely holding back the tears.

Daphne simply said, "Oh Russ," and got up and gave

---

[39] "Enquiring minds want to know" was the slogan of the National Enquirer™ Magazine.

him a hug too.

Next, Thorndike and "Benjamin Disraeli Jr." each received bag of Rocco & Roxie's™ Jerky Sticks and Russ gave one to each of them. They headed off in different directions to enjoy their treats.

Russ opened a present from Detective James and his wife and held it up for everyone to see.

"The Shillelagh Makers Handbook, by John Hurley" Lou read out loud for everyone's benefit. "Wow. Looks like a fun book. Can I borrow it when you finish?"

"Louis Langlois" Bernadette snapped.

"What" Lou said, honestly confused, "that's a compliment, right Russ?"

Once more "around the horn" and Russ opened another book, "The Thirty-Nine Steps" by John Buchan. It was from Nathan and Mariell and was one of Russ's favorite mysteries.

"Thank you both" he said sincerely, "it's a true classic!"

Daphne got the next gift and it was from Russ. He had been known to give her earrings or necklaces for her special occasions, so when she saw the small case she assumed it would be more beautiful jewelry.

Instead of earrings she found a strangely shaped object.

Charlie was sitting next to Daphne and they looked at the object together.

"It's a key" Charlie said suddenly, "it's a new car key." The key was an "extra" key, cut at a local shop, and without the name brand.

When a confused Daphne looked up, Russ was pointing to the side-door of Caledonia, the door with the covered drive for drop-offs and pick-ups. She jumped up and screamed, then ran out of the Main Hall and down the hallway to the door, where more screaming was heard. Charlie was right behind her and Nathan, Mariell, Ben, and Veronica all followed quickly. Soon enough more screams were heard, these accompanied with talk and joyous laughter.

Daphne had taken good care of her late mother's old front-wheel drive minivan but it had 250,000 miles on it so Russ thought a new 4-wheel drive vehicle would be a good gift in Vermont.

"You can't help yourself can you?" Arnold said to his old Navy Buddy.

"You know me, Arnold."

"I sure do. Nature's Nobleman."

In a few minutes Daphne came running back, followed by the pack of young people. She threw her arms around Russ.

"Thank you, thank you, thank you" she said breathlessly. "It's beautiful."

"It" was a new Ford Bronco™, "Outer Banks" model, 4-wheel drive, in ruby-red metallic.

After everyone got seated again Nathan handed Russ a small gift.

"Another book" guessed Ben, as Russ opened it. It was from "that darned Dan Garn," "The Postman-Poet of the North Country." It was an underwhelming, ragged edged, over-used volume entitled "The Protocols of Spy Craft."[40] Russ couldn't help but laugh uproariously at how his friend and fellow spy had gotten back at him.

"Hilarious" Lou said, "did you know they're selling little bronze replica statues of him in Jericho? Making a mint I hear. That guy is a real character!"

"That's an understatement" Bernadette replied to her husband. "You know I suspect him of being a spy!"

At this several heads turned in unison, all thinking the same thing." Nathan, Ben, and Lara, all knew the truth about Russ, and Lara knew about Dan Garn.

"Yeah" Lou said facetiously, "but you think that transit driver named Steve is a spy, and who else was it, oh, yeah,

---

[40] "The Protocols of Spy Craft," originally "Spycraft," published between 1942 and 1945 this "secret" document became the "Bible" of American and British intelligence services through modern times.

that famous artist who lives down on 'O' street, by the Power Company, what's her name?"

"Judy" Bernadette said impatiently, "Judy O'Flaherty-Carruthers."

"Yeah" said Lou, "I knew it was O'Something-or-Other, I swear she thinks everybody's a spy. At least she's stopped saying you're a spy, Russ, and that's a welcome relief."

Russ laughed and everyone followed his lead.

"I wonder what Lou would think if I told him Bernadette was 100% correct about that transit driver and the famous artist?" Russ thought to himself. "How does she do it?" he wondered. "Is it really the spy novels? Whatever it is she has a nose for picking out spies, no getting around that."

In the hope of changing the conversation Nathan gave Russ another gift. It was in a big box that looked like it had been wrapped by a lumberjack in the Pacific Northwest, sometime back in the early 1900's.

"To Russ, From The Ramsays, All of Them" it read.

"Chief Ramsay is a good man" Daphne said.

"Be careful" Lou said, "if you aren't careful Bernie will say she suspects him of being a spy."

Laughter followed, at least until Russ pulled the first item out of the box, then the "Oohhs and Aahhs" began.

"What is it" Veronica asked curiously.

"That is a Scottish kilt" Professor Duncan said, "and if I'm not mistaken that's the 'Ancient Tartan of Clan Macpherson.' Its hand-stitched too, and beautiful."

"You're right" Russ said in a quiet voice, "it's the Ancient Macpherson."

For all his love for Scotland and his Scottish heritage, Russ Personette had never owned a kilt. Now he did and it was magnificent. A tag attached to the kilt said, "This kilt was made by The Tartan Shop™ using 8 yards of tartan.[41]

---

[41] The Tartan Shop™ at amanda@scotclans.com

Russ opened the last gift. It was from Harley Shaw and Russ guessed it was some kind of wall sign because of its long, flat shape. To his surprise it was a custom car license plate in heavy black gloss enamel, gold trim, and golden letters that read "Professor P."

"That must be for the Aston Martin" Arnold said quickly.

"Yes, indeed" Russ agreed with a broad smile. "What a guy" he said with a chuckle, "what a guy!"

After all the presents had been opened, Veronica recruited everyone into picking up the wrapping paper, bows, ribbons, and boxes for recycling.

"Wait" Arnold called out in the midst of the cleanup, "save me a piece of that 'Wicked Witch – Cheery Santa' wrapping paper, that will come in handy some time."

"Hahaha, you Scoundrel!" Russ said flatly. He'd secretly hoped never to see that paper again and Arnold knew it.

While everyone cleaned up the Main Hall, Lara took his hand and leaned close. She wore a deep burgundy hip-length blouse with silver points like tiny stars, and earrings and necklace of brilliant Garnet. She was the most lovely thing in his life and his eyes told her more than his words could have said.

"Darling" she whispered, "I know you said you weren't much of a 'Matchmaker' but looking around this room I have to say, you have been a very busy boy!"

Meanwhile, Thorndike sat across the room on a Chippendale chair once owned by J. P. Morgan and tended to his ablutions. After all, cleanliness is next to catliness.

# The End

Thank you for reading

## "The Professor Who Drove an Aston Martin"

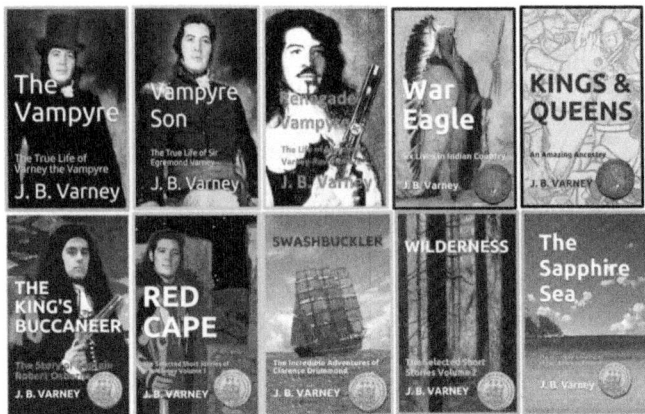

# Other Books by J. B. Varney

## Red Cape
Book 1 of the Collected Short Stories

## The Wilderness
Book 2 of the Collected Short Stories

## The King's Buccaneer
A Novel of Intrigue set in the 1700's

## Swashbuckler
A High-Seas Adventure in the Pirate Age

## The Sapphire Sea
The Adventures of a Retired Couple

## The Vampyre
The True Tale of Varney the Vampyre

## Vampyre Son
The Adventures of Sir Egremond Varney

## Renegade Vampyre
Coming soon

## War Eagle
The Nonfiction Biography of a Sioux Chief

## Kings & Queens
A Genealogical look at one American Family

available at amazon.com

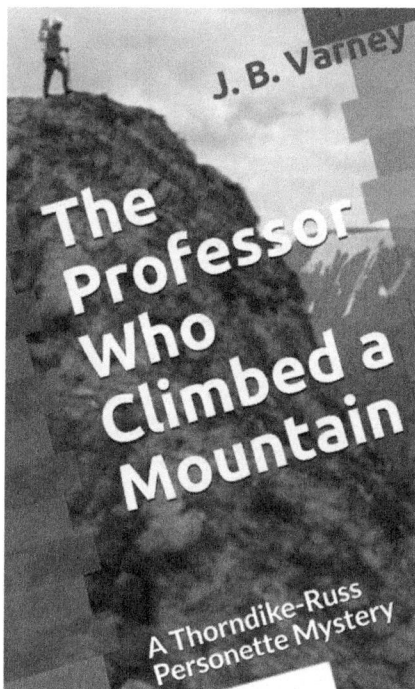

J. B. Varney

The Professor Who Climbed a Mountain

A Thorndike-Russ Personette Mystery

## So what on earth comes next for Thorndike & Company?

Will that rascal Thorndike finally retire and enjoy a life of domestic bliss in his beautiful new home at Caledonia with Benji, Winston, Princess Charlotte and Sunshine? Or will he lead Russ, Lara, Captain Ramsay, Detective James, Agent 36, Ben & Nathan, Special Agent Awmiller, and the erstwhile Postman, "that darned Dan Garn", on another series of wild "Cock-a-leekie Soup Adventures"?

Find out more in J. B. Varney's next novel.

# THE PROFESSOR WHO CLIMBED A MOUNTAIN

# ABOUT THE AUTHOR

J. B. Varney is a life-long writer who credits the late Lillian Jackson Braun, author of the "Cat Who" series, with inspiring him to write cozy mysteries designed simply to be fun entertainment!

He is a descendant of early Vermonters, among them many from Chittenden County itself. He and his family have had many pets over the years, including a cat much like the indomitable Thorndike, and a Cockatiel named "Sunshine"!

His goal in writing "The Cat & The Professor Mysteries" is to give lovers of pets, history, and mystery, more cozy mysteries to warm their hearts!

*Bon Voyage!*

Printed in Great Britain
by Amazon

53798166R00148